P9-DHN-444

THE ETRUSCAN CHIMERA

Berkley Prime Crime Books
by Lyn Hamilton

THE XIBALBA MURDERS
THE MALTESE GODDESS
THE MOCHE WARRIOR
THE CELTIC RIDDLE
THE AFRICAN QUEST
THE ETRUSCAN CHIMERA

THE ETRUSCAN CHIMERA

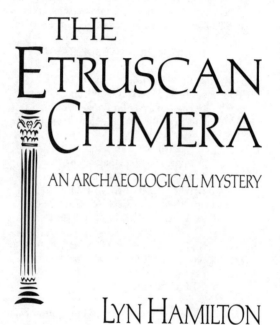

AN ARCHAEOLOGICAL MYSTERY

LYN HAMILTON

BERKLEY PRIME CRIME, NEW YORK

This is a work of fiction. Names, characters, places, and incidents
either are the product of the author's imagination or are used
fictitiously, and any resemblance to actual persons, living or dead,
business establishments, events, or locales is entirely coincidental.

THE ETRUSCAN CHIMERA

A Berkley Prime Crime Book
Published by The Berkley Publishing Group,
a division of Penguin Putnam Inc.,
375 Hudson Street, New York, New York 10014.

Visit our website at
www.penguinputnam.com

Copyright © 2002 by Lyn Hamilton.
Jacket art by Tony Greco & Associates.
Text design by Kristin del Rosario.

All rights reserved. This book, or parts thereof, may not be
reproduced in any form without permission.

First edition: May 2002

Library of Congress Cataloging-in-Publication Data

Hamilton, Lyn.
    The Etruscan chimera : an archaeological mystery / Lyn
Hamilton—1st ed.
        p.   cm.
    ISBN 0-425-18463-3 (alk. paper)
        1. Antique   dealers—Fiction.   2. Archaeological   thefts—
Fiction.   3. Etruscans—Antiquities—Fiction.   4. Antiquities—
Collection and preservation—Fiction.   5. Italy—Fiction.   I. Title.

PS3558.A44336 E87 2002
813'.54—dc21

                                                    2001058974

PRINTED IN THE UNITED STATES OF AMERICA

10   9   8   7   6   5   4   3   2   1

For Celia and Jan

PROLOGUE

THE MAN WIPED THE SWEAT FROM HIS *brow and sighed. By all the gods, it was hot here by the kilns. He could only dream of a place in the hills where the air sighed in the cypress trees, or of the sea, almost near enough to see here in Velc, from the highest treetop, but not so close that its breezes cooled his face.*

He had chosen the vessel with care. He'd tested several, feeling their weight and their balance as he made a pouring motion and running his fingers across the surface to feel for imperfections in the clay that would destroy his work in the final firing. This one was perfect.

He'd thought long and hard about the subject, too, how best to capture the heroic struggle, the fight to the death between two bold antagonists, how to place the black figures against the red background to best effect on the softly rounded surface.

The choice of subject had been easy, the one he'd heard first from some Greeks who toiled in his workshop, his son's favorite tale, the story the boy had asked to hear every night before sleep. He could recite it, almost without thinking, these many years later. About how Proteus, king of Argos, plotted against the brave and beautiful Bellerophon because Proteus's wife, the lovely but deceitful Antea, her advances spurned by the noble Bellerophon, had told the king terrible lies. How Proteus, enraged, had sent Bellerophon with sealed orders to Lycia, where the Lycian king, upon opening the tablet, had learned that Bellerophon was to die. How he had sent the young hero on an impossible mission to kill the dreaded chimera, a monstrous creature with the head of a lion, the hissing tail of a serpent, and a goat in between, who with every fiery breath scorched the Lycian soil.

How Bellerophon, guided by the gods and aided by winged Pegasus, had triumphed. Flying over the monster, he'd shot a bolt of lead down the throat of the terrible beast. Melted by the creature's own fiery breath, the molten metal seared her entrails. How in agony, the monster died.

The man picked up his tools, and after a moment's hesitation, touched the surface. This one he was not doing for the workshop, not for the wealthy families who snapped up his work for their loved ones' tombs. It would not be for sale. This would be his masterpiece.

PART I
THE GOAT

ONE

ROME

It struck me, as the cell door clanged shut, that the road to hell is paved, not so much with good intentions, nor even a single violent, murderous act, although that, too, occurred. No, the road is a series of small choices, almost imperceptible rents in the moral fabric, that, taken together, over time, like drops of water on stone, erode our sense of right and wrong.

In my case, the journey began with a beast that could not possibly have lived, much less taken human form, and a man some still say didn't exist. The creature was a chimera, the kind of monster that lurks in your subconscious, rising up to haunt your sleep. The man was Crawford Lake.

Lake was one of those people who, like former presidents and Hollywood legends, are saddled with a two-word descriptor permanently attached to their names. In Lake's case, those words were *reclusive billionaire.*

I will leave the explanation of the latter word to the financial analysts, who have of late enjoyed something of a feeding frenzy over the carcass of Lake's once-powerful empire, a rather hydralike conglomerate with tentacles insinuating themselves throughout the so-called global economy. I can, however, speak with some authority on the first word, and I can assure anyone who wants to know that *reclusive* doesn't half cut it when it comes to describing the man.

Indeed, when I first met him in his apartment in Rome, Crawford Lake had not been seen in public in at least fifteen years. The media was reduced to using photos taken, I swear, by the same people who purport to have spotted Bigfoot and the Loch Ness monster, grainy snaps of a shadowy figure disappearing in the distance, or, if not prepared to pay the price the paparazzi demanded for these pictures, suspect though they might be, to reproducing Lake's school yearbook portrait. Even in those youthful days, Lake exhibited a tendency to secrecy, but perhaps, being the sixties, the scraggly hair that pretty much hid his eyes was merely a fashion statement. Why he would want to live that way I didn't know at the time, but I suppose I assumed that anyone as rich as he was could be as antisocial as they pleased.

Still, from my perspective, he took it too far.

"Surely this isn't necessary," I told my escort, as he beckoned me to turn around so that he could tie a dark scarf across my eyes.

"No, I suppose not," he said, smiling not at me but at his own reflection in the car mirror. He was an attractive young man, and he knew it, with perfect teeth, dark skin and eyes, dressed in a rumpled linen suit and shirt, with a flash of gold chain at his chest, one of those young Italian men who find themselves rather fetching and think the women of the world should, too. "But then," he added, placing the cloth over my eyes, "if you knew where my employer lives, I'd have to kill you."

I wasn't entirely sure he was kidding. The scarf securely in place, he tapped the glass between us, and the limousine pulled away. My hotel was on a side street off the top of the Spanish Steps, and I tried to figure out—what else was there for me to do, sitting there blindfolded?—where we were going. I gave up, however, after several turns and stops and starts in the traffic. After about ten minutes or so by my estimation, the car stopped, and I felt myself being led up a couple of steps, then into an elevator that rumbled slowly upward, then just a few more steps and, as a door closed behind me, the blindfold was removed.

I was standing in a room that almost defied description, filled as it was with so much to look at. Heavy, dark green curtains were drawn across the large windows and securely fastened in a way that prevented me from seeing outside and thereby gaining some clue as to where I was but still allowed a bright shaft of sunshine into the room near the top of the window. There was a jumble of furniture, most of it ornate but rather worn, and almost every inch of the place, walls, tables, even the floor, was covered with objets d'art. The most striking feature was two large frescoes, faded in spots, probably nineteenth-century, depicting bucolic Italian scenes. There were gold cupids, dozens of them, all over the place, and piles of old books on the floor and on every table, lovely old ones with leather covers and gold titles embossed on the spines. On top of some of these piles rested small sculptures, most of them bronze. A coffee table was awash in vases—urns in black and red, possibly Greek, but also perhaps Etruscan, and several in a burnished black material called bucchero—and a couple of very nice marble busts of eminent Roman citizens.

It was almost as good as a museum. In just one glance I could see Greek, Roman, and Etruscan objects, Meissen porcelain figures, what looked to be a stone head from Cambodia, several oil paintings on the few inches of wall not covered with frescoes, baroque mirrors, a wooden horse, probably late eighteenth-century, and not one, not two, but three chandeliers, not in Murano glass, as one might expect in this part of the world, but rather crystal, probably eighteenth-century Bohemian.

Two things surprised me about the room. First was that there was just way too much of it. And I'm not a neatness freak. As anyone who has seen either my antique shop or my house can tell you, *less is more* is hardly my decorating credo. I like a certain amount of clutter, different objects and styles playing off each other. This, however, was just over the top, the marriage of a compulsive collector with a bottomless pot of cash.

Secondly, most of it was what people in my line of business rather condescendingly call *stuff*, which is to say that there were no really exceptional—by which we normally mean breathtakingly expensive—pieces.

There was a painting over the mantelpiece that was clearly a copy—the original was well-known and in an art museum. The other pieces were good, but there were few that would have cost him much over $25,000, not one that would have cost him over $75,000. I'd have been happy to sell Lake just about anything in the room, but there was nothing there that would indicate the kind of financial resources a man like Lake would have, and not the collector that I knew Lake to be. He regularly made the news in collector's magazines and was clearly prepared to pay millions if he had to for something he wanted. None of it was in evidence here.

As I struggled to take it all in, a handsome man of about fifty, with a nice head of dark hair sprinkled with gray and the kind of perfect tan that makes you think tanning beds or extended holidays on a private yacht briskly entered the room. I searched in vain for vestiges of the rather retiring young man of the yearbook photo. Lake's self-confidence had evidently soared in the intervening thirty years or so. No doubt acquiring a net worth of six billion dollars will do that for you. He also looked young for a man who'd come of age in the sixties, but I put that down to the fact that he had the resources to take good care of himself.

"Lara McClintoch," he said, extending his hand. He was standing in the shaft of sunlight, which gave a kind of halolike quality to him, which I found amusing. "I'm Crawford Lake. Thank you for coming. I apologize for all the drama and for keeping you waiting. I hope you will forgive me. Unfortunately, I find such secrecy necessary. I was attending to some business when you arrived, and given I am so rarely here in

Rome, I needed to get it done. Now, tea? Or perhaps something stronger?"

"Tea would be lovely," I replied, thinking that the fact that Lake used the apartment so infrequently explained both the art and the rather airless quality the place had. He rang a bell, and a maid appeared instantly, as if she'd been hovering in the hall, awaiting a summons.

"Tea, please, Anna," he said. "And some of that lovely lemon cake of yours."

"Right away, Mr. Lake," the woman said, inclining her head slightly, as if bowing to lesser royalty.

"Well, what do you think?" he said, waving his arm around the room. "Do you see anything you like?"

"The alabaster vases are exquisite," I said carefully.

"Fourteenth century," he said. "Not very old, but yes, lovely, aren't they? What do you think of the paintings?"

"The frescoes are superb," I said. "I have been admiring the oil over the mantelpiece," I added, choosing my words carefully. "I'm wondering where I've seen the original. The Louvre, perhaps?" It had surprised me, indeed, to see what was obviously a copy among all this exceptional art, and I wanted Lake to know I knew a copy when I saw it.

He frowned. "This is the original," he said. "But you are correct in one respect. The copy is in the Louvre."

"Oh," was the best I could muster. To my relief, tea arrived in a stunning silver tea service and, as promised, slices of lemon cake on a Sevres porcelain plate.

We engaged in small talk for awhile, he pointing out a number of objects in the room and telling me how he'd acquired them, while I made appreciative sounds.

I knew that Lake was South African originally, but his accent was what I think is called mid-Atlantic, a slightly British, slightly American sound that he must have worked hard to acquire. Everything about him was very polished, in fact, which came as something of a relief, given my sleepless hours of the night before when I'd imagined a cross between a Howard Hughes–type recluse, with long hair and toenails, and a pathologically shy computer nerd of some kind.

"Now to business," he said at last, struggling for a moment to find an empty place on which to set down his teacup. "No doubt you're wondering why I asked you here."

I nodded. I was delighted to be invited, to be sure, but perplexed as to why.

"I need you to purchase something for me," he said. "A work of art. Very old. From someone in France. You'll get a commission, of course, and I'll cover all your expenses. Will you do it?"

"I'm flattered to be asked," I said cautiously. "But if you will forgive me for being so blunt, why me? Why not send a member of your staff?"

"They don't know antiquities," he said with a dismissive wave. "I'm told you do."

"Mondragon, then," I said, referring to a well-known art dealer. "He often buys for you, does he not? And he knows antiquities rather well."

Lake looked impatient. "You will no doubt understand that when my name is associated with an important purchase, the price invariably rises," he said slowly. "Way beyond its true value."

"The Apollo," I said.

"The Apollo," he agreed. "Aplu or Apulu to the

Etruscans. Regrettably, yes. I see you do your homework, Ms. McClintoch."

I did my homework, all right, mildly patronizing
though his comment might be. Not that research on
Lake was difficult to do. His financial escapades were
regularly featured in just about any newspaper you'd
care to mention, as were some rather aggressive art
purchases. There was no question he was very rich.
But he couldn't buy everything. He'd gone after a
2,300-year-old statue of Apollo, a gorgeous piece of
work, Etruscan as he'd indicated, and he'd lost to a
Texas collector who probably didn't have Lake's resources but who had proved adept at outflanking him
on this particular acquisition. Before that, Lake had
been on just about every art magazine's one hundred
top collectors list on an annual basis. Post-Apollo,
however, he seemed to pretty much have abandoned
the field to others.

"It wasn't worth half what Mariani paid for it," Lake
said, referring to the proud owner of the Apollo. "I still
have regrets. Having said that, you will understand, I
think, that I did not reach this rather enviable financial
position by paying more than anything is worth, even
for something as wonderful as that. I need someone
who will not be linked to me in any way to purchase
the object I wish."

"Which is?"

"We'll discuss that in a moment."

"You've explained why you want to deal with someone new, but not, I think, why you chose me."

He shrugged ever so slightly. "I do my research.
You've just demonstrated you do yours. I'm told
you're honest, know your stuff, and that you're per-

sistent, if not stubborn. I admire persistence. It is a quality we may share. Furthermore—I hope I do not offend you in saying this—your business is not well-known internationally. McClintoch & Swain is not"— he hesitated—"the kind of firm with which I would normally do business."

I could hardly disagree, being reasonably certain that McClintoch & Swain, the shop I co-own with my ex-husband Clive Swain, was pretty much unknown beyond a two-block radius of the store, let alone internationally.

"Do you know what a chimera is?" he asked abruptly.

"A mythological creature, isn't it? Part lion, part snake, part something else."

"Goat." He nodded.

"Goat," I agreed.

"You do not disappoint me, Ms. McClintoch," Lake said. "You could have said it was a term used by scientists for any hybrid, plant or animal, or you could have said it was a name for a creature that changes its appearance at will. But you picked the right one, as far as I'm concerned. Now, do you know the Chimera of Arezzo?"

"The bronze chimera in the archaeological museum in Florence, you mean? The one found in Arezzo in Tuscany?"

"Yes," he said, reaching for a large envelope on the table beside him and then placing a photograph in front of me. "Lovely, isn't it? Bronze, late fifth or early fourth century B.C. One of the truly great pieces of Etruscan art. We owe its discovery to Cosimo de Medici. He rather fancied himself as an archaeologist. It is said that he cleaned the finds himself, a painstaking bit of work. He found the chimera in 1553, and also the Arringatore, the Orator, in 1566, both Etruscan. I expect he undertook the work because he loved it. But it also suited his political aspirations. His successor was declared dux magnus Etruscus, great Etruscan leader, did you know that? Not enough that Cosimo was declared grand duke of Tuscany in 1569. Silly really, the dux magnus Etruscus business, given that the Etruscans had been defeated by the Romans more than two thousand years earlier, but I suppose it speaks to the power the glorious past has over us. Magnificent work of art, is it not? Look at the power in the head and haunches of the lion, the menace in the serpent tail, and the intractable nature of the goat, so evident."

No question about it, the Chimera of Arezzo was indeed a showpiece of Etruscan bronze work. It was a beast with the head and haunches of a lion, a second head of a goat, and a tail ending in a serpent's head that curved around and looked about to bite the goat.

Interesting, though, that Lake was going on about Cosimo de Medici. Like the Medici family, Lake had made his fortune in banking—conventional financial services at first, but then moving aggressively and early into Internet banking—and he shared with Cosimo both aspirations to empire and a rather ruthless way of dealing with his adversaries. Where Cosimo had expelled all his rivals from his city of Florence and had annexed the neighboring city of Siena, sending his enemies to be beheaded or imprisoned in terrible dungeons, Lake had initiated and successfully completed a couple of really hostile takeovers of rival companies. Lake, allegedly a fan of all things Italian, had called his company Marzocco, after the heraldic lion of Florence. It is said that the defeated enemies of that city were once required to kiss the rear end of a statue of the animal, and figuratively speaking, that was pretty much what anybody who came in conflict with Lake eventually had to do.

On a more positive note, both Lake and de Medici, although separated by almost five hundred years, were significant patrons of the arts. Still, it was difficult to see where this conversation about art and empire was going. There was no way the Arezzo Chimera was up for sale, and I sincerely hoped he wasn't thinking I'd break into the archaeological museum in Florence to get it for him.

"It's so lifelike, isn't it?" he mused. "Even if it could never really exist. I mean, look at it. Doesn't it seem to be about to strike at something, a fight to the death?"

"Something or someone," I agreed. "Bellerophon, wasn't it, the hero who killed the chimera?"

"Brava," he said. "Again, you do live up to your advance billing, Ms. McClintoch. Bellerophon, indeed. Homer's *Iliad*, book six. The creature, a horrifying beast that breathed fire, was said to live in Lycia in Asia Minor, and yes, she—have you noticed how many of the monsters of ancient mythology were female?—was killed at last by the hero, Bellerophon. A Persian Saint George in some respects. I suppose the chimera could be an early version of a dragon myth. Do you recall how Bellerophon managed this rather daunting task his enemies had set for him?"

"Didn't he fly over the creature on a winged horse and shoot an arrow with a plug of some kind on it that was melted by the chimera's breath? Something like that, anyway."

"That's correct. I see you know your mythology as well as your antiquities. Bellerophon was given the winged horse Pegasus by his father Poseidon, god of the sea, and flew over the chimera. He put a plug of lead on the tip of his arrow and shot it down her throat. It melted and seared the entrails of the chimera, killing her. She would have died in agony. Rather ingenious, wouldn't you say?"

"No doubt," I replied. There was something about his tone that bothered me, the rather gleeful spirit in which he recounted the tale, and his emphasis on the fact that the chimera was a she. Could it be that the billionaire had a misogynistic streak? "Look, this is all very interesting, Mr. Lake, but I still don't know what you want from me."

"Why, Bellerophon, of course," he said to me, placing a second photo in front of me. It showed a rearing winged horse with a man astride it, about to shoot an arrow. The photo was not as clear as the first, more of the home rather than the professional variety, but I could see it was an impressive piece of sculpture. Lake moved the two photos together, and it did, indeed, look as if the Arezzo Chimera was snarling up at the rearing horse and rider.

"What about the dimensions?" I said. "I can't tell from these photographs."

"Perfect," he replied. "The Arezzo Chimera is only about thirty-two inches high, rather small for a monumental sculpture, really. The Bellerophon is about six and a half feet. Towers over her."

"I don't recall any indication that there was a Bellerophon statue with the Chimera," I said rather dubiously, but I could feel myself getting excited.

"Ah, now this is where it gets interesting," Lake said. "I searched the city archives of Arezzo for that time period, the 1550s," he said, then paused abruptly as if he'd misspoken himself. "Rather, to be more accurate, I should say I had the archives searched for me. There is a reference to a large bronze like the Chimera being discovered outside the city gates on November 15, 1553, along with several smaller bronzes. There's a later notation to the effect that the tail was missing.

"Giorgio Vasari—Cosimo de Medici was his patron, and Vasari recorded many of his exploits—writing in 1568, says it was found in 1554, a year later than the archival records. He also mentions the missing tail. Some say Benvenuto Cellini replaced the tail—Cellini was an artist supported by de Medici—but I doubt that's true. In any event, the Chimera is not my interest. The Bellerophon is. I believe there are enough indications that there was more than one large bronze found in Arezzo, and given the legend and this photo, I think there's a good chance I've located it. I want this one, Ms. McClintoch, and I want you to get it for me. Are you up to the challenge?"

"Well, I . . . what would you want to do with it once you had it, Mr. Lake?" I asked.

"What would I do with it? Oh, I see what you mean. My intention is to turn it over to the museum in Florence. The Chimera, while magnificent, is not all that impressive by itself, I'm sure you'll agree. A question of scale, really. But with Bellerophon, the two pieces as they were meant to be will be truly astounding. They deserve to be together."

"That's a very generous gesture, Mr. Lake," I said. It was not unheard of, in Lake's case. I did recall he'd donated some very fine antiquities to various museums over the years, but still, I was on my guard.

"Yes and no," he said, with a rather disarming smile. "To be honest, I am launching a new high-tech fund here in Europe, and I want to make a positive impression, something that will make people sit up and notice, and then, of course, buy in. I think finding the Bellerophon and then donating it to the archaeological museum might do that for me. Wealthy philanthropist spends ten years tracking down missing Bellerophon, buys masterpiece for Italy, et cetera, et cetera. Then a couple of days later I launch the fund. Not entirely unselfish, of course, but still worth doing, I hope you agree." He spoke with the authority of someone who expects everyone to agree with him, and I found, somewhat to my surprise, that I did. Did it matter what motivated him? The important thing was that the Bellerophon be reunited with the Chimera and that everyone have an opportunity to appreciate them.

"I ask you again. Are you up to the challenge?" he said. "I'll pay you and pay you well. You'll get a commission on the purchase—we can discuss how much—and I will cover all your expenses. I have taken the liberty of opening a Swiss bank account for you, electronic, and my bank, of course, and if you agree, then ten thousand U.S. dollars will be deposited in it to defray expenses. Now," he said, naming a commission rate, "would that be worth your time?"

I've never actually figured out what my time is worth, believing that dividing the rather paltry profit McClintoch & Swain turns from time to time by the number of hours I put into the business would just depress me. However, while I prefer not to discuss money in general, and my commission in particular, I will say that there was no question that the sum would be more than my time would normally fetch.

Still, I hesitated, and he, poor man, took that to mean the amount wasn't enough. "If you can keep the selling price under two million, I'll up your commission another percentage point. Under a million and a half, one more."

"I'm sure that will be satisfactory, Mr. Lake," I replied in as neutral a tone as I could muster. My heart soared like a hawk, actually. Even if no one ever knew that I had been Lake's purchaser, this would be my entrée into a level of the art world I'd never thought I'd see. And for a good cause, too: uniting the Chimera with the missing hero.

"Good," he said, handing me a piece of paper. "Anything else?"

"What if I can't get the Bellerophon, for whatever reason?"

"I reward success, not failure, Ms. McClintoch. However, I do try to be fair. The ten thousand I will deposit in your account should more than cover your out-of-pocket expenses, and I will consider it nonrefundable, no matter how much or how little of it you spend. Is that satisfactory?" I nodded.

"Then, here is the account number and password. I suggest you memorize both and throw away the paper."

I looked at it. The bank was Marzocco Financial Online, and the account number was l4M24S—one for the money and two for the show. The password was easy, too. It was Chimera. I tore up the piece of paper and handed the scraps back to Lake. "Got it," I said. "Now, who has the Bellerophon?"

"I believe, on fairly good authority," he said, "that it's in the hands of a collector in France by the name of Robert Godard. I've never met the man, but I think he's had it for a few years now. It may even have been in his family for a generation or two. I'm not sure Godard knows what he's got, the missing half of the Arezzo bronzes, I mean. I'm sure he knows it's good. He's a collector, after all, but he may not have put two and two together, as it were. Probably thinks he has a rather unusual equestrian statue. I'd like it to stay that way. It will keep the price down."

I nodded. "I'm not entirely sure myself that the two pieces go together," Lake went on, "but I believe they do, and when we see them side by side, I think it will be clear they do."

"You say Godard has had the bronze for a long time. What makes you think he'll sell it now?"

"My sources tell me he's ready to sell. Financial hardship, is, I think, the term that comes immediately to mind." He must have seen something in my face. "I've heard you have a somewhat suspicious nature," he said.

Who, I wondered, *had he been talking to about me?* I wouldn't characterize myself as suspicious, just cautiously skeptical, that's all, what I'd call a healthy attitude in a business that occasionally appeals to people with baser motives and where the phrase *caveat emptor,* buyer beware, is a useful phrase to remember. What I'm trying to say is that fakes abound in the antique trade. I like to think I haven't been had very often.

"I had nothing to do with his current situation, I assure you," Lake said. "He brought it on himself. I merely hope to profit from it. Godard is a collector who doesn't know when to stop. I do." He looked about the room for a moment, at the jumble of art and artifacts, and then permitted himself a small laugh. "Although I'll grant you this may not be apparent at first glance." I laughed, too. I rather liked the man.

"Do you know where I can find him?"

"The best way to contact him is through a dealer, a freelance type—he doesn't have a retail operation—by the name of Yves Boucher. You can get in touch with Boucher in Paris. Antonio will give you his number," he added. I gathered Antonio was the rather pretty young man who'd accompanied me to the house. "I suggest you go to Paris right away, as early as tomorrow morning if possible. Antonio will give you some cash to cover your expenses until the money is transferred. It will be there this evening. You can check anytime tomorrow. Antonio will also give you a phone number where he can be reached. He'll be our go-between. When you've gotten in touch with Boucher and then Godard, and have some idea of the price range, you can call Antonio. Once we've agreed on the price, I'll transfer the money to your account. You understand I don't want my name associated with this in any way, do you not?"

"I do," I replied. "You have my word that your name will never be mentioned."

"Thank you," he said. "And you have mine in this matter." I'd heard that Lake was one of those people who closed multimillion-dollar deals on the strength of a handshake. I decided if it was good enough for him, it was good enough for me. Heaven knows I'd had occasion to discover from time to time how worthless signed contracts could be.

"You'll have to arrange the bank transfers," he went on. "It will all be in your name. But I'll ensure the money is there. Don't worry about that. You'll probably have to give them a deposit on it. Just let Antonio know. Now I must get back to work, although this is much more interesting, and I'm afraid you will have to submit to the rather theatrical device of the blindfold again. I do apologize for it," he said, extending his hand and smiling rather engagingly. "Anna will see you to the door."

"Do you mind if I use the facilities before I go?" I said, trying to look embarrassed. "All that tea . . ."

"But of course," he said. "How thoughtless of me. Anna will show you the way."

He rang for the maid. "I will get it, by the way," he said, as we awaited Anna's arrival.

"The Bellerophon? Of course you will," I said.

"The Bellerophon, yes. But I meant the Apollo. Mariani finds himself in some financial difficulties. I confess this time I had a hand in some of them. He'll have to sell it any day now, at much less than he paid for it, and rather closer to what it's worth. It's a matter of time. I'll be there." The tone was mild, but there was no doubt in my mind that there was a ruthless mind behind it. I found myself feeling a little sorry for Mariani, and, for the first time, more than a little apprehensive about my own dealings with Lake. I didn't think he'd brook failure on my part. It also occurred

to me that at least where Etruscan statuary was concerned, Lake, like Cosimo de Medici before him, rather
aspired to the title of dux magnus Etruscus himself.

The feeling lasted for only a moment, however. "It's
been a pleasure, Ms. McClintoch," he said. "I'm glad
we'll be doing business together." He gave me another
lovely smile, and despite my misgivings, for a fleeting
second or two, I found myself hoping our relationship
would be a long and mutually rewarding one. He nodded in my general direction, then disappeared down the
hall.

Anna not only accompanied me along a rather
gloomy hallway, the doors on either of it shut tight
against prying eyes like mine, but also waited outside
the door. The window was frosted glass on the bottom,
but not on the top, and as quickly and quietly as I
could, I stood on the toilet seat and peered out. I found
myself looking out on to a rather spectacular rooftop
garden, with cascading flowers and shrubs, a small table with two chairs, and off in one corner, the dominant
feature, a statue of Michelangelo's David, life size. I
smiled to myself. I was sure if I asked Lake about it—
which I couldn't, of course, given my subterfuge—
he'd tell me the David in the Accademia in Florence
was the copy, the one on his roof the genuine article.
Craning my neck, I could see down the street a little
to some café umbrellas and the letters FECIT on the
edge of a high building. I was almost certain I pretty
much knew where I was.

I stepped down carefully, flushed the toilet and ran
the water for Anna's benefit, then opened the door. It
was time to check out of my hotel and get myself to
Paris to pick up the trail of Bellerophon.

TWO

PARIS

I AM NOT A DISHONEST PERSON, NOR, IN spite of later events that might lead one to think otherwise, am I a fool. I've been in this business long enough to know that one has to be very careful when dealing in antiquities. Suspicious by nature of opportunities that look too good to be true, I put in a call to customs authorities in both France and Italy first thing the next morning, and then went on-line to check the various databases of stolen art. There were no reports of a missing bronze statue of Bellerophon nor anything remotely resembling it that I could find. I then did another on-line search of some of the major auction houses. Still nothing. Satisfied, I checked my new bank account, pretty much the best one I'd ever had. True to his word, Lake had seen to it that $10,000 was deposited in it.

I wasn't surprised. A great deal had been said about Lake's ruthlessness and drive, his obvious need to succeed at whatever he did. But I had never heard him described as disreputable in any way. If anything, even his rivals would grudgingly admit to his integrity.

Checks made to my satisfaction, I called Clive and told him I'd acquired the farm furniture and pottery from Tuscany we needed for the cottage we were doing north of Toronto, and that I was taking a short detour to Paris to do a sweep of the flea markets for old linens and such.

I toyed with the idea of telling Clive the truth, that we had an assignment from none other than Crawford Lake himself, but I'd given my word on it, and I was reasonably sure Lake would not entirely approve of taking Clive into my confidence. For all his faults, which I'm happy to tell anyone about any time they ask and sometimes even when they don't, it has to be said that Clive is a tireless promoter of our business. He also is a name-dropper of some distinction, believing as he does that the more famous our clients, the more famous we, too, will be. I didn't think he'd be able to contain himself if he knew that we now had a billionaire on our roster of customers.

"Some guy called," Clive said. "Antonio somebody or other. I think he works for D'Amato," he added, referring to our Italian shipper. "They seemed to have misplaced the name of your hotel in Rome, so I gave it to him."

So that was how Lake had tracked me down. I'd been wondering, although not that much. I figured anyone with the resources at his disposal that Lake had could do just about anything he put his mind to. I hadn't gone to Italy to see him; quite the contrary, in fact. I'd been on an annual buying trip in Europe to pick up some furniture for the store: Tuscany was particularly hot right then—you know, rather worn wood furniture, tile floors, roughly finished ocher-colored walls, diaphanous curtains blowing in the breeze, that sort of thing—and we'd been asked to furnish a couple of places, one in the country, one in town, in Tuscan style. It looks easy, but it's not. It requires attention to detail and some really good pieces to pull it all off. Clive is the designer, I'm the antiques expert. He comes up with the ideas, and I go and find whatever it takes to make it happen. In many ways, we make an odd—I'd say any divorced couple in business together is by definition odd—but reasonably effective team. In addition to the Tuscan houses, I also had a buyer who was always interested in whatever Italian antiques I could find. Like Lake, he was an avowed collector of almost anything Italian, most particularly eighteenth-century Venetian glass. So I'd gone to Venice, swung through Florence and Siena, and ended up in Rome.

"Did he get hold of you all right?" Clive asked.

"Yes," I replied. "Everything's taken care of."

"Good," he said. "Well, have some fun in Paris while you're there. Sit in the sun at some Left Bank café, watch the world go by for awhile. Take a week, why don't you? We can afford it."

"You haven't been rearranging the store again in my absence, have you?" I said suspiciously. Usually Clive wants me to hustle right back and help him with the shop.

"I have not," he said, sounding hurt. "You shouldn't always think the worst of me, Lara. I just noticed you've been looking tired lately. Alex and I can manage here for a few more days," he added, referring to Alex Stewart, my friend and neighbor who helps out in the shop. At least with Alex there, I could relax, knowing he wouldn't let Clive do anything too awful. And, as Clive pointed out, whether he knew it or not, we could afford it, all right. Lake's advance would more than cover my time in Paris, and if I could get the Bellerophon, I'd be coming home with a new Internet bank account and lots of cash.

"That's nice of you, Clive," I said in a conciliatory tone. "I think I'll take you up on it. I'll let you know where I'm staying in case you think of something else we might need from Paris while I'm there."

As Lake had pointed out, I like to do my homework. I consider myself first and foremost a furniture expert, although in the business I'm in, I need to know something about a lot of things. More than anything else, I rely on years of experience and the kind of sixth sense one acquires along the way about what's good and what's not. I couldn't say I was an expert in Etruscan antiquities, but I did know where and what to look for. First I went to the Villa Giulia in Rome, one of the premier Etruscan collections, and had a really good look at what was there. Along the way, I picked up a pile of recommended books on the subject, a couple on Etruscan art, another on the Etruscans themselves, an archaeological study, and then, just for fun, D. H. Lawrence's *Etruscan Places*, some essays on travel the author undertook in the 1920s to Etruscan sites.

What I found interesting was how much, yet how little, we know about the Etruscans, or the people we have come to know as Etruscans. It is unlikely they ever referred to themselves that way. That name came from the Romans, who referred to their neighbors, occasional allies, and in the end, intractable enemies, as Tusci or Etrusci. The Greeks called them Tyrrhenoi, after which the Tyrrhenian Sea is named. The Etruscans called themselves Rasenna, or Rasna.

Their language, a rather unusual one that, unlike almost all other European languages, did not have Indo-European roots, has been deciphered to a large extent, but when it comes right down to it, there is very little to read, other than inscriptions on tombs and such. They may have had, indeed must surely have had, a rich body of literature, but it is lost to us, so what we know about them comes from archaeology or the writing of others: Greeks and Romans for example, whose own particular biases are reflected in their accounts. They also must have had a complex ritual and religious life, because we know that long after the Etruscan cities came under the domination of Rome, Roman citizens were still calling upon Etruscan haruspices, diviners, to aid them in important deliberations and decisions. The number and elaborate nature of their tombs indicate that there was a social structure, including a wealthy elite, but that also they believed in an afterlife. What exactly they believed, however, is, to a large extent, shrouded in the mists of time.

What we do know is that people who shared a common language, customs, and beliefs, dominated a large part of central Italy, what is now Tuscany—the word itself speaks to its Etruscan roots—part of Umbria and northern Lazio near Rome between about 700 B.C.E. until their defeat and assimilation by the Romans in the third century B.C.E. Their territory was essentially bounded by the Tiber River on the south and east, and the Arno to the north. To the west was the Tyrrhenian Sea. They lived in cities and used rich metal deposits along the Tyrrhenian shore to develop extensive trade by land and sea. In time, a loose federation of twelve cities, the Dodecapolis, grew up. The ruling elite of these cities, city states, really, met annually at a place called Volsinii to elect a leader.

During their heyday, before the birth of the Roman republic, there were Etruscan kings of Rome—the Tarquins—who, between 616 and 509 B.C.E., were instrumental in building the city that would ultimately defeat them. The last king of Rome was Tarquinius the Proud, who was expelled from Rome in 509 B.C.E. From that time on, Rome and the Etruscans were enemies, fighting over every inch of ground.

In the end, the Etruscan federation could not hold against the might of Rome. For whatever reason, the cities did not band together to protect themselves, and one by one, they fell. Their cities were abandoned, or fell into ruin, or were simply replaced by others, until they were reborn, in a different form, as medieval cities, some of the loveliest in Italy: Orvieto, Chiusi, Cortona, Volterra, Arezzo, and Perugia among them.

As mysterious as these people may have been, I noticed that many had opinions on them. Indeed, I would say that the Etruscans presented a blank slate, in a way, on which later people found a convenient resting place for their own hopes, beliefs, and desires. Cosimo de Medici was hardly the first to use people's rather vague notions about the Etruscans for his own purposes. A Dominican friar who went by the name of Annius of Viterbo, determined, in the fifteenth century, that the

Etruscans, a noble and peace-loving people, according to him, had helped Noah repopulate the earth after the Flood. To prove his point, he argued that their language was a version of Aramaic. Despite his rather outlandish views, Annius's theories may have helped save some Etruscan antiquities from destruction by the church as pagan symbols. The Etruscans could have used Annius a century later, when something like six tons of Etruscan bronzes were melted down to adorn a church in Rome.

Lawrence, of *Lady Chatterley's Lover* fame, also thought the Etruscans were his kind of people, in touch with nature and their natural selves. He saw phallic symbols everywhere on his visits to Etruscan sites and wrote glowingly of what he saw to be their refreshingly natural philosophy. On the other hand, the philosopher Nietzsche, who arguably knew something about angst, called them gloomy—*schwermutigen*—although what made him think that was not clear. The art critic Berensen dismissed all Etruscan art as being non-Greek and therefore unworthy, even though, if I'd interpreted what I'd read correctly, Greeks living in Italy had been responsible for some of it, and some of the art prized as Greek and Roman had later been revealed to be Etruscan. By the end of my reading, it was pretty clear to me that views expressed about the Etruscans said more about the holder of those opinions than about the Etruscans themselves.

My last stop in Italy was Florence, for a look at the famous Chimera of Arezzo itself, now housed in its own room in the archaeological museum. Lake was right. As public sculpture, it was not particularly impressive. At only about thirty inches or so in height, it needed the Bellerophon to make it into something you could picture sitting in front of a temple, for example, or in a public square. But it was a magnificent piece of art. Using the lost wax method of manufacturing, the artist had managed to show the muscles beneath the surface, the ribs through the skin. The animal had already been wounded, and you could even see the blood spurting from the wound in its haunches. But still it—she—fought on, ferocious in combat, the snake head swaying, the goat's head rearing up, and the lion, its mane erect, roaring in rage. The sculptor had cut an inscription into the wax model before the bronze one was formed. The inscription on one of the front legs read, according to the notes I had, *tinscvil*, making it a gift to Tinia, the Etruscan Zeus. I had seen what I needed to see. I called Boucher and arranged to meet him late the afternoon of my arrival, two days after my meeting with Lake, at the Café de Flore.

I booked myself into a lovely Left Bank hotel, rather nicer than the place I usually stay, but there was all that glorious expense money in the bank, and I did, after all, have to keep up appearances. They couldn't know Lake was my buyer, but they needed to know I could afford to move in these social circles. My check of the auction house catalogues told me I wasn't going to get the Bellerophon for less than a few million dollars, and that only if I got lucky. Still, Lake clearly knew he was going to have to pay big for it, and even if I couldn't get it for the lowest sum he mentioned and get the extra commission, I was going to do quite nicely, thank you.

Yves Boucher turned out to be a tall, thin man with short salt-and-pepper hair, nice cheekbones, and the

requisite arty appearance: black jeans and boots, a collarless white and black striped shirt, and a black leather
vest. He was seated at a table on the sidewalk, reading
a newspaper, a glass of Pernod in front of him, when
I arrived. I ordered a Kir Royale, for the equivalent of
about twelve dollars, a ridiculous extravagance, but I
was already enjoying being in Crawford Lake's employ.

I wasn't quite sure what to think of Boucher at first.
Not that I could point to anything specific that bothered
me. He was pleasant enough, rather courtly and old
world, really. He had a habit of placing his right hand
against his chest, palm flat, fingers splayed, when he
spoke to you, as if expressing heartfelt sincerity and
conviction with every word. He was soft spoken, and
from time to time he'd have to lean forward to speak
to me, as the roar of the traffic on Boulevard St. Germain threatened to drown out his words.

"Robert Godard," he said, reflectively. "Unusual
man. Not easy to deal with, you'll understand. Rather
anal, you know. Hates to part with anything. Despite
the fact he needs the money, it will be difficult to get
him to sell the equestrian bronze. I believe he will, but
only if he likes you."

I had not realized this was a personality contest, although I understood the situation. Collectors tend to be
rather possessive people, some obsessively so, and if
they need to part with one of their treasures, they usually like to sell it to someone they feel appreciates what
they have.

"Where can I find him?" I asked.

"Good question," he said. "He moves around quite
a bit and can be a little cagey about where he is at any

point in time. I have a cell phone number where I can contact him. I'll set up a meeting for you." By this, Boucher meant he wanted in on the deal. Well, there was money to spare.

"And your terms?" I asked.

"Oh," he said with a wave. "I don't charge very much for making contact. We'll talk about that later."

"I'd prefer to talk about that now," I said. "My client wants the bronze but doesn't have unlimited funds." A slight fib, but I suppose I could argue that even billionaires have their financial limitations.

"One percent of the selling price," he said. Assuming the Bellerophon sold for a couple of million, that was a $20,000 phone call he was going to make, but I didn't know how to get in touch with Godard any other way.

"And if the deal doesn't happen, despite the introduction?"

"A flat fee. Five thousand."

"Okay," I said reluctantly, hoping Lake wouldn't consider Boucher part of my expenses but would reimburse him directly. Boucher let his hand leave its apparently permanent position on his chest to briefly shake my hand.

"Canadian, is he?" Boucher went on, signaling the waiter to bring us another round.

"Who?" I said.

"Your client," he said.

"He moves around," I said.

"What business is he in?"

"E-commerce," I said. I figured that didn't narrow the field down much.

"Not one of those revolting sixteen-year-olds who've

made millions setting up Internet companies in their parents' basements, I hope," he said. "So brash. So American, really. I suppose it fits though. The kid probably wants to put a bronze statue of a horse on the front lawn. I wonder if his mother will permit it." He looked at me closely to see my reaction.

I laughed noncommittally. Both of us were playing this pretty close to the vest. "So, when do you think I'll get to meet Godard?"

"I'll call him this evening," he said. "And get in touch with you at your hotel as soon as I've made contact. I assume you want to meet him as soon as possible?"

"I do," I said.

"Fine. I'll be in touch. Is your schedule relatively free?"

"Relatively," I said. "I have some other acquisitions I need to make when I'm here, but I'll do my best to accommodate M. Godard's schedule." I wasn't about to let Boucher think this was my only reason to be in Paris or the biggest transaction I'd ever made.

"Good. I'll set something up with him and let you know when and where," Boucher said. He signaled for the bill. I reached for my handbag. "Allow me," he said, as the bill arrived. "You're a guest in Paris."

He then made a big show of patting various pockets and looking embarrassed. "My wallet," he said at last. "I must have forgotten it. How embarrassing!"

"It's my pleasure," I said, reaching for the bill. I didn't believe him for a moment. The bill was about fifty dollars for four drinks. Thank heaven for Crawford Lake. Having said that, there was a bright side to it. If Boucher was broke, then he'd certainly want to see that I got to meet Robert Godard.

"I'll get the next one," he said, handing me his business card. I doubted that very much. The card was pretty simple, just his name and a phone number. Apparently he, Lake, and Godard all shared an aversion to having anyone know where they lived. I gave him my card, which is rather more fulsome, writing my hotel number on the back.

"I'll be in touch," he said. "If you're not at your hotel, I'll leave a message."

We shook hands again, and Boucher disappeared into the crowd.

I treated myself to a nice dinner at a tiny restaurant on the Isle St. Louis, compliments once again of Crawford Lake. I was back in my hotel room when the phone rang.

"Yves Boucher," the voice said. "I've been in touch with Godard. He's waffling, as I expected, on the bronze. Says he wants to think about it for a day or two. Don't worry, he'll come around. Just stay in town, and I'll be back in touch in the next day or so."

It was disappointing, to be sure, but not the worst thing that had happened to me, having to cool my heels for a day or two in Paris. I wondered if my partner, Rob Luczka, could get a decent last-minute fare and a few days off to meet me. But then, did it matter how much it cost? I needed to get used to having money for a change. Rob and I never had anything remotely like a romantic weekend in Paris. Maybe it was time we did. I dialed his number.

Rob Luczka is a sergeant in the Royal Canadian Mounted Police. We've been friends for a number of years now, and recently got a little closer. I don't know how to characterize our relationship, nor even what to call him. My partner? Sort of. My spouse? Not really. Would we ever get to the spouse stage? I have no idea. I value his friendship more than I can say. I also enjoy his company a very great deal. But move in together? I don't know about that, either. Sometimes I just like to curl up in an armchair in front of my fireplace all by myself, put on the kind of music I like and he hates—because of my travels I rather enjoy Andean flute and some obscure forms of gamelan music and the like that drive him bananas—or watch weepy videos like *Stella Dallas*, wear my rattiest bathrobe, and just bliss out. I expect Rob has his own equivalent of these things too. He likes cop movies—of course—the blacker the better, and football. Not that I think this makes us an unusual couple or anything, and so far, it's working fine.

If I'm a little ambivalent about the status of our relationship, there is one part of it about which I have no reservations whatsoever, and that is his daughter Jennifer. I adore her. I take her side almost all the time, the cause of some tension between us, and would happily have her around on a permanent basis. She's transferred to a university closer to home and is around most weekends now.

It was Jennifer who answered the telephone. I got caught up on all her news—new clothes, a new beau, and the professor she thought was an idiot—and then asked about her dad. "He's on an assignment," she said. My heart leapt into my throat. RCMP assignments, in my opinion, are almost always dangerous, if not downright life threatening, although Rob says I overdramatize everything. When I first met him, he had a desk job, having been hurt in a drug bust, but he now had a clean bill of health and was back "on assignment." It made him happy. It drove me nuts.

"I hate this part," I said.

"Me, too," she said. We both thought about this for a few seconds. "He said he'd be away a few days."

"Well, don't worry," I said.

"You neither," she said.

"Call me if you hear anything," I said.

"Yes," she said.

"Have him call me when he gets back," I said.

"Okay," she said.

"Don't worry," I said.

"You said that already," she said.

"Everything will be fine," I said.

"I know," she said. "Love you."

"You, too. Bye." So much for a romantic interlude. Now that I'd had this conversation, I sincerely hoped I'd get to meet Godard soon so I could go home and worry myself sick there instead of worrying myself sick in Paris. I mean maybe Rob's assignment was a stakeout somewhere, where all he had to do was record someone's comings and goings. Or maybe he was investigating some white-collar crime where the only possibility of violence would be someone throwing a pen at him. Or maybe not. Why, I wondered, had I taken up with a policeman, rather than, say, a banker or a civil servant?

Get to work, Lara, I told myself. *It's the only thing to do. You told Clive you were going to do a sweep of the flea markets and the antique stores, so that's what you're going to do.*

The next day, after a night primarily spent fretting over the two Roberts, Luczka and Godard, I started out on the Right Bank, with the Louvre des Antiquaires on the Place du Palais Royal, where I picked up a couple of very fine pieces of furniture, at fine furniture prices, regrettably, but my brush with wealth in the person of Crawford Lake seemed to have dulled my more parsimonious instincts. Then I headed for Le Marais, and some dealers in St. Paul near La Souris Verte, followed by a shop selling lovely old silver by weight on Rue des Francs Bourgeois, before collapsing into a chair in a café in Place des Vosges. Then it was across the Seine to the Champ de Mars, and the Village Suisse's collection of antiques dealers. After that, it was over to the Louvre to look at all things Etruscan, so I could be the expert Lake expected me to be, and then, for good measure, and thinking I still wouldn't be able to sleep, I took in a performance of Verdi's Requiem at the Eglise St. Roch on the Rue St. Honoré. There was no message from Boucher when I got back, rather late, to my room.

The following day being Saturday, I headed for the flea markets—Clignancourt and Montreuil—zipping on and off the Metro and walking for miles. I didn't come up with much, just some nice old linens, but it kept me moving and not thinking, which was the real point of the exercise. At some point, as I was zipping about Paris, I realized that I was being followed. Crawford Lake may have done business on the strength of a handshake, but he was hedging his bets. Antonio the Beautiful was following me everywhere. As irritating as this might be, I resolved to make the best of it. Antonio believed at first, I think, that I didn't see him, but my cheerful wave disavowed him of that. He waved back but kept his distance, which was fine with me. After my wave, however, he made no pretense of hiding.

On Sunday, I went first to the flea market at Vanves to see an antiquarian book dealer I know, picking up a 1924 edition of Sir Richard Francis Burton's *The Kasidah* for a client who collects Burton. Then I went to check out the *boquinistes* on the banks of the Seine, finding two very fine maps that I was pretty sure my favorite map collector client, a man by the name of Matthew Wright, would be happy to see.

In between all these jaunts, I drank gallons of coffee and read piles of newspapers. As far as I could see, the news in Europe was pretty much the same as it had been last time I'd been over. According to the papers, the Italian government had once again declared war on organized crime, their last effort, presumably, having been as unsuccessful as all previous attempts. French truck drivers had declared war on their government, as had British farmers on theirs, and Irish fishermen, eager to join in the fray, had declared war on Spanish fishermen, who they claimed were fishing illegally. Some relief from all this bellicose behavior could be found in a story about an arts administrator in Germany who had denied that his comments about a rival's race had been anti-Semitism, but instead a glowing comment on the diversity of the new Germany, and another about an Italian businessman by the name of Gianpiero Ponte who had left his Milan office of a Friday afternoon, and rather than going straight home to his wife and children, had driven instead to his weekend home in Tuscany. There Signore Ponte had either fallen, jumped, or been pushed over the edge of a cliff. While death by misadventure had not been ruled out—there was some rather lurid speculation on that subject—an investigation into his business affairs had begun, and it appeared that he had suffered some rather serious financial setbacks in the days before his fatal plunge. Photos of his grieving widow, the rather lovely Eugenia Ponte, and his gorgeous children, were much in evidence.

The one moment of excitement, if not fear, in the midst of days of increasing boredom peppered with worry about Rob, occurred as I was window shopping on a little street off the Boulevard St. Germain. Before I knew what was happening, I was swarmed by a group of Gypsies, one of whom grabbed at my handbag. I backed up against the wall and held tight to my bag, but I couldn't figure out how to get away from them. I did the only thing I could think of: I started yelling. In a matter of seconds, help came in the person of Antonio, who waded into the crowd and pulled me free.

"*Multo grazie,* Antonio," I said.

"Very bad," he said in careful English. "You must watch more carefully."

"Can I buy you a drink?" I said. "Or a coffee or something? To say thank you?"

"I am not supposed to have intercourse with you," he said. "No speaking," he added, no doubt because of the startled expression on my face.

"But it is important for me to practice English," he said. "We speak English, okay?"

"Okay," I said.

"Then it is possible for us to have a drink together. Do you think there is Italian wine?"

"I'll ask," I said. The waiter looked horrified. "French wine only, Antonio," I said.

"Is okay," he said, but he didn't look any too happy. I ordered a nice Côtes du Rhône.

"How goes your work here?" he asked after a few tentative sips.

"Slowly."

"Yes," he said. "Do you think we will be many more days here?"

"I sure hope not."

"Me, also," he said. "I'm not certain about that man you had meeting with," he added, putting his hand over his heart in Boucher's favorite mannerism. "I think he wants to be success, but always, he fails. It is not good to be with men like him. They pull you down. You become like them."

"That's an interesting observation, Antonio," I said, and it was. Antonio was not only good-looking, he was also rather perceptive. He'd pretty well summed up Boucher, and he'd done it from a considerable distance. "But Mr. Lake wants me to deal with him, so what else can I do?"

"I know," he said. "You are not married?"

"No."

"You have a boyfriend, though."

"Yes, I do. He's a policeman."

"A policeman! That is dangerous work. It is a worry?"

"Yes. I'm worried right now."

"Too bad. I worry also, about my girlfriend. Her work is not dangerous, like your policeman. She is a bank teller. But still, I worry. Do you have photo of your policeman?"

"You know, I don't," I said. "Perhaps I should have."

"Too bad. I have a photo," he said, taking a rather dog-eared picture from his wallet. "Here."

"She's really lovely," I said, studying the photograph of a rather conventionally pretty young woman. "What's her name?"

"Teresa," he said. "And she is lovely. That is the problem. She is like the most beautiful flower, and there are many bees who admire her. I am afraid that while I'm away, another bee will take my place."

I tried not to smile. "Antonio, you are very good-looking yourself," I said. "I'm sure she will be glad to see you when you get home."

"Looks are not enough," he said. "Teresa is feminist." We both thought about that for a moment. "That is why I have taken this work, to watch for you," he said. "My employer pays very well. Teresa is very interested in money."

"You don't work for Mr. Lake on a permanent basis, then?"

"No," he said. "From time to time only. This time only until you have done what he wants."

"I'll try to do that just as quickly as possible," I said.

"That will be very good," he said.

"So what do you do when you're not working for Mr. Lake?"

"Many things. I am an actor, with the Corelli Ponte agency. It is very important agency in Rome," he added, having judged correctly by my vacant expression that I had no idea about Italian agencies. "But usually there is no work, so I do many things: cook, waiter. But I hope one day to be famous. Like Giancarlo Giannini, you know. Work in Italy, but also Hollywood. That would make Teresa very happy. It is for this reason I must practice English, and why I have intercourse with you now."

"You know, Antonio," I said. "Given that this is an English lesson, I think that *intercourse* expression . . . perhaps you should say *have a conversation*, or *speaking* instead. Technically it is correct, but your meaning might be misconstrued." He looked slightly baffled. "Misunderstood, I mean. Someone might interpret it a different way."

"Like what?"

"I was afraid you'd ask me that question. Well, um, now it tends to mean having sex."

"Ohhh," he said, slapping his forehead with his palm. "That is very bad. I was taught that in school by my teacher of English, Signora Longo. She was very old, and we, the other boys and I, were certain she was a virgin. Perhaps she knew only the old expressions, or," he said, smiling suddenly, "she knew more about life than we thought."

We both laughed. "It is good you tell me this. I save you from Gypsies, and you save me from being miscon-strued. Very excellent new word for me. Before, we are associates only. Now I think we are friends, no?"

"We are friends," I said.

"Being a friend is a responsibility, I think."

"Well, yes, I suppose, but it's also . . ."

"A joy?" he said.

"Yes, exactly," I said.

"I think so, too," he said.

We finished our wine. "And now," he said, "we will return to before. You work. I watch you."

"Okay," I said. "Thank you again for coming to my rescue."

"It was for me a pleasure. Also speaking with you in English. Thank you for French wine," he said. "Is not so bad."

"*Prego,* I said.

When I got back to the hotel, there was finally a message from Boucher saying that he'd been in touch with Godard again, and things were looking up. Godard was coming to Paris in the next day or two and would probably see me. Boucher would be back in touch with something more concrete as soon as he could.

By this time, I had done absolutely everything I could think of to do in Paris and was starting to get a little impatient, if not downright irritable, although there was absolutely nothing I could do about it. I had no idea what the fellow looked like, where he lived, or anything else except that he apparently had an Etruscan horse that he might or might not be prepared to sell, and that he would probably speak to me sometime, somewhere.

Boucher called again that evening. "Look," he said in a whisper. "I'm in the Café de la Paix with a friend of Godard's. Why don't you wander over here and happen upon me, if you see what I mean. You know. Chance encounter. Here he comes. I've got to sign off." The phone went dead in my ear.

I hailed a cab and headed for the café. "Hello Yves,"

I said, coming up to the table. "Fancy meeting you here."

"Lara!" he said, rising from his seat. "Good to see you. Pierre, this is the woman I've been telling you about, the antique dealer from Toronto. Lara, this is Pierre Leclerc, a colleague of mine from Lyons. Pierre is an antique dealer as well. How fortunate we should run into each other." He placed his hand against his chest and just oozed surprise and pleasure. He was so good at it, I decided I would never be able to trust the man.

"Won't you join us?" Leclerc said, pulling out a chair rather gallantly. The two men were a study in contrasts. Where Boucher favored the casual turtleneck and black jeans look, Leclerc was the well-dressed dandy, in tan suit, cream shirt, and lovely gold and brown tie with matching puff, and some rather expensive-looking gold cufflinks. They were also quite different in style, Boucher favoring an air of sincerity, or at least he tried to, while Leclerc had a rather oily charm.

"Kir Royale, isn't it?" Boucher said, signaling the waiter and ordering both mine and another round for the two men. I wondered whether I'd now be buying drinks for three. We engaged in small talk for a few minutes—the weather, Paris traffic, that sort of thing— until finally we got around to the subject at hand.

"Do you have a shop in Lyons, Pierre?" I asked.

"No," he replied. "Not anymore."

"He's a broker," Boucher said.

This made me nervous. In fact, the antiquities market in general makes me nervous. There is always the question of authenticity, where antiquities are concerned. There are so many fakes, and it's not always easy to tell. There is also the rather tricky question of provenance, where the objects came from, and whether or not they were acquired legally. Collectors' appetites, and by collectors I mean both individual and institutional, museums and the like, are fed by a shadowy group of dealers and brokers who find the desired objects. From time to time, people of rather dubious reputation get into the field. I had the horrible feeling I was in the presence of one now.

"Are you in the market for anything in particular?" Leclerc asked, adjusting the French cuffs on his impeccable shirt and straightening his cufflinks, which were rather ostentatious, two rather large gold disks.

"My client is interested in a bronze Pegasus," I said. "He's the horsy type," I added. "Collects with that theme in mind." I had no reason to think this was true, but I wanted to steer clear of the word *Etruscan*, which I was reasonably sure would narrow the field of collectors and put the price up. "I've heard that a Robert Godard might have such a thing, and I'm trying to get in touch with him through Yves here."

"I know Godard," Leclerc exclaimed. "Rather well, in fact. I've supplied him with several pieces in the past." He paused for a moment and then gave me an impish smile. "Perhaps we could do business together." His knee pressed against mine. I could not help but wonder what kind of business he meant.

"Godard is playing a little hard to get," Boucher said.

"I thought you said he was on his way to Paris," I said. "Arriving tomorrow or the next day?"

"He's changed his mind," Boucher said. "He's like that."

"He does become difficult to deal with from time to time," Leclerc agreed. "Doesn't like to part with anything. But he is in a selling mood right now. Approached properly, I think you might be successful in convincing him to part with it. Now, will you please forgive me? I must make a telephone call."

As he left, his hand brushed the back of my neck.

"He wants a cut," Boucher said.

"How do you know?" I replied. "He didn't say anything."

"That's why he's gone to the telephone. He's giving us time to discuss it."

"I thought you were going to put me in touch with Godard," I said.

Boucher looked pained and pressed his hand harder against his chest. "That's what I'm doing," he said. "That's why I set up this meeting. Leclerc is someone close to Godard. You don't have to include him, of course, but he will certainly make everything move a lot faster. It's entirely up to you."

"How much?" I sighed.

"I don't know," he said. "He may want a percentage. If you're lucky, though, and he likes you—I think he does, by the way, I saw him looking rather admiringly at you when you came in—he might take a flat fee, say ten thousand. If you're really lucky," he added.

"I'm going to the ladies' room," I said. "Be right back."

What I really wanted was time to think. I went outside, pulled out my cell phone, held it to my ear, as if making a call, and then looked back through the windows to the table. Across the street, Antonio sat with a cup of coffee on the table in front of him. He flashed a grin, his beautiful teeth evident even from where I stood. I looked back to the café I'd just left. From the street, the interior was quite visible. Leclerc returned, and the two men sat, heads together in a conspiratorial way. Boucher said something, and they both laughed. I knew, somehow, that the joke was at my expense.

Suddenly, all the sleepless nights, and waiting, and worry caught up with me, to say nothing of the pressure of working for Lake. I went back to the table. "Sorry, gentlemen, but I have to go. I've had a call from an agent in Amsterdam," I said. "He has something I know my client will be very interested in: painting of a horse and rider, Flemish. I'll have to try to get a flight out first thing in the morning. Perhaps I'll swing by here on my way home, and we can talk again. Yves, I think you owe me a drink," I smiled. "So thanks for the Kir Royale." I stomped out of the place, hailed a cab, and went back to the hotel, leaving them, I hoped, in some disarray. With any luck, I'd forced the issue. Because I was sick and tired of waiting for Godard.

THREE

VICHY

WE REACHED THE OUTSKIRTS OF VICHY about four o'clock the next afternoon. It had taken most of the day to get there, partly because I was determined not to appear overeager, but also because Boucher had insisted on coming with me, a fact I found rather irritating, despite the fact I'd apparently won the war of nerves. My snit of the previous evening had had the desired effect: I'd had about ten minutes' sleep— at least that's the way it felt after a night spent alternately fuming and plotting how I'd find Godard myself and convincing myself that Boucher would come through now, if he believed my little subterfuge—before the telephone jarred me awake.

"I've located Godard," Boucher had said without so much as a hello. "He's back home now. He was difficult to persuade, but I explained the situation. We can see him today. We'll have to get a move on, though. It will take the better part of the day to get there."

"Really?" I said, squinting at the clock. It was only seven in the morning. "I'm not sure I can put off the Amsterdam people. They're expecting me this evening." Despite the fact that I'd emerged victorious, I wasn't giving him any satisfaction.

There was a pause. "It's up to you, of course," Boucher said. "But Godard is a difficult man to get an appointment with, as you already know, and he'll see us later today or tomorrow morning if we can't get there today."

"And *there* is?"

"Vichy. He has a chateau in Vichy. Didn't I mention that?" Of course he hadn't. He hadn't given me even the smallest clue as to Godard's location. "I've managed to get us an invitation to his chateau."

"Okay," I said. "I'll see what I can do. I can't get in touch with the agent in Amsterdam for an hour or two. His office won't be open yet. I'll call you back as soon as I make contact and let you know either way."

"We'll need a car," Boucher said. "Mine's unexpectedly in for repairs."

Just like your wallet, I was tempted to say, but didn't. This would have to be all sweetness and light until I'd actually met Godard. "Let's worry about that if I can reschedule Amsterdam," I said. "I can always rent one if necessary."

I left Boucher to cool his heels for a couple of hours, the same way he'd been making me wait, while I found a car to rent and checked out of the hotel.

"You should have joined forces with Leclerc," Boucher said as we headed down the highway. "He's got really good connections."

"So, did he get this appointment with Godard, or did you?" I asked through clenched teeth. Boucher was definitely getting on my nerves, chattering away as the miles rolled past.

"I did, of course," he replied, sounding wounded. I couldn't see, given I had my eyes glued on the road ahead but also on the rearview mirror, looking in vain for some sign that Antonio had picked up my trail, but I knew Boucher had his hand on his heart again. "But it's not a good idea to get on Leclerc's bad side. I wouldn't be surprised if he's already in Vichy. He knows Godard really well, you know, can get in to see him easily. I'll bet he's there right now negotiating the purchase of the horse."

"Why would he do that? Does he have a buyer for it?"

"He may do," Boucher said, after a pause.

"What are you trying to tell me, Yves?" I snapped, but I knew the answer before the words were out of my mouth.

"You," he said sadly. "I'm afraid he'll get it and resell it to you at a much higher price. Most unfortunate."

There was no sign of Leclerc, nor of Antonio, as I turned off onto a country road. It had been a long, hot summer in Europe, but it was coming to an end. The trees were yellow now, with only brief patches of green, and the fields had all been harvested. The sun was still warm, but there was an edge to it, and dark clouds on the horizon signaled the arrival of autumn rains. It was beautiful, though, and I wished I was there with someone other than Boucher, and for a purpose other than business.

After several miles of driving through the countryside, we turned onto a long drive lined with tall poplars that, in the late afternoon sun, cast stunning shadows across the road and beyond. At the end of the drive, past two large stone sphinxes that stood guard, was a storybook castle, a gorgeous chateau, all turrets and crenellations. A silver Renault was pulling away as I parked and got out of the car. It stopped abruptly, the door opened, and I heard my name.

"What are you doing here, Dottie?" I said as soon as I saw the driver.

"Looking for treasure, of course," she said, air kissing me on both cheeks. I found myself enveloped in a cloud of expensive perfume.

"You haven't met Kyle, have you?" she said, gesturing to a rather attractive young man at least ten, maybe fifteen years her junior. He smiled prettily and shook my hand, saying nothing, and all the while gazing adoringly at Dottie, who did look rather smashing in a short, tight leather skirt over toned and tanned— Dottie knew how to look after herself, I thought enviously—legs and a leopard print scoop-neck top that showed a fair amount of cleavage. "The boy toy," she mouthed at me. "Isn't he gorgeous?" she said, sotto voce. "Lovely pecs," she added.

He was lovely, no doubt about it. He was built like a football player, or maybe a bouncer—very broad shoulders and slim waist—with heavily moussed blond hair that failed to control a rather adorable cowlick. Mind you, Rob had reasonably good pecs, too, and he had the advantage of being smart, well-read, a reasonably good conversationalist as guys go, and just about my age. I suddenly wished more than anything that he were there.

"Gorgeous," I murmured.

"I saw Clive a few months back," she said. "At the Winter Antiques Show in New York, if I remember correctly. I hear you're back in business together. How . . ." She paused for a moment, searching for the right word.

"Risky?" I said. "Or maybe foolhardy?"

"No, darling," she said. "I was thinking something more like sophisticated, civilized, something like that. So unlike my awful divorce from Hughie. He's still being quite horrid about everything. But who cares? I'm having much more fun than he is, the old turnip." She linked her arm through Kyle's and smiled engagingly. Kyle gave me a lovely lopsided grin. My, he was cute.

"And this is?" she said turning in Boucher's direction.

"Oh, sorry," I said. For a pleasant second or two, I'd forgotten he was there. "Yves Boucher, a dealer from Paris. This is Dorothea Beach. She specializes in French antiques. She has a wonderful shop in New Orleans."

"Delighted, I'm sure," she said.

Boucher bowed and kissed her hand. *"Enchanté,"* he said. Dorothea had that effect on most men.

"Boyfriend?" she mouthed at me as Boucher bent over her hand. I shook my head vehemently. "That's good," she whispered.

"You're here to see Godard, obviously," she said

aloud, inclining her head in the general direction of the chateau. "Regular parade through the place. Pierre Leclerc was leaving just as I arrived. You know him, don't you? Paris dealer? I can't stand the man. He kept pressing himself against me in the most revolting way." The lovely Kyle looked vaguely peeved. I wondered if he could speak, and then decided it didn't matter. "Oh dear," she said. "I shouldn't have said that. I hope he isn't your best friend or anything." I indicated she would get no argument from me on the subject of Pierre Leclerc.

"Strange bird, that one," Dottie said. "Godard, I mean. It doesn't take a genius to see he has to sell, I offer him a fair price, but then he says he'll think about it. I don't think he likes me. Oh, I hope you're not after the same thing I am," she said suddenly. "Are you?"

"I doubt it," I said. "I'm not in the market for furniture right now."

"That's a relief, sweetie," she said. "I'd hate to have to fight you for it, but fight you for it I would. I'd rather lose to you than Leclerc, of course, but I just desperately want it. Gorgeous dining set. Solid wood. Not even a whiff of veneer. And sixteen—sixteen!—chairs. Late eighteenth-, early nineteenth-century. Stunning. I was just drooling over it, trying not to let on, of course. Maybe I should have been more effusive. Maybe he's one of those types who only sells to people he thinks love the stuff as much as he does. Although if he sells it to me," she said, pausing for breath, "he'll be eating dinner off a TV table, poor thing." She shrugged. "I'll come back tomorrow as he's suggested and try to be more ingratiating. I hope I don't have to

kill him to get it. What did you say you were looking
for?"

"Equestrian statue," I said. "Pegasus. Bronze."

"I saw that," she said. "It's . . . well, big. Probably
very good, too, but I don't know anything about bronze
statues. If you want it, I hope you get it. If I were you,
as a strategy, I'd gush all over that horse. The coy
approach doesn't seem to work with Godard. If you're
staying in town, perhaps we can get together for a bite.
Right now, Kyle and I have to find something to do to
pass the time, don't we, sweetheart?" She put her arm
around his waist and grinned at me. "Hope to see you
later, Lara. Clive told me you have a new boyfriend,
and I want to hear all about him."

As she got into the car, she turned back one more
time. "Nobody answers the door, by the way. It's open.
You just go right in. Hang a left at my dining set, and
keep going straight on. He was in his study when I last
saw him. You'll pass your horse on the way."

I turned back to Godard's place as the tires on Dorothea's car spun in her haste to get to whatever activ-
ity she and Kyle had in mind. The chateau was
spectacular, but close up, it had an air of neglect. The
hedges needed pruning rather badly, and the gardens
were overrun with vines and weeds. Over to one side,
a sheep and a couple of lambs were tethered to stakes,
and a few chickens were scratching in the dirt. If it
was a fairy tale castle, then perhaps it was Sleeping
Beauty's, waiting for her prince, as the forest grew up
around her.

Still, it was a chateau. While I had no idea what
kind of fortune it took to keep a place like this up, no
doubt it was a considerable sum. Perhaps that ex-

plained the troop of antique dealers through the place
that day, one of whom, to my extreme annoyance, was
Leclerc.

Despite Dottie's advice, I did try knocking. As predicted, this elicited no response, so after a minute or
two, I pushed open the door. It creaked, just like in the
movies. I would not have been surprised to see some
aged retainer shuffling his way to the door, but there
was no one. The door had been cut into one of the
round turrets, and so I found myself in a quite pleasant
circular vestibule tiled in white and black marble, with
a very old brass chandelier. From there one went directly into the dining room, with rounded walls and
leaded glass windows up very high. Dottie's table and
chairs were, as she said, gorgeous. I found myself
wishing I hadn't told her I wasn't interested in the furniture. This table and chairs would make quite a statement in the main showroom at McClintoch & Swain,
of that there was no doubt. At the far end of the table
lay the remains of a meal, a half-drunk glass of red
wine, some crusts of bread, and a plate. All the chairs,
sixteen of them, were lined up against the walls rather
than around the table, including the chair one would
have expected at the set place. Presumably they'd been
placed that way so that potential buyers could get a
good look at the table, but it all seemed rather forlorn.

The next room was the living room, I suppose, although it could have been anything. Dottie had said
Godard would be eating off a TV table if she bought
the dining suite, and she was right about that. While
the markings on two very large but threadbare carpets
on the floor hinted that the room had once been well
furnished, now there was only a small and rather

homely settee under the window and across the room from it, in front of a magnificent stone fireplace, one chair and a little side table and lamp not beside the chair, as one would expect, but across from it. Marks on the wall over the mantel indicated that something, a mirror perhaps or a large painting, had once hung there. On top of the side table and piled up beside it were several books. It was a peculiar arrangement, with the chair to one side of the fireplace and the lamp and the books and the table on the other. All of a sudden I knew what the explanation was, and knew too, with certainty, that Boucher had been stringing me along with tales of Godard's travels.

Saying nothing to him but promising myself I would at the earliest opportunity, I stepped into the gloom of the next room. It was very dark and rather damp. It was undoubtedly the oldest part of the chateau, the fortified tower, several stories high, with slits for weapons rather than windows. Fourteenth century, I'd guess, although it took me a minute to take it all in. This was where Godard kept his treasures, or at least some of them. A number of glass shelving units were lined up in rows on one side, and in here rested a large number of terra-cotta pots.

A large sculptural piece had been clamped to one of the stone walls, and over to one side, in all its glory was Bellerophon. The winged horse was rearing up, and the rider, leaning forward, was aiming his weapon at something below. Far above me, a couple of birds were flitting about, and I realized that the slits in the walls had not been glassed in, and that the tower was very much in its original state. I started toward the horse but heard a voice from the next room speaking in a low murmur. "We'd better go and talk to Godard first," Boucher said.

A man much younger than I expected, about thirty or so, sat at a desk talking on the telephone. He had a thin face, its pallor accented by dark, long hair, pulled back in a ponytail. He wore a white, collarless shirt, open slightly at the neck, and a black, loose fitting jacket. In front of him on the desk were several large tomes, one of them open in front of him. Behind him was a computer turned on. I turned to Boucher. "Travels all over the world, does he?" I said, looking him right in the eyes.

"I didn't know. I've never actually met him," Boucher said, looking away. "I've only talked to him on the telephone."

The sound of our voices, however low, made Godard look up. "Not you again," he said rudely, looking right at Boucher. Boucher shifted nervously. "I thought I told you not to come back."

"Never met?" I said under my breath. "Perhaps he's mistaken you for someone else."

"Are you with him?" Godard said, looking at me with some hostility.

"No," I replied. I would have plenty of time later to count the lies I'd told the week or so since I'd met Lake, but at the time, I barely noticed what I'd done. "I believe I was here first," I said to Boucher, as if I'd just met him. "So perhaps you wouldn't mind waiting your turn outside." Boucher, slimy liar that he was, beat a hasty retreat.

"What do you want?" Godard said to me, his hand over the phone. He wasn't exactly welcoming, but the hostility in his tone dropped perceptibly as soon as Boucher left the room.

"I understand you may have some antiquities that you are willing to sell," I said. "I wondered if that is the case, if I might have a look at them. I'm an antique dealer from Toronto," I added, placing my card on the desk in front of him.

Godard stared at my card for a few seconds. "Give me a minute," he said at last, gesturing to a chair nearby. "I'll be finished this call in a minute. You were saying . . . ?" he said into the phone. "No, there's nothing I want to sell right now."

That didn't sound too promising. I didn't take the proffered chair which, like the rest of the room, was piled high with books. The study was lined with shelves, each crammed with books, some new, some old, some very old and probably valuable. The world's great literature was represented here, from Shakespeare to Victor Hugo, in several languages. Judging from the volumes nearest me, however, Godard's primary interest was in the occult. Dolores Chapman's *Conversations with Nostradamus* sat next to Nostradamus's own writings, *Centuries* and *Prognostications*. There were several tomes on astrology and foretelling the future, another one that, if I remembered correctly, promised to explain all the mysteries of Revelations. Over by the window was a telescope, which tied in rather nicely with the astrology books. I didn't care what he read nor what he believed in, but with the dark gloom of the tower behind me and this pale and rather sickly young man and all these books around me, I was beginning to wish I was outside catching the last few rays of the late afternoon sun, even if it meant dealing with

Boucher. Still, I was going to have to establish some rapport with him if I hoped to get the Bellerophon.

The call went on for only a minute or two longer, but Godard was not yet ready to talk about the collection. "I need another minute here. Alone. Go and have a look, why don't you? Pull the cord by the door."

The cord by the door turned out to be a long string that, when pulled, turned on a few lightbulbs that had been strung about the room. It felt a little bit like being in a dungeon, with the poor light and the cold stone of the walls. But while you might take issue with the ambiance, the collection was well worth a closer look. There was terra-cotta in abundance: kraters, bowls, jugs, amphorae. There was plenty of the black bucchero and painted pottery of different styles: red figures on black, white figures on red, and black figures on red, just about every permutation and combination in Greek- or Etruscan-style pottery one could ever hope to see. There were also bronze hand mirrors, incised on the back with scenes of gods and animals. All were top notch, as far as I could see, and a few definitely museum quality.

The very large sculptural piece on the wall I decided was a temple frieze, in terra-cotta. On closer examination, it showed a man on a winged horse, spearing a creature with two heads and the tail of a snake.

Lake had said he thought that perhaps Godard didn't know what he had in the Bellerophon, but seeing this collection, I was convinced that wasn't so. The clincher was a small case toward the back of the room, which held a single object only. It was a black figure hydria, a ceramic water jug, beautifully painted. It was smaller than average, maybe fifteen inches high, round on the bottom and tapering to a slim neck and the flaring out again, with three handles, one on each side for carrying it, and a third for pouring. Almost every inch of the neck and lip was covered in decoration, swirls, and so on, and on the rounded part was a scene showing a man on a winged horse battling a creature that was part lion, part goat, and part snake. Godard collected Bellerophon and the chimera.

"Sorry to keep you waiting," Godard said, maneuvering his wheelchair between the glass cases carefully. "Have you seen anything here that interests you?" He looked different, but I couldn't put my finger on why.

"Everything is quite exceptional," I said. "Can you tell me what you want to sell?"

"I don't want to sell any of it," Godard said.

"Then perhaps I am wasting your time," I said. And he mine, of course.

"I said I didn't want to sell any of it," Godard said. "I didn't say I wouldn't sell it. No doubt you noticed my somewhat constrained circumstances. Most of the furniture and paintings are gone. There is nothing else. Have a look. If you see something you like, and it's something I'm prepared to part with at this very moment, then perhaps we can do business."

I supposed that was something, but, being cautious, I did not go right up to Bellerophon. Instead, I stopped at the chimera hydria. "This is obviously special," I said.

"It's not for sale," he said.

"How about this?" I said, pointing to a bronze mirror.

"It's not for sale, either." This was sounding pretty hopeless, but I couldn't see myself going back to Lake and telling him I couldn't get what he wanted, so I soldiered on.

"I can certainly understand your feelings about these objects," I said, doggedly trying to win the man over. "This is a very fine collection, and it would be difficult to part with any of it. How did you come to acquire it?" A touchy subject that one. Provenance is a really important concept in antiquities and essential in proving that objects have been legally acquired, or at least acquired long enough ago that you won't be in any trouble with various authorities.

He looked as if he wouldn't answer, but then he said, "My father did most of the collecting. He spent summers in Italy—Tuscany—and made the acquaintance of some fellows who helped him collect. Probably *tombaroli*," he said with a slight smile. "I assume you know what that is."

"Tomb robbers," I said.

"Correct. In any event, no matter how he acquired it, it was a long time ago, and so all seems to be aboveboard now. There was an expert out here two maybe three years ago, before my father died, anyway. He took detailed photos and everything. If there'd been any problems, I'm sure he would have said something. My father also collected, purchased pieces at auctions and so on. I have all the receipts."

"And you?"

"I pretty much just sell it," he said.

By this time, I'd managed to reach the horse. Taking a small pocket flashlight out of my bag, I began to study it carefully, as Godard watched. It was bronze, certainly, and the right size. I checked out the front legs, then the back. Carved into a back leg was Etruscan writing. *"Tinscvil,"* I said, muttering aloud. Just like the Chimera of Arezzo. I'd looked at it carefully enough and had even tried to copy the writing on the chimera's paw.

"What did you say?" Godard said, wheeling up to me.

"Tinscvil," I said. "Dedicated to Tinia, or Zeus, isn't it?"

"You read Etruscan," he said.

It is a measure of how far gone I was, enthralled by the prospect of all that lovely money from Lake, and determined to convince Godard to sell, that I did what I did then. I didn't lie, exactly. I just said nothing. Or rather I just murmured something that Godard took to be assent, something like *hmmm.*

He looked at me for a moment, and then pointed to a rather peculiar-looking object in one of the cases. "Do you know what that is?"

Strangely enough, I did. Several of the books on the Etruscans I'd consulted had shown pictures of something similar, and I'd noticed it because it was so odd. "It's a bronze model of a sheep's liver, isn't it?" I said. "Etruscan haruspices, diviners, used them to foretell the future."

"That's right," he said. "You can see the sixteen sections of the sky around the outside, and there are fifty-two names of divinities on it." He opened the case and took the object out, stroking it with one hand as he held it with the other. "People scoff at divination," he said. "But they shouldn't. The Romans believed in it. They left nothing to chance. Nothing. Before every battle, before every important decision, they called on Etruscan haruspices. They knew."

"Well, the Romans were certainly successful," I said.

"Exactly," he said, failing to notice the tinge of sarcasm in my voice. He put the bronze liver back in the case.

"Are you by any chance a member of the Società?" he asked.

This one I couldn't fake, but still I wasn't entirely straightforward. "No, I'm afraid not," I said. I assumed he meant an academic organization of some kind, or an archaeological society.

"But you know about it, of course. The chimera hydria."

"Hmmm," I said again.

"I don't know if there are any women in it, but that does seem a little old-fashioned, even by Italian standards, and come to think of it, the Etruscans themselves wouldn't have objected, would they? The Greeks may not have allowed women at their symposia, but the Etruscans rather welcomed them. Would you like me to put your name forward? You read Etruscan, and you certainly know Etruscan antiquities. You picked all the best stuff in the room in a matter of minutes. It's early days for me, of course, given that I've only been a member for a few months, but you never know. I'd give anything to go to the meeting," he said. "But I am a trifle constrained in what I am able to do," he said, gesturing to his legs, wrapped carefully in a blanket.

"That's most unfortunate," I said. I meant whatever had happened to his legs, but he took it differently.

"It is," he said. "I have waited so long to become a

member. My father died a couple of years ago. I'm Cisra, by the way."

"How do you do," I said.

"Not too well, as you can see," he replied. "I have two weeks to raise the money and to figure out how to get there. If I could afford some help and perhaps a van equipped with hand controls, I might make it. I hope so."

"That's too bad about your father," I said.

"Yes," he said. "Left me in something of a financial pickle, as you can see. But at least I got to be Cisra. It's not automatic, you know."

"What isn't?" This was the most baffling exchange, and I needed to get him off the subject, whatever it was, and back to the sale of the Bellerophon.

"The name. It's not hereditary or anything. Someone has to die before you can get in. The numbers in the Società are limited, as I'm sure you know, to twelve plus one. But there's bound to be a spot now that Velathri's gone."

"Velathri?" I said.

"You know," he said. "Velathri. Volterra. I'm surprised you don't recognize the Etruscan name for it."

Volterra I knew. It was a town in the northwest part of Tuscany. Etruscan city, too, if I remembered correctly. As far as I could recall, though, it was still there. "Oh, right," I said. "Of course. Sorry."

"Gianpiero Ponte," Godard said, as if I was being really dense. "Surely you read about it. It was in all the papers."

"You mean the businessman who went over the edge of a cliff somewhere or other?"

"Volterra!" he said. "That's my point. Velathri is now vacant, and you might get it."

"Oh," was all I could muster.

"I could consult the liver to see if you stand a chance. I've studied the sheep's liver for four years now, ever since this happened," he said, pointing to his legs again. "I think I'm ready to use a real one now."

I thought of the sheep and the adorable little lambs outside and cringed. There was now no question in my mind that Godard was what Clive would call a few sandwiches short of a picnic. Not in terms of his intelligence, perhaps. If he'd read only a few books in his library, he was smart enough. But his grasp on reality seemed a little tenuous. I could see now that I looked at him more carefully that his pupils were dilated. Drugs, I thought, either for severe pain, quite possible, given his circumstances, or others of the more recreational kind.

"Have you ever tried using a medium, by the way? I tried reaching my parents and grandfather that way, but it didn't work. I have a good feeling about this, though. As far as I'm concerned, that is," he went on. "All the signs are positive. Maybe that's why you're here. Yes, that is almost certainly it. The signs told me someone would come to help me get to Velzna, you know, Volsinii. I suppose you use the Roman names. They told me you were coming. Of course it would be somebody who reads Etruscan. I wouldn't sell to anyone else. It must be you. I'm building my tomb. Would you like to see it?"

"Sure," I said. *Good grief,* I thought.

"Come along," he said, leading me back to his study.

"I'm interested in the horse," I said, determined to

stay the course no matter how bizarre it got.

"Bellerophon, you mean?"

"Yes. Bellerophon." There seemed no reason to be coy on that subject anymore. "Did you sell it to Leclerc already?"

"Who's he?"

"Pierre Leclerc. He was here earlier this afternoon. Fancy suit. Cufflinks, that sort of thing."

"The cufflinks!" he said. "Yes. Fantastic! I wonder where he got those. That name's not right, though, is it? Leclerc? Close though. Le-something. Le Conte, isn't it? The horse, though. Did he ask about it? I can't remember. I didn't sell him anything. I don't like him. I'm quite sure he isn't the one. Here we are." He leaned over and pulled aside a carpet to reveal a trapdoor. "Get ready to be amazed, shocked, dazzled, whatever."

I looked down into pitch darkness below. "I don't think I want—"

"Of course you do," he said. "Give me a minute. I'll go first." He wheeled his chair back and grabbed a rope attached to a pulley on the wall behind him, pulled the rope and himself over near the edge, then slipped out of his wheelchair and, after lowering the chair down, pulled himself into a makeshift harness and eased himself down as well. "Come on," he said. "Take the ladder. We'll talk about Bellerophon down here. And you'd better bring that flashlight of yours. The light seems to have blown out."

What I do, I thought, *to serve a customer.* Reluctantly, I climbed down the ladder. When I reached the bottom, I panned the flashlight around the space and gasped as the face of a man, one who looked exactly like Godard, stared back at me.

"Fabulous, isn't it?" he said.

"Fabulous," I agreed, catching my breath. And it was, in a way. I was in a room about twenty feet long and ten wide. There were two stone benches to either side of me, and an archway straight ahead. The ceiling was decorated in red and green and cream squares. Beyond the arch, the walls had been painted with scenes of a party, at least that was what I thought it was. A man, the one who looked like Godard draped in a dark red toga, lay stretched out on a couch of some kind, while various women, bearing platters of fruit and jugs of wine, lined up to serve him. Other men—I counted twelve in addition to Godard—also reclined on couches, some with women beside them. To one side of them, a door had been painted on the wall.

In the background was the chateau—I recognized it immediately—surrounded by fields where little lambs gamboled. Beyond that stretched a forest. Other men dressed in tunics were hunting with bows and arrows. Another was playing a stringed instrument of some kind. The predominant color was red, but there were swirls and leafy vines that snaked their way around the picture, birds, painted in blue and white and green, flew through the trees and around the people, caught in the sweep of my flashlight. Above the archway, two leopards faced each other, fangs bared.

Over to the right in the outer room where I was standing, three people were shown sitting in three chairs, staring straight ahead. The perspective wasn't perfect, but the faces were very lifelike.

"My mother and father," he said, following my glance. "And my grandfather. Do you like it?" he said.

"It's . . . extraordinary," I said.

"It is, isn't it?" he said. "It's modeled on Etruscan hypogeum tombs like the ones at Tarquinia," he said. "The frescoes are contemporary, of course, although I tried to give them an authentic feel."

"You painted this?"

"I did," he said. "It's my project."

"But a tomb!" I said.

"Well, why not?" he said. "I'm not going to last long anyway. It helps me while away my final hours. I started it while I could still stand, but as you can see," he said gesturing to one wall where the top was bare, "I need help to finish it. Can you paint, by the way?"

"I have absolutely no talent that way at all," I said. It may have been the first truly honest statement I'd made since I got there.

"Too bad," he said. "I'll go up first, and if you don't mind, you could attach the wheelchair to the rope when I send it back down."

"About Bellerophon," I said, as I climbed out of the basement.

"I can't sell it to you," he said. "I know I should, but I just can't do it. Not to you. Not to the one who's going to get me to Velzna and the Fanum Voltumnae."

"How much would it take to make you change your mind?" I asked.

"I won't change my mind, but I need a hundred and fifty thousand dollars. That's all. I could get a van for that and cover the cost of finishing my tomb and putting me in it. Do you see anything else you'd like here that you'd be prepared to pay that much for?"

"The chimera hydria," I said.

"No, no!" he exclaimed. "Anything but the hydria, please. It's the last thing I would part with. What about the temple frieze? It's pretty spectacular, don't you think? Would you pay one fifty for that? It's worth it, you know. A good price."

"Yes, it is. I'd have to consult my client, though."

"Okay, but do it soon. I need it to get to Velzna. Do you think he'll want it?"

The telephone ringing in his office saved me from having to answer.

"I'd better get that," he said. "It may be about the arrangements. You can use my name as a reference, by the way, if you want to replace Velathri. Hold on a second," he said, grabbing the telephone.

"Why don't I come back tomorrow?" I said.

"A hundred and fifty thousand," he said grabbing my arm, and pressing the receiver to his chest. "It's a very good price. You must buy it. I know I have very little time left. That is what the portents tell me. I must go to Velzna and the gathering of the twelve before I die. Promise you'll come back."

I fled the room just as fast as I could. It was dark outside, and Boucher was dozing in the car. The chateau now looked rather sinister, with very little light flickering in its windows, a massive black hulk against the night sky. I drove quickly into town, dumped Boucher as soon as I got there, and then found myself a hotel room. After a long, hot shower, an attempt to wash away that awful day and place, I went downstairs for a drink. The hotel was situated on a nice little square, and the bar/café spilled out of the lobby onto the street. I bought the local papers, and, over a glass of wine, combed through them. It took me about three minutes to find what I wanted. I was ready to head out to find Boucher.

"Yoo-hoo! Over here," a voice called out, and I spied Dottie and Kyle having a drink in a café. At a table nearby, Boucher sat with Leclerc, or was it Le Conte? It wouldn't surprise me in the least if he used more than one name, given my impression of his insalubrious dealings. Both men looked grumpy. I wondered if Boucher had been able to find himself a cheap place to stay, and whether Leclerc really was intent on outwitting me. A couple of tables farther on was my friend Antonio the Beautiful, who smiled and waved as Dottie did. Funny how they all turned up in the same place, especially Antonio, whom I'd not caught sight of at any point during the several hours' drive from Paris to Vichy, but who obviously had managed to follow me, just the same. I went over to Antonio first. "I need to speak to your boss," I said. "Right away."

"It will take me awhile," Antonio said. "But I will arrange it. He'll call you either very late this evening or first thing tomorrow at your hotel," he said, checking his watch. "I hope this means I will be seeing my beautiful Teresa soon."

"I think so," I said. He brightened visibly and gave me his very best smile.

"I think our relationship is at an end," I said next to Boucher, setting the newspaper on the table in front of him. I ignored Leclerc, who didn't acknowledge me, either.

"But you promised me at least five thousand dollars," Boucher said.

"Your presence could well have cost me this deal," I said. "Five thousand is rather more than your contribution is worth."

"I don't understand your attitude toward me," he said, placing his hand over his heart.

"Oh, I think you do," I said, tapping the newspaper. He didn't even have to look at it. He knew exactly what I was referring to: a classified ad inviting anyone who cared to come, to a sale of contents at a certain chateau just outside Vichy.

"I wouldn't be quite so sure the horse is yours," Leclerc said, dropping all pretense at charm. "Godard is quite unhinged, as I'm sure you noticed. He's invited me back for a chat tomorrow. We'll see who prevails here, won't we."

"Yes, we will," I said.

"That's more like it," Dottie grinned as I sat down. I had a couple of hours to kill, and Dottie was almost certainly going to be way more entertaining than Boucher.

"What is more like it?" I said. I was exhausted, and a little depressed by my day.

"That one over there," she said, gesturing toward Antonio, who was paying his bill. "Clive told me you have a new boyfriend."

"No, Dottie, he's not my boyfriend, either." I sighed.

"Too bad," she said. "He's one of the most gorgeous young men I have ever seen." Kyle thought about that for a minute or two and then frowned.

FOUR

"GODARD WON'T SELL," I SAID TO LAKE.
"Then offer him more," he said. "I want that horse."

"It's possible I could talk him into selling it for one hundred fifty thousand, if you insist," I said.

"A hundred fifty thousand what?" he said.

"Dollars."

"You're joking. Is that all? I thought I'd have to pay millions. So what's the problem?"

"It's a fake."

There was a pause on the line. "Are you sure?" he said.

"Yes."

"What makes you think so?"

"Workmanship, primarily. The quality of the work is not even close to that of the Chimera of Arezzo. I'm making the assumption that the same artist, or at least the same atelier, would have made both pieces, so you should see some similarities between the two, and the workmanship would be equally competent. It's not. Then there's the Etruscan inscription on the leg. It looks the same as the one on the Chimera, and indeed says the same thing. However, the Chimera was made using the lost wax method."

"What?" he interrupted.

"Lost wax," I said. "An exact image was carved in wax, then the hot metal poured into the mold containing the wax chimera. The wax melts, the metal cools, and presto, a bronze statue."

"Yes, yes," he interrupted. "I know. Get to the point."

"The point is that the inscription on the Chimera, the dedication to Tinia, was carved into the wax before the statue was made. The inscription on the horse, on the other hand, was etched into the leg after the bronze was cast. I think the statue may well be a hundred years old or so, but someone, an enterprising sort, carved the inscription on the horse's leg rather recently, hoping to make it appear rather older than that.

"I see," he said. "Disappointing."

"Yes," I said. "I think Godard knows it's a fake, too, and has decided to do me a favor and not sell it to me, despite the fact he really needs the money."

"I see," he said again. "Well, did he have anything else you think I might be interested in? There must have been something. My new fund launches in two weeks. I need a big splash here."

"There's one particularly interesting terra-cotta. It's a hydria, a water jug, black figures. Strangely enough, it actually shows Bellerophon killing the chimera. You could get that for one hundred fifty thousand, too, and it would be worth it."

"I don't collect chimeras, you know," he said.

"I understand that. But you would probably be interested in a piece by the Micali painter."

There was a pause. "I don't think so," he said. I was a bit surprised at that. He didn't seem to even recognize the name. Sometimes, through careful study, it's possible to identify the work of a single artist, even hundreds of years after the fact. The painter, or sculptor, or whatever, uses a particular technique or the same symbol over and over. There are at least three such artists from Etruscan times, one called the Bearded Sphinx painter because of the use of that image, another the Swallow painter, and the most famous of them all, the Micali painter, named for the man who identified the work. The chimera hydria showed all the signs of the Micali painter, a rather energetic style, not particularly refined, and some very nice swirls around the top of the vase. It would take an expert to be sure, but it was certainly worth a gamble.

"Anything else?" he said.

"If you're interested in big, there's a terra-cotta temple frieze. It also depicts the chimera myth. I think it's probably authentic."

"Get it," he said.

"Godard may not want to sell it."

"Get it anyway. A hundred fifty is what I'll pay."

"I'll try," I said.

"Don't try," Lake said as he hung up. "Do it."

It was still relatively early when I headed downstairs to find myself some coffee. Dottie, dressed in a very smart red leather suit and surrounded by expensive luggage, was at the front desk.

"Hi," she called. "Hoped I'd see you before I left. We've decided to check out. Heading farther south: Provence. Bound to be some fabulous finds there, although overpriced, no doubt. Still, people pay just about anything for something old from Provence, even if it is farmhouse furniture that's seen better days. I can't understand it, when they could have Louis XVI. I'm going to stop by the chateau first to see if Godard will reconsider. If not, then I'm on my way. I decided in the middle of the night that I can't waste time fretting over the ones that got away, no matter how fantastic. Now where is that Kyle?" she asked, looking out on to the street. "I sent him on an errand this morning, and he's taking rather longer than he should. Oh, there he is," she said, as the Renault pulled up in front of the hotel. "Gotta go, sweetie. Come to New Orleans anytime. You can stay with me."

"Bye, Dottie," I said, as she hugged me. "Maybe I'll see you in New York this winter. It's my turn to go to the antique fair."

"Bring the new boyfriend," she said. "I'm dying to meet him. I'll bring whomever I happen to be with, and we'll make it a foursome." Kyle, who obviously had missed this last remark, waved prettily.

There was no sign of Antonio the Beautiful nor of any of the others, to my general relief, so I sat in the café and ordered a croissant, apricot jam, and coffee. The air was crisp but the sun pleasant, and I tried to get myself into a more positive frame of mind by refusing to think too much about what I was doing there, and what unpleasantness might await me out at the chateau when I went back to try to buy the temple frieze.

Several unbidden thoughts kept presenting themselves, however much I might try to ignore them. One was Lake himself. I'd thought Lake was a significant collector, knew him to be, in fact, from all the reports of his purchases, and the fact that he was on all the biggest collector lists worldwide that there were. For a man who spent a lot of money at it, he didn't seem to know that much about what he was collecting. The collectors I knew took some pride in knowing as much as they possibly could about their passion. It bothered me that someone like Lake wouldn't know the Micali painter, and even more so that he hadn't seemed to know about the lost wax method of manufacture, although he'd recovered quickly when I had explained it. It wasn't something I'd expect everyone to know, of course, but Lake collected bronzes, at least a few of them, notably the Apollo he'd missed, and now the Bellerophon. I couldn't help remembering the collection at his apartment in Rome: all that stuff, expensive but not exceptional, and all over the map, literally and figuratively speaking. This said to me that either he did it for the show, not because he was truly interested in what he was collecting, or he was pathologically inclined to acquire things, regardless of taste. Both of these possibilities diminished him in my eyes.

My reverie was interrupted by the unwanted arrival of Yves Boucher. "Leclerc has gone to the chateau," he said as he pulled out a chair and sat down without asking. "I saw him leave about forty-five minutes ago. He's really annoyed with you. I'm sure he's going to get that horse."

"Perhaps," I said.

"He'll be in touch soon," he said. "To gloat, and also to sell it to you at a much higher price."

"I can hardly wait to hear from him," I said.

"I was always on your side, you know," Boucher said. "I know you think I wasn't, but I was. I still am. In fact, I could try to negotiate a very small increase on his part. He and I are still on pretty good terms."

"I don't think so, thank you," I said.

"Why not?" he said. "If I could get him down to say, five percent, that, together with my flat fee of five thousand, wouldn't be too bad. I'm sure Leclerc will get it for a good price, maybe better than you could do, and so you wouldn't in the end be paying any more for it."

"No, thank you," I said again.

"But why?" he repeated.

"I'm no longer interested in the horse," I said.

"I feel you're not being completely open with me," he said, hand over heart. "There's something you're not telling me."

"Well, that's certainly the pot calling the kettle black," I said. "You have been stringing me a line ever since we met. Godard was jet-setting about the world, was he? He'd changed his mind, he was being difficult. Leclerc is the only person who can get me an appointment with Godard. Wasn't that it? The man is in a wheelchair, and he's holding a contents sale! How stupid do you think I am?"

"I brought you here. You wouldn't have found Godard if I hadn't."

"Actually, I've been thinking about that. If I hadn't been given your name as a starting point, I could have tracked Godard down. It would have taken me a day or two, but I have contacts, and collections like his tend to be known in the circles I travel in. I could probably have done it in less time than it took you to bring me down here. What were you making me wait for? The first day of the sale?"

"I really was having trouble getting you an appointment with Godard. He's not quite well, mentally I mean, as anyone can see, but I thought he'd come around eventually, and I didn't want you to lose heart. I didn't know about the contents sale, either. I really believed Leclerc could help you. I'll grant you he's not the most pleasant person to deal with, but he has purchased objects from Godard, paintings and so on, over the past several months. I was as much the dupe as you were in all of this. Maybe more. But I was told to see to it that you got to meet Godard, and that was what I was trying to do."

"Who told you?"

"Told me what?"

"To see to it I got to see Godard?" I said, impatiently.

"I can't reveal that."

"Well then, this conversation is at an end."

"Look," he said. "I need the money. You promised me a flat fee of five thousand dollars if the deal didn't go through."

"No," I said.

"I will try to get you the horse," he said.

"It's a fake," I said.

"What?" he said.

"F-A-K-E, fake," I said. "You probably knew that, too."

"No," he said, swallowing. "I didn't. Really and truly." For once he didn't put his hand on his heart. He was probably telling the truth.

"Then you're not much of an antique expert, are you?"

"Perhaps not," he said. "But the man who asked me to set this up . . ."

"And who might that be?"

"I can't tell you," he said. "I already said that. But he knows his stuff. I cannot believe . . ." He sat staring at the table.

"Will you give me a lift back to Paris?" he said at last.

"No, I'm not going back to Paris," I lied. "You'll have to take the train."

"I don't have enough money," he said. "Look, is there anything I can do here to earn my commission."

"You could tell me who got you into this."

"I assume it was your client," he said.

"No, I don't think so. I doubt very much my client contacted you directly."

"Then I'll tell you who my contact is, if you tell me the name of your client."

"Do you want to be paid something, or don't you?"

"Five thousand?"

"Twenty-five hundred."

"Four," he said.

"Twenty-five hundred," I said. "Final offer. Considering all that's happened, I really have no obligation to give you anything at all. You can give me a blank check of yours, canceled of course, and I'll see to it that the money is transferred today."

"How do I know you'll do that, once I've told you?"

"Because where I come from, a person's word is good. I realize that is a foreign concept to people like you and Leclerc, but there it is," I snapped.

"Vittorio Palladini," he said.

"Who's he?" I said.

"Italian lawyer. Big collector. Not particularly discriminating. Rather *nouveau riche*, if you know what I mean. Don't tell him I said so. He just started collecting about three years ago. I sometimes help him find stuff. You really don't know him, do you? He's not your client?"

"Did he pay you a commission?" I asked, ignoring his question.

"No, he said you would."

"Well you've been screwed all round, haven't you?"

"Yes," he said. "That is certainly true. I was offended, you know, that Palladini wasn't using me. But this is a tough and unforgiving business, I'm sure you'll agree. He, the secretary, asked me if I knew Godard. I did, even if he doesn't like me, so I said yes. I called Godard, but he hung up on me, told me not to call again. I kept at it because I was afraid I'd lose Palladini as a client. He buys a lot of stuff, most of it from other people, but every now and then I get lucky. That's when I had the idea of bringing in Leclerc. Will you really pay me?"

"Yes," I said. The fellow was so inadequate, I found myself feeling sorry for him. But I had no intention of paying for nothing. "But first, tell me more. Did this Palladini person contact you directly?"

"Of course not," he said. "He's too big a personage for that. His secretary did. But I have found a few things for him in the past, so I did what I was asked. Also, I needed the money, as I've already admitted. Business hasn't been so hot lately. I'm out of my league here, I know."

"So this Palladini's secretary just said that you were to see that I meet Godard. Nothing more?" I said.

"Yes," he said.

"Okay," I said. "The money will be in your account later today. You can check it this afternoon. I'll say good-bye now," I said, picking up the bill. I wasn't going to leave money on the table with Boucher around.

"Au revoir," he said. "And thank you."

I went back to my room, got out the laptop, and reluctantly transferred twenty-five hundred dollars to Boucher's account, sent a few E-mails of my own to the store and to Jennifer Luczka, checking on her and asking if she'd heard from her dad. At this point, I just wanted to go home. I wished I'd never heard of Lake, never been dazzled by all his money, never had to deal with pathetic people like Godard and Boucher, nor miscreants like Leclerc.

It was in this rather melancholy frame of mind that I headed back to the chateau. It was late morning, and I was reasonably sure that Leclerc would be long gone. Indeed, I waited an extra hour to make sure of it. I didn't think I could stand another encounter with the man. Dottie would have come and gone by then as well. I hoped she got the furniture, but I thought if she hadn't, and given that the sheep's liver had said I was the one, I might have a go at Godard about that. If I got it, then the trip might have been worthwhile. I'd let Dottie know, of course. I wasn't that mean-spirited.

She might pay me a small commission if she still wanted it. If not, it would make a rather fine display at McClintoch & Swain.

By the time I arrived, the sun had gone behind the clouds, and a rain shower was passing through. The autumn colors that had seemed so beautiful in the sun were now a rather dreary and sere yellow. The sheep and the little lambs were gone, and my heart sank. It was all so unspeakably dismal, I could hardly get out of the car.

I knocked rather perfunctorily, not really expecting anyone to answer. Once again, the door creaked unpleasantly as I pushed it open.

"Monsieur Godard," I called into the gloom. "It's Lara McClintoch. I'm back, as promised." There was no reply.

I stepped into the dining room and gasped as a mouse scampered across the room. There was no sold sign on the dining room table. Dottie had apparently been unsuccessful in convincing Godard to part with it.

I went into the living room. There had been a fire in the fireplace, but it was now merely smoldering, giving off a rather unpleasant odor, as if someone had doused it.

"Monsieur Godard," I called out again. The place was absolutely silent. I crossed the threshold of the tower. The horse was still there. I walked up to it and saw a sold sign. *Leclerc,* I thought with some satisfaction. *I hope he paid a bundle for it.*

My enjoyment was short-lived however, because the very next thing I saw was a sold sign on the floor beneath the temple frieze. "Oh no," I groaned. "What will I do now?" I didn't think Lake would be too impressed with me when I called him back to tell him I'd lost the temple frieze, too.

The Micali painter: Lake hadn't been very interested, but perhaps that was because he didn't know what it was and could be persuaded. I turned to the glass case. The case was open, and the chimera hydria, the object that Godard had said was the very last thing he would part with, was gone. I suddenly had a very bad feeling about the place, a sense that something awful had happened. Perhaps it was just too quiet, I don't really know, but my feet felt like lead as I stepped into the study. The trapdoor was open, and Godard's wheelchair lay on its side nearby. I knew there was something wrong with that, but it took a second or two for me to remember that he had let the chair down on the rope before he descended himself.

I looked down into the basement but could see nothing. "Halloo," I called down, but all I could hear was my own voice sounding rather tinny in the space. With absolute dread, I grabbed my pocket flashlight and aimed its weak beam down into the darkness of the tomb. Godard lay sprawled, his body contorted in an awkward position, with his useless legs partly under him, his eyes still open, mouth contorted in a hideous grimace of fear or perhaps rage, as blood seeped from a wound at the back of his head.

FIVE

VOLTERRA

"GODARD IS DEAD," I TOLD LAKE.

"Dead!" he exclaimed. "This wasn't supposed to happen."

"No," I said. That was a ridiculous thing for him to say, but still, it was a shock.

"You didn't give him any money did you, before he passed on?"

"No."

"Well, that's something, anyway. At least I won't lose that. Hold on for a minute, will you?" He put his hand over the receiver, and I could hear muffled voices, but none of the conversation.

"Sorry," he said, coming back on the line. "I was attending to some other business. That Etruscan hydria you spoke of: I don't suppose you could just go back and get it? I don't mean steal it or anything. But you could leave a check for, say, five thousand dollars, payable to the fellow, and it would look as if we'd bought it."

"Mr. Lake!" I said. "The man has died in a dreadful accident! And anyway, the hydria was gone."

"Gone, did you say?"

"Yes."

There was another pause and again the sound of muffled voices.

"Okay then," he said, coming back on the line. "We're going to have to regroup here. I've got less than two weeks now. Where are you?"

"My hotel room in Vichy. I've been talking to the police. I think they'll let me leave soon."

"Good. Have you got a car?"

"Yes."

"All right then. As soon as they let you get on your way, head south. I'll meet you at my villa in northern Tuscany."

"Wouldn't it be faster to drive back to Paris and fly to Milan or Rome?"

"You'll take the rest of the day getting the car back to Paris, and you'd have to rent a car in Milan or Rome, anyway. Why don't you just get in your car and drive."

"Okay," I said.

"What happened to him, by the way?" Lake said, rather late, in my opinion.

"He fell into his basement. He was in a wheelchair. . . ."

"I didn't know that," Lake said.

"No. He had rigged up a method for getting down into the basement, lowering his wheelchair down and then himself. I guess that was what he was trying to do when he fell."

"What did he need to go into the basement for. Wine, or something?"

"He was painting his tomb."

"Oh," Lake said after a pause. "So he ended up dead in it, did he?"

"I'm afraid so."

"Unfortunate timing," he said.

I decided right then I didn't like Lake, not one bit. He was insensitive, didn't know a thing about antiquities, and was all round, a jerk. But by now I had spent rather a lot of the expense money: Boucher's twenty-five hundred, the airfare, the lovely hotel in Vichy, and the even lovelier one in Paris, the car rental, well it was shrinking rapidly, and the only way to recoup was to find something, anything, for Lake. If I told anyone, most particularly Clive, what had happened, they'd think I was an idiot. There seemed nothing for it but to carry on.

"I'll drive as far as I can today, then come the rest of the way tomorrow."

"Good," he said. "I'll see you there. I'll hand you over to my assistant now, to make the arrangements."

I drove as far as Nice that day, staying at a little inn just north of the city that Lake's assistant, an anonymous woman, had recommended. There would be a room reserved there for me, she'd assured me, which was just as well, because it was about ten at night when I pulled into the parking area. It appeared I was the last to arrive, because I had to sandwich my car into a very tight spot between a red Lamborghini with Italian plates and a bright yellow umbrella tossed in the back window, and a dark green Passat with a scratch on the back fender and a broken taillight. For a minute I debated whether or not to park out on the street, thinking that I might be accused of scratching the Passat or worse yet, putting even the smallest of nicks in the Lamborghini, but I decided I was just being paranoid after a particularly bad day. I could tell by the parking lot that this was going to be another of those expensive places Lake favored. There wasn't, with the exception of the Passat and my rented Opel, and perhaps the silver Renault a little farther along, a car there you could buy for under eighty thousand.

And in fact, the hotel was really lovely but also very expensive, as anything Lake had anything to do with seemed to be. It occurred to me that while I had enjoyed staying in rather nicer than usual hotels when I first came into Lake's employ, I now just resented the expense. I disliked it even more when, as I crossed the lobby, I heard my name being called out, and once again saw Dottie and Kyle. It shouldn't have been a surprise, given the Renault in the parking lot, but I was surprised, nonetheless, and not particularly happily. I liked Dottie, but I was in no mood for socializing.

"I can't believe the way we keep running into each other, Lara," she said. "What a nice surprise. Won't you join us for a drink?"

"I don't think so, Dottie. But thanks. I'm really tired, and—"

"I'll bet you are," she said. "That's rather a long drive, isn't it? Have you had dinner? No? Well, you must eat something. The food here is fabulous. The dining room's closed, but we can order you something in the bar."

I was too tired to argue and allowed myself to be led to a chair in the bar.

"Did you get the horse?" she said.

"No," I said.

"I didn't get the furniture, either," she said. "That's why we came down here, to do some more shopping. Did he just refuse to sell it to you?"

"I didn't get a chance to ask him," I said. "He was dead when I got there."

Dottie was so startled, she knocked over a glass of water, sending ice cubes across the table. None of us said anything as a waiter rushed over to repair the damage. "What happened?" she said when we were left to ourselves again. "He was perfectly all right when I saw him. Quite chatty and friendly, in fact."

"He fell into the basement."

"My goodness," she said. "Oh dear," she added, frowning. "How would that happen?"

"There was a trapdoor arrangement under the carpet in his study. He had a system for getting down, but I guess it didn't work."

"Oh dear," she said again. "You didn't find him, did you?"

"I'm afraid so," I said.

"You poor thing," she said. "No wonder you look so pale. I'm so sorry. Waiter, a single malt scotch for my friend." She paused for a moment. "You know what he said to me yesterday when I asked if he'd consider selling me the dining room furniture? He said he wouldn't because he had no more need of it. What do you make of that?"

"I don't know, Dottie," I said. I just didn't want to talk about this, and it seemed it was the only thing

Dottie did. She was so entranced by the subject she wasn't touching the food in front of her.

"And you know what else? He said he was going to someplace . . . *V*, something or other."

"Velzna," I said.

"That's it. What do you think that is?"

"I have no idea," I said.

"I'll bet it's someplace like Valhalla," she said. "He was hinting he was going to commit suicide, and I didn't even notice. I feel just terrible."

"He just fell, Dorothea," Kyle said, reaching over and patting her knee. "He couldn't walk. You shouldn't be worrying like this." These were the first words I'd heard him utter, other than hello, and much to my surprise, the man made a lot of sense.

"I expect Kyle's right," I said. "We should just try to forget it."

"I suppose," she said. "Are you planning to stay here for a couple of days? It would be a good idea, after what you've been through."

"I don't think so," I said. "I think I'll head for Italy. Tuscany."

"Tuscany!" she said. "That sounds nice. Maybe we'll go there, too."

Kyle shrugged.

"Where in Tuscany are you going?"

"Volterra," I said. I didn't really want to tell her, but she was so persistent. "To start, anyway."

"Volterra," she said. "I don't know it. Is it nice? Would you recommend it?"

"I haven't been there before," I said, "so I'm not sure. I just thought I'd go and see if I could find a nice place to stay and take a bit of a break, just like you."

"Volterra," she said. "Maybe we'll head for Tuscany, too."

The next morning, I was on my way early, having persuaded the inn to give me a decent breakfast and pack me a lunch. The bellhop placed my luggage in the trunk and a box lunch and a couple of bottles of water in the backseat, and then I headed down the highway for the border between France and Italy. It was a decidedly dreary day, with rain off and on, making the drive difficult and tiring. Shortly after I got under way, the water bottles started rolling around in a most irritating way, and the smell of the lunch was making me slightly nauseated, so I pulled over at a rest stop. I had a coffee, then opened the trunk to put the water and lunch box in.

The trunk, which until that moment I'd assumed contained nothing more than my suitcase and a spare tire, now held a cardboard box. I thought that I must have opened the wrong car, somehow, or worse still, driven away with somebody else's in Nice, but after a moment of some disorientation, I realized the key fit and it was clearly mine. Had I left the trunk unlocked, and the hotel made a mistake and given me someone else's belongings? I pulled open the box to find something wrapped in a hideous bubblegum pink blanket, which I removed, looking for clues as to the owner. I tugged on the edge of the blanket, and the Micali chimera hydria rolled out.

My heart almost stopped. I stood in the rain, staring at that thing for the longest time, until a family returned to the car next to mine, and I closed the trunk quickly and got into the car.

After the family pulled away, I got out again and

opened the trunk, hoping rather irrationally that in the
interim the hydria had disappeared. It hadn't. I
wrapped it up carefully, got back in the car once again,
and sat thinking about my current circumstances. In a
nutshell, I was approaching the border with an antiquity for which I had no papers. I could call the police
from the gas station, but what would I say? That I'd
found an Etruscan hydria in my trunk but had no idea
how it got there? I could take the hydria back to Vichy
and try to stick it back in the glass case in the chateau,
but, even in the unlikely event I could get back in the
chateau, that option would take many hours of driving,
and Lake was expecting me in Tuscany that night. That
some person or persons unknown had put this hydria
in my car for a reason that could not have been positive
did not occur to me at the time, which speaks to the
state I was in.

The only thing I could think to do was to keep on
going, hope I wasn't caught with it, and get to Lake's
place, where surely between the two of us, we could
work something out.

With the European Union, border crossings in Europe are rather more perfunctory than they used to be,
with most people simply being waved through. Holders
of foreign passports are treated somewhat more strin-
gently and are occasionally pulled over and their ve-
hicles searched, but relatively rarely. I thought the
chances of making it through were reasonably good. I
considered trying to hide the hydria under the floor of
the trunk or the passenger seat, but if caught like that,
I'd look guilty. It was too large to put in my suitcase,
but I put my luggage back in the trunk, along with the

lunch and the water to provide cover. Then, in a state of high anxiety, I started for the frontier.

I always think when I have to clear customs and immigration anywhere, that the line I'm in is inevitably the slowest, with either the surliest or the most suspicious agent, and there was no doubt this was the case on this occasion. As my car inched forward, and several cars ahead of me were pulled over, I got more and more frightened. I thought of changing lanes but decided this might call attention to myself. I started making up stories about how the wretched thing had managed to get itself into my trunk. Would my name now be in police computers, given that I'd called for help when I found Godard's body? Worse yet, would they somehow know this hydria had belonged to Godard and think I'd stolen it or, heaven forbid, that I'd pushed him into the basement when he'd interrupted me during the robbery?

My hands were shaking as I handed over my passport, and I suppose noticing this, the guard ordered me to pull over to one side. A rather severe-looking woman came out of the building and demanded I open the trunk. I pushed the button in the glove compartment, and then stood beside her, trying to look as if I hadn't a care in the world as she peered into the car. Miraculously, after a few seconds, and a couple of prods at my suitcase, and even a tug at the blanket, she slammed down the trunk lid and waved me on my way. Perhaps she thought anyone with sufficiently poor taste to have a blanket that color could not possibly recognize anything worth smuggling. A mile or two down the highway, I pulled over and threw up on the side of the road.

I was still feeling absolutely ghastly by the time I reached Volterra, the town close to where Lake had his villa. Lake had told me to check into another inn, lovely, I'm sure, not that I was in any frame of mind to appreciate it, and, as usual, expensive. It had taken me all day and well into the evening to get there, but despite my fatigue, as soon as I got to the room, I unpacked the chimera hydria, removed the lampshade to give me more light, and had a good, close look.

It was absolutely beautiful, even more so than I'd thought when I'd seen it in the gloom of Godard's chateau. The scene, Bellerophon killing the chimera, was painted with real élan, embellished with swirls around the neck and base. I loved the feel of it, the smooth surface, so perfectly burnished, the weight and the balance, things most of us don't get to enjoy, given our only opportunity to experience such antiquities is behind glass in a museum. The hydria was in perfect condition, without so much as a crack, let alone a repair, so good, in fact, that I wondered if it were a fake. I was disabused of this notion, however, after I placed a call to the shop.

"Hi Lara," Clive said. "Enjoying your little holiday?"

"It's lovely, Clive," I said. "Would you happen to have the Interpol CD handy?"

"It's here somewhere," he said. "Why?"

"There's something I want to check," I said, "so do me a favor and load it up, will you?"

"Okay," he said a minute or two later. "What am I looking for?"

"A hydria," I said. "Etruscan. Depicting Bellerophon and the chimera."

"Who or what is a Bellerophon?" he said.

"Hero on winged Pegasus who killed the chimera, which is . . ."

"I know," he said. "That thing with way too many heads."

It took several minutes of combing through the list of stolen antiquities before Clive said, "Give me a little more of a description of the hydria, Lara."

I did. "I think it's here," he said. "That was a pretty detailed description you just gave me. It's supposed to be painted by some guy called Micali—actually I think Micali is the name of the person who identified him, not the painter him- or herself—or one of this guy Micali's followers. Done around 500 B.C. You wouldn't by any chance have this thing in your possession, would you?"

"No, Clive," I said. "A vision of it came to me in a dream."

"I can never tell when you're being facetious, Lara," he said. "But if you do have it, it's stolen, from a museum in the archaeological zone of Vulci, wherever that is."

"Mmm," I said. This situation just kept getting worse.

"If you do have it," he said, "you'd better call the French authorities."

"Italian," I said.

"I thought you were in Paris," he said.

"I was," I replied. "Now I'm in Italy."

"Well, wherever you are, you'd better turn it in. According to the UNESCO resolutions on the subject, if you acquired this chimera thing in good faith, you're entitled to compensation for it. You did acquire it in good faith, did you not? You didn't say, steal it, or anything, did you?"

"No, I did not steal it, Clive." I sighed. "Thanks so much for that vote of confidence."

"Sorry," he said. "I just worry about you sometimes, Lara. Rob called, by the way. He says to tell you to stay out of trouble."

Right. Leaving aside the fact that it was way too late for that, what would have been wrong with "Tell Lara I love her," or "Tell her I miss her terribly every minute she's away"?

"He also said to tell you he misses you," Clive said. "I suppose I should have mentioned that first."

"Good-bye, Clive," I said. "If Rob calls again, tell him I miss him, too."

It was at this point that I hatched what I thought of as Plan A. I would get the hydria to Lake. He would then have one of his minions call a news conference on his behalf, or whatever it was he'd been planning to do with the bronze horse, and announce with a flourish that he'd managed to track down an Etruscan antiquity, probably by the Micali painter or one of his followers, that he believed to have been stolen. There'd be a nice speech about returning it to the museum where it belonged, where all could enjoy it and appreciate the rich heritage of the Etruscans and so on.

The plan wasn't perfect. There'd be questions about where he found it, and I needed to come out of this with a clean reputation and a nice commission, even if I hadn't paid anything for the hydria, and we'd both have to count on the fact that no one would recognize it as the hydria in Godard's place. I might be able to say that I bought it from Godard, at Lake's request.

Now that Godard was dead, who was going to argue with me? With a bit more refinement, I hoped Plan A would work. It had to. There was no Plan B.

I put the carton with its precious contents back in the trunk of the car to keep it out of sight of the prying eyes and possibly clumsy hands of the housekeeping staff and settled in to wait for Lake to contact me.

I didn't hear from him that first evening. I tried calling the number he'd originally given me, Antonio's cell phone, but there was no answer. I left a voice mail message to say I'd arrived. The next morning, I sat in the lounge of the inn drinking tea with lemon and slowly eating toast, hoping my stomach would settle down, waiting for Antonio to show up. After a couple of hours of this, I couldn't sit still anymore and headed out.

Volterra is a really spectacular place, a medieval town set high up, maybe 1,800 feet on high cliffs, the *balze* as they're called, over two huge valleys, with views in every direction. It's about thirty miles from the sea, which you can occasionally see, and it can be a pretty wild and windy place. It has narrow cobblestone streets that have a claustrophobic feel to them as the buildings on either side hang over the street. It has gorgeous public buildings, the Duomo and several churches, and here and there you can find reminders of a much earlier Volterra, the Velathri of the Etruscans and the Volterrae of the Romans.

D. H. Lawrence, visiting during a cold and rainy April, found Volterra to be a gloomy place, cold and damp, the people rather sullen. On that day, however, the sun was shining, and although, because of the steep and narrow streets and the buildings that shielded them, sunlight rarely reached street level, hovering instead over the red tile rooftops and the crenellations of the grander buildings, I found it all rather beautiful.

Realizing that I was hungry at last, I sought out a trattoria on a steeply sloped street near the center of the medieval part of the city, the Piazza dei Priori. It was late, the place was empty except for a couple of men at the back, and the server, a rather robust woman who obviously loved to talk, hovered after she brought my *insalata mista*, a lovely green salad with carrots and radicchio.

"Just here for the day?" she asked.

"A couple of days," I said. "I arrived yesterday and may stay a day or two longer."

"Most people just come for an hour or two, on their way to or from San Gimignano," she said. "There are nicer places to stay in Tuscany than Volterra."

"I think it's beautiful here," I said.

"You wouldn't think so if it was raining or really windy."

"Perhaps not," I said. Why argue? I just wanted to eat.

"You're not with the media, are you?" she asked a few minutes later as she brought a steaming bowl of *pasta al funghi*, mushroom pasta.

"No," I said, tucking into the food. "Why would you think that?"

"That Ponte business," she said. "The reporters, the police. What an affair!"

"Ponte," I said. "Is that the fellow who—"

"Jumped off the *balze*," she nodded. "You should have some wine with this," she said. "I'll bring you a nice glass of Vernaccia de San Gimignano."

"Okay," I said. I wasn't going anywhere.

"I saw him that very day," she said, placing the glass in front of me. Vernaccia is one of my favorite whites, so I took a sip and smiled. "Good?" she said. I nodded.

"He walked right past here," she said. "I was outside sweeping the street in front of the place. He walked down the hill and through the gate, the Porta all Arco. Have you seen it yet? No? You should. It's Etruscan, the bottom part, anyway, and the heads. They're supposed to be Etruscan divinities of some kind. Tinia, I think, plus a couple of others. They're guarding the town. Anyway, Ponte—we all know him here—he has a splendid villa, vineyards, everything, very fancy, on the road between here and San Gimignano. Later on, when I was going home, I saw him just standing there, outside the gate, looking over the wall. He'd been there for at least an hour. They found him the next morning at the foot of the *balze*. I say he killed himself. Why else would he just stand there looking out from the gate? I suppose he decided it wasn't high enough there to kill him, so he went over to the high cliffs, waited until dark so no one would see him, and then threw himself over the side. Lots of people jump off the cliffs there. They say suicidal people are drawn to that spot. Perhaps it's the sound of the wind calling out to them. Although why Ponte would want to, with that beautiful wife and children. You never know about a marriage, though, do you?" She turned to a call from one of the men at the back. "I'd better go. Enjoy your meal."

"I believe you've just been introduced to the Volterrans' love/hate relationship with their city," a man seated a couple of tables away said to me, as the woman retreated. I turned to look at him. He was very nicely dressed, a business suit with exquisite Italian tailoring, not terribly attractive, perhaps, but one of those Italian men who seem quite comfortable with themselves. He'd arrived a few minutes after I had. "Don't let her put you off your food," he added. "It is a lovely place, and all that nonsense about the *balze* is just that. Nonsense."

"Are you from here, then?" I said.

"No. Rome. I'd like to live here," he said. "But my wife is Roman, through and through. She'd much rather breathe pollution and gas fumes than be out in the country. We do have some property here, though, a vineyard and some olive trees, so I get to come here from time to time to check on them."

"I've always dreamed of having some property here," I said. "One of those wonderful old Tuscan farmhouses, a few acres of vines."

"Well then," he said. "My card. I know people in real estate I'd be happy to put you in touch with."

"I'd like to be serious about it, but no, I fear it's a dream only." I looked at his card. His name was Cesar Rosati. "Here's my card as well," I added.

"Antique dealer. How interesting," he said. "Are you by yourself, by the way?"

"Right now I am," I said. "But I'm meeting friends shortly." Not true, but I usually find it pays to be cautious in these kinds of situations. It was nice to have somebody to talk to, though. I'd been on the road for a long time, now, and I'd spent way too many evenings by myself in a hotel room watching CNN and eating room service food, which even in Italy isn't so hot.

"Do you mind if I join you? Talking across two tables seems rather unfriendly," he asked.

Why not? I thought as I gestured toward the seat opposite. "The Rosati Gallery," I said, looking again at the card he'd given me. "No doubt I should have heard of it, but I haven't."

He smiled. "There is no reason you should have. It's more a hobby than a business, and we can't compare ourselves with the fabulous collections in Rome. Like the Vatican, for example. It would be foolhardy, if not downright tempting fate, to try to compete with an organization with God on its side." We both laughed. "I'm semi-retired really. I used to be a banker. Now I just dabble in a few things. The gallery I do for the pleasure of it. My wife's family has some wonderful art, and we've opened a part of our home to the public."

"I must come and see it," I said. "What kinds of art do you have?"

"My wife prefers sixteenth-century sculpture, but her family has collected for well over a hundred years, so there's something for everyone: Etruscan right through to some twentieth-century paintings. It's small by museum standards, of course, but a very nice private collection. If you're in Rome, I hope you'll call me. I'll show you around personally."

"So, a gallery in your home," I said. "That must present some challenges. Security, and so on. With Etruscan artifacts, for example. There's probably a big market for those." I found myself asking the question, even though I wasn't sure I wanted to know the answer right at that moment.

"There is, indeed. It's a disgrace, really, how many Etruscan antiquities have been stolen or bought and sold illegally. We have very good security, of course,

but we did have one break-in. Funny you should mention Etruscan artifacts. Only one object was stolen, a
really gorgeous Etruscan kylix, nothing else. You
know what I mean by kylix, do you? A two-handled
drinking cup? Probably the Bearded Sphinx painter.
I'm sure it was stolen on demand. Someone wanted
that piece, and only that one, and hired someone to get
it."

The woman returned with Rosati's order, raised her
eyebrows slightly when she saw he'd moved, and
asked if we'd like some more wine. We said we did.

"It bothers me," Rosati said, as she left us. "The way
she talks about Gianpiero Ponte. I couldn't help over-
hear her talking to you about him. I knew Ponte. I
wouldn't call him a friend, exactly, but he was a close
acquaintance, and I dislike hearing people gossiping
about him. Who knows what makes a person do what
he did? Not the sounds of the *balze*, certainly. He had
a lovely wife and family, and it's a terrible tragedy."

"I'm sure it is," I said.

Despite that gloomy subject matter, I spent a reasonably pleasant hour of conversation with Rosati over
a second glass of wine, a *tartuffo*, and an espresso, all
of which improved my sense of well-being no end. He
made a few suggestions about sights in the area he
thought I'd be interested in seeing and was obviously
pretty knowledgeable about Tuscany as a whole. I
learned some more about the market for Etruscan antiquities, although nothing, really, I didn't know by
now. My one complaint was that he left his cell phone
on and took three calls while he was sitting with me.
I may be old-fashioned, but I really dislike listening to
people talk on the phone while they're sitting in a res-

taurant, particularly if they're at my table. He made an appointment with one caller, had a mild disagreement with the second, and brushed off the third. Then he placed a brief call to someone to tell them where he was.

At some point in the conversation I mentioned where I was staying. "Lovely place," he said. "If your friends haven't arrived, perhaps we could have dinner together at the hotel this evening. I promise I won't bring my cell phone," he added. "I can tell you don't approve."

I hesitated for just a second too long.

"No pressure. I'm sure you're busy," he said. "Why don't we leave it that I'll be in the dining room at eight. If you're there, wonderful. If not, it's no problem. I have no other plans."

"I expect I'll see you then," I said. Why not, really. It was better than room service again.

I checked for messages at the hotel. There were none, so I decided I might as well do some sightseeing. Plan A would work, I told myself. I just had to be patient and wait until I saw Lake again. By late afternoon, quite by accident, I found myself by the *balze*. The cliffs have something quite primordial about them, sheer drops and yawning crevices, where the wind whistles and groans far below. I knew what had created them. Soft yellow sandstone on top, they are a gray clay lower down. The water that falls on Volterra seeps through the surface stone, pooling in the clay below and destabilizing the ground. From time to time, great masses of the cliffs simply collapse into the depths below. The *balze* are, in many ways, starkly beautiful, but I could see that they'd be a place people would feel drawn to if they were desperate, or depressed, or just tired of life. I thought of Ponte, a man I'd never known, and Godard, one with whom I'd spent only the better part of an hour, both gone, perhaps both of them by choice.

Precariously near the edge of the cliffs stood the remains of an old building. Its walls were cracked and broken, and it looked forlorn, abandoned to its fate, as the edge of the *balze* crept nearer. Soon it would follow the Pontes of this world, the ancient walls and necropolises of the Etruscan city, and other much more recent buildings that had crashed into the dark chasms when the earth gave way beneath them. As I looked at it, I began to feel as if that abbey and I were alike somehow, that I, too, was standing helpless, unable to move, waiting to be pulled into the abyss. I wished I'd never met Crawford Lake nor been dazzled by his money and my own ambition. Annoyed with myself for being so deeply affected by the place, I pulled myself away to head back to the hotel, which seemed to me, with its bright lights and people, to offer a sort of sanctuary.

As I entered the grounds, though, I was fast disabused of that notion. The hotel had two small parking areas, one to the side of the hotel, the other around the back. I parked on the side, beside a red Lamborghini, the same one I'd parked next to in Nice, given the yellow umbrella in the back window, and entered the hotel by a side door. As I did so, through a hole in the hedge, I was startled to catch a glimpse of carabinieri in the back lot. To my horror, they were opening the backs of cars and peering in, shining flashlights against the dim light. I pulled back a little into the shadow of the hedge and thought what to do. The police were searching trunks. When they got to mine, unless I got it out of there, they'd find a stolen Etruscan hydria. I'd have to make a dash back to my car, drive off before they got to it, and find somewhere else to hide the hydria until I could contact Lake. I turned back toward the car.

At that moment, a dark green Passat with a broken taillight and a badly scratched fender pulled up to the unloading spot near the front door, about three or four cars from mine. The driver got out and signaled for a bellhop. As he did so, he turned slightly, and by the lamp at the entranceway, I saw who he was: Pierre Leclerc, or perhaps it was, as Godard had thought, Le Conte. This seemed just a little too much of a coincidence for me. Whatever his name was, he'd been in Vichy, and while I hadn't seen him, the damage to the car also placed him in Nice at the same hotel as I was. At some point between the time I'd seen the hydria in the glass case in Godard's chateau that first afternoon and the rest stop on the highway between Nice and the Italian border, the hydria, stolen not once, but twice, presumably, had turned up in my car.

Leclerc reached into the car, popped the trunk, and signaled to the bellhop to bring his bags in, as he went up the steps to reception. The boy took out two large suitcases and used his elbow to push down the trunk lid. Perhaps because of the damage to the back, it didn't catch, and the trunk bounced open a few inches as the two men disappeared through the hotel's front door. I really didn't think about what I did next, moving almost on automatic pilot. I looked about me quickly, saw no one watching, then in quick succession strode the few steps to my car, got the carton out of

PART II
THE LION

SIX

AREZZO

The hotel I chose in Arezzo was rather more modest than the places I'd been enjoying heretofore on this jaunt through Europe for Crawford Lake. If anything, it was a little down at the heels. Like many of the lesser establishments in Italy, it was decorated in red: red curtains, red bedspread, red tiles in the bathroom. Usually, this kind of decor offends my aesthetic sensibility. That's an occupational hazard for someone like me who deals with beautiful places and objects on a daily basis: We are a little hard to please in this regard. Here in the tiny *albergo* off the Corso Italia, Arezzo's main street, however, I felt much more at home than I had in Lake's lovely and expensive boutique hotels. Obviously, I'm a shopkeeper, not an aristocrat, at heart.

In addition to the questionable color scheme, there

was the hot water, when there was any, that clanged noisily as it made its way through what surely were prehistoric pipes, and the sounds in the next room, the rhythmic creak of the bedsprings and the grunts and groans of a rather energetic couple, came through the walls as if they were cardboard, which maybe they were. Still, the place had one overwhelmingly positive feature: No one, with the exception of Antonio, assuming he picked up his voice mail messages, knew I was there. I'd been very careful about that. I'd called the car rental agency and convinced them that the car they'd leased to me stalled all the time and insisted they give me a new one, which they did. Then I called the hotel in Volterra and told them that I would be checking out earlier than anticipated. I went back to the room and as quickly as I could, packed my bag, settled my bill, paying for an extra day so there would be no argument, and then disappeared—at least I hoped that was what I'd done—into the sunset.

I'd pulled out a map and at random picked a town that was far enough away from Leclerc and the carabinieri but close enough to Volterra that I could still meet Lake wherever and whenever—and I sincerely hoped it would be soon—that he called. The town I chose was Arezzo.

The hotel had several advantages from my perspective. The staff was pleasant enough but not too familiar or, worse yet, curious, and the clientele was, by and large, transient: backpacking students and the occasional businessman who stayed only briefly. It also had a nice little breakfast room—it became the bar later in the day—and in it they served a decent cappuccino and a better than average breakfast of cold cuts, cheese, fruit, and lots of croissants and bread.

"Would you mind if I sat with you?" a voice asked the second morning I was there, as I was drinking my coffee and searching the newspaper in vain for any mention of a stolen Etruscan vase or the arrest of the man I knew as Pierre Leclerc. "The dining room is rather crowded, and I'm afraid there doesn't seem to be a free table."

I wanted to say no. A couple of days before, I'd been eager for some company. Now, given what had happened, all I wanted was to be left alone. I looked up to see a woman of perhaps sixty or sixty-five, gray curly hair and sunburned complexion, clad in jeans and a flowered shirt. She was tiny, an inch or two under five feet, with the delicate features that make me feel, although I'm average just about everything, like a galomphing giant. I found I couldn't bring myself to snub her. "Please," I said, gesturing to the empty chair across from me.

"Espresso, please," she said to the waiter. "Don't let me interrupt you," she said. "Go right ahead and read your paper."

"I'm finished with the first section," I said. "Would you like it? It's in Italian."

"I would, indeed," she replied. "And Italian is fine. You have saved me a few lire today. Thank you. I confess I'm watching my pennies. On a pension of sorts. I usually watch and see if anyone leaves one, then I pounce on it."

"My pleasure," I said. I turned back to the newspaper, hoping she wouldn't talk. I was disappointed.

"Are you touring around Tuscany?" she asked.

I set down the paper. It was hopeless. "Yes, I am,"
I said. Tourist was as good an explanation of my presence as anything. "How about you?"

"In a manner of speaking," she said. "I've been here
in Arezzo for about a month now. No reason to go
home, so I stay on."

"There are lots worse places than here," I offered.

"Indeed there are. I love it here. I even like this little
hotel. I wish they'd use another color for the rooms
though. I feel as if I'm staying in a bordello."

I laughed. "My sentiments exactly."

"Well, if you have nothing planned for today," she
said. "You can always come and help me look for Lars
Porsena."

"Who?" I said.

"You know," she said. " *'Lars Porsena of Clusium/
By the Nine Gods he swore.'* "

" *'That the great house of Clusium/Should suffer
wrong no more,'* " I said. "I can't remember the rest
of it."

" *'By the Nine Gods he swore it,'* " she said. " *'And
named a trysting day . . .'* "

I joined in, and we finished it together. " *'And bade
his messengers ride forth/East and west and south and
north/To summon his array.'* " We both laughed.

"I know I recited that in grade school, but I can't
remember who wrote it, and I don't think I ever knew
who Lars Porsena was."

"Thomas Babington Macaulay," she said. "That
would be Baron Macaulay to you. *Lays of Ancient
Rome*, published in 1842. Not much as poetry goes,
but it has a certain schoolboy charm, wouldn't you

say? We also have the baron to thank for Horatius at the bridge."

"I know that one, too," I said. *"'With weeping and with laughter/Still is the story told/How brave Horatius kept the bridge/In the brave days of old.'* How's that?"

"Brava," she said. "I have only just met you, and already I know you are a woman of education and refinement. Even if you don't know who Lars Porsena was."

"I don't know where Clusium is, either."

"Clusium is Chiusi, just a few miles south of here. Several Tuscan towns are mentioned in the poem. Even Arezzo here, by its Roman name. *'The harvests of Arretium/This year, old men will reap.'* Volterra, too. Volterra was called Volaterrae by the Romans. The Etruscans called it—"

"Velathri," I said.

"You do know about the Etruscans!" she said. *"'From lordly Volaterrae/Where scowls the far-famed hold/Piled by the hands of giants/For godlike kings of old.'"*

"Stop!" I groaned. "No more Macauley, please. 'Where scowls the far-famed hold.' What could that possibly mean? No, don't tell me. I want to know who Lars Porsena was."

"An Etruscan who tried to reestablish Etruscan rule in Rome sometime around 500 B.C.E. It is quite possible that he was successful, but if he was, it wasn't for long. His son was defeated at the battle of Aricia shortly thereafter. Porsena's supposed to be buried in an absolutely fantastic tomb, complete with labyrinth. It's never been found, although many have claimed to discover it. Giorgio Vasari was one who did. He was

positioning, if that's the word, his patron, Cosimo de
Medici. You know who he is, I presume?" I nodded.
I most certainly did. Indeed I'd been lectured on the
subject by none other than Crawford Lake, but I
couldn't tell her that.

"Vasari was trying to persuade people that Cosimo
was the new Lars Porsena. In any event, Vasari was
wrong, I suppose about Cosimo, but certainly about the
tomb. The tomb wasn't found then, and it hasn't been
found since. For some reason, I took it into my head
that I would come upon it first. It's supposed to be
near Chiusi, Clusium, that is, which is just a few miles
south of here. In fact it's supposed to be under Chiusi,
'sub urbe Clusio,' according to Pliny, who also said it
was three hundred yards wide with a labyrinth, and
topped by pyramids.

"There are tunnels under the city that some say are
part of the labyrinth but I think were just drainage or
water systems. I decided that the tomb could be just
about anywhere in the area. I mean what did Pliny
know? He was writing long, long after the event. I
looked around Chiusi for a few weeks, then moved up
to Cortona—that would be Curtun to the Etruscans—
and then here. I'm working my way north. The wonderful thing about this project of mine is that many of
the Etruscan cities evolved over the centuries into some
of the most beautiful hill towns in Tuscany and Umbria, if not all of Italy. You're welcome to come with
me. I mean it. It's not too difficult, doesn't cost anything, gets you to some glorious countryside, and it's
rather entertaining, in a way."

"I'm afraid I have a couple of things I must get done
today," I said. I'd just confessed I was at loose ends,

so this rang false, but if she was offended, she didn't give any indication.

"Maybe another time," she said.

"Yes, it sounds like fun," I said. I didn't tell her I'd already seen one Etruscan tomb too many. As I spoke, she quickly slipped a roll, a pear, and some cheese into her bag.

"I guess you saw that," she said. "I load up on breakfast. It saves me stopping for lunch. No, I suppose I should be truthful. It saves me having to buy my lunch. I'm on a rather strict budget."

"That's okay," I said. "I remember only too well doing that in my student days and even well beyond."

"Thanks," she said. "I'm Leonora Leonard, by the way. Ridiculous name, I know. Thank heavens women don't have to change their names when they get married now, so they don't have to be saddled with a name like that. Please call me Lola."

"Okay, Lola," I said. "I'm Lara. Lara McClintoch."

"Lara and Lola," she said. "I think we're going to make a good team."

"Perhaps we are," I said as I got up to leave. "See you later."

I tried Antonio's cell phone. Still no answer, much to my annoyance, so I stomped out of the hotel. I'd told Lola that I had things to do, and I suppose I did, although nothing of any urgency. I checked out a couple of antique stores on the Via Garibaldi, got myself some money from a bank machine, had some lunch, and then did a little grocery shopping. I treated myself to a rather fine bottle of Tuscan wine, a Rosso de Montalcino, plus bread, cheese, and some prosciutto and melon. It was starting to rain, and I thought if it really got miserable, I'd have a picnic in the room that evening.

My heart was in none of these activities, and I thought that perhaps I should have gone looking for Lars Porsena's tomb with Lola. As unlikely a task as it was, it seemed to serve more purpose than simply marking time, which was exactly what I was doing, waiting for Lake to call. I decided I might as well go back to the hotel and have a nap. Sleeping might make the time go faster.

As I approached the hotel, I saw a shape I recognized. It was Antonio, I was sure, and I went dashing after him. He was well ahead of me, moving along the Via Cavour toward the Church of San Francesco, and while I called his name, he didn't appear to hear me. He turned right onto Via Cesalpino, striding uphill quickly toward the Duomo, the high point of the town, with me in hot pursuit. I was gaining on him when he reached the top, but he got into a car parked there and drove off as I came puffing up. I watched in dismay as the car turned the corner a block or so from my position, heading down the Via San Lorentino, presumably for the city gate.

I dashed back to where I had parked my car, and although I knew it was hopeless, I tried to follow him. I got caught in traffic near the city gate and sat pounding the steering wheel in frustration. From there, the road out of town went steeply downhill, then on to the main road between Arezzo and Cortona. There was no sign of Antonio's car. He could have turned either north or south, and for no particular reason, I chose south. The road was not all that busy, but the visibility was obstructed by the rain and the fog that was rolling in from the fields on either side of the road. I passed a couple of sodden people on bicycles and one on foot. After several minutes of this, I decided to give up and turned the car around to head back to town.

I was almost back to town when I passed the person on foot a second time, and this time felt a twinge of recognition. I was in such a bad mood that I tried to ignore it and drive on, but a hundred yards or so past the hapless walker, I stopped, pulled over to the side of the road, and backed up.

I leaned over to open the passenger door. "You look like someone who could use a ride, Lola," I said.

"You have no idea how grateful I am for this," she said after she'd climbed in and I pulled away. "Looking for Lars was not particularly entertaining on this occasion, I must say. I am soaked right through to my undies." She was shivering as she spoke, and I turned up the heat. Her trousers were covered in mud up to her knees, and she had a smudge on her cheek. The rain had made its way past the collar of her windbreaker, and there were streaks of wet down her flowered shirt.

"No tomb today, I guess," I said.

"Not today," she agreed. "Have you seen any of the Etruscan tombs?" she asked. "You really should, you know, while you're here."

"I've seen an Etruscan tomb of a sort," I said. "Someone I met in France was painting his own tomb in the Etruscan style, modeled on the tombs in Tarquinia. I've only seen pictures of the real thing, but this one looked pretty authentic."

"Painting his own tomb? Where would he be doing that?"

"In his basement," I said.

She laughed out loud, a deep, rumbling laugh that seemed to come from her toes. "Another victim of Etruscomania," she said. "Has to be. It's an incurable mental disease, I'm afraid, although I haven't heard that it's been properly documented as such by the medical profession. But what do they know? I'd like to meet this person."

"Unfortunately, he's dead," I said.

"What happened?"

"He fell into the tomb—from the main floor."

"Oh," she said. "That's terrible." Then she started to giggle, and much to my amazement, I did, too.

"It's really not funny," I said, gasping for breath.

"No, indeed it is not," she agreed between fits of laughter. "It just sounds so ridiculous. I've always said that Etruscomania is a terminal condition. I've just never thought of it quite that literally."

"He was absolutely bonkers, I have to tell you. He just kept maundering on about the Etruscans, and some Società he was a member of," I said.

"An academic group of some kind?"

"I have no idea. There can only be thirteen members, twelve plus one, whatever that means."

"One for each Etruscan city state, I'd think," she said. "The Dodecapolis. It was a loose federation of Etruscan cities. They met every year at—"

"Velzna," I said.

"Yes," she said. "Velzna or Volsinii to the Romans. I think you know more about the Etruscans than you're letting on. There are any number of organizations that get together to study the Etruscans. If it's not expensive, I'd probably like to join."

"Somebody has to die before you can get in," I said.

"Then maybe I don't want to join. Come to think of it, though, there's a vacancy, isn't there, now your friend is dead? Maybe someone killed him so they could take his place. Now there's a thought," she said.

We both dissolved into giggles again. "This really is silly, isn't it?" I said.

"Silly but creepy," she said.

Lola's teeth were chattering by the time we got back to the hotel. "You've caught a chill," I said to her, sounding like my mother. "I think you should go to your room and have a hot bath right away."

"Good idea, but there is a flaw. There's no hot water this time of day," she said.

"That's true," I said. In fact, the only way to get a hot shower was to leap out of bed the moment you heard the pipes clank, about six in the morning. That's when the water got turned on, or at least got up to a half-decent temperature. After that, it was pretty much tepid, if not downright cold, water for the rest of the day.

"Too bad," I said. "Are there any messages for me?" I said, turning to the young man at the desk.

"No," he said, checking my box.

"Are you sure?" I demanded. "Did someone not come and ask for me this afternoon?"

"I wasn't on duty," he said.

"Then could you check with someone who was, please," I said.

The boy, with some reluctance, opened the door behind the counter and poked his head around the corner. "There was," he said a moment later. "A man. We rang your room when he came, but there was no answer.

He didn't leave a message. He said it wasn't urgent, and he'd come back later."

Not urgent? It was, from my point of view. "Did he say when?"

"I don't know," the boy said. I glared at him. He poked his head around the door again. "No," he said. "He didn't."

Annoyed, I turned back to Lola. She was taking some olives from a small bowl on a table in the lounge. I was about to go to my room in a snit and leave her to fend for herself, but she looked so pathetic in her muddy, rumpled clothes that I couldn't do it.

"I have an idea," I said, taking her arm. "How does a glass or two of a really fine red wine sound to you? A little cheese, a little bread, and maybe even some prosciutto and melon."

"You're toying with me," she said.

"It's in my room," I whispered, signaling we should be quiet so the kid at the desk wouldn't hear.

"I'm your slave for life," she said.

We went up the stairs to the second floor arm in arm, then down the hall to my room. I unlocked the door and flipped the light switch. As I did so, I caught sight, out of the corner of my eye, of a flash of bubblegum pink blanket.

"Oh, my," Lola said. "What is that?"

SEVEN

CORTONA

LONG AGO, I HAD A GROUP OF FRIENDS who enjoyed a running gag. One of us had received, as a birthday gift from her mother-in-law, one of the ugliest platters ever produced. That Christmas, the original recipient of the monstrosity wrapped it up in an elaborate fashion and gave it to another member of the group. Soon the platter was being passed from one friend to another in more and more ingenious ways. It arrived in pizza boxes, was slipped into kitchen cupboards when no one was looking, hidden in garden sheds, or taped to the back of a box of laundry detergent when no one was looking. It was even placed in a toilet tank. You just never knew when that unpleasant object was going to turn up in your home. Contemplating the chimera hydria, swaddled in its pink blanket on my bed, I thought of that platter. The only difference was that one was a gift from a relative with no taste. The other was a priceless, stolen, twenty-five-hundred-year-old antiquity.

"It's gorgeous," Lola said. "Can I have a closer look?"

"Ah, sure," I said.

"It almost looks real," she said. "I mean, it looks authentic. Except it's so perfect. If it were old, it would have some flaws, cracks and things like that, wouldn't it? Wherever did you find it?"

"A student made it," I said. "An art student in Rome. I ordered a few more. We'll put them out and see how they do, and if they sell well, I'll reorder. I co-own an antique shop in Toronto, you see. Did I mention that?" Amazing how the lies were just tripping off my tongue these days.

"An antique shop! How lovely!" she said. "I've always wanted to do something like that."

"It would look good with the antique furniture we sell," I said. "If someone was looking for accessories and such."

"Yes, I can see that," she said. "Good idea. But he—is it a he or a she?"

"Who?" I said.

"The art student."

"It's a he." One has to be vigilant when telling tales. "He hasn't signed it."

"Hasn't he?" I said. "You're quite right, he hasn't."

"He should. You wouldn't want to be stopped by customs," she said. "Someone who doesn't know anything about it, thinking it's an antiquity."

"That's good advice," I said. "I'll make sure he signs the others I've ordered."

"This one, too, if you can send it back to him. Isn't it illegal to even possess certain antiquities in Italy? I'm sure I read that somewhere. Or maybe it was India. In any event, you can't be too careful."

"Point taken," I said. I really wanted to scream at her to shut up, but then the phone rang.

"Hello," the familiar voice said. Lake was almost whispering. "Is that—"

"Lara McClintoch speaking," I said rather formally for both Lake and Lola's benefit.

"Look, it wasn't supposed to go this way," he said.

"No, it wasn't," I agreed. "Would you like to set a time and place for us to meet, Signore Marchese?" I said.

"Who? I see: You're not alone, are you?" he said.

"No, I'm not," I said, smiling at Lola and gesturing at the bottle, while digging a corkscrew out of my purse with my free hand.

"Have you got the chimera vase?" he asked.

"Yes, I do."

"Good. I think it's our only chance."

"I agree," I said. I'd have to tell him about Plan A.

"Where and when should we meet?" I repeated.

"Do you know Cortona?" he said.

"I know where it is, if that's what you mean. Not intimately, though."

"Do you know the Tanella di Pitagora?"

"No."

"Someone's coming. I've got to go. Meet me at the Tanella di Pitagora at seven A.M. tomorrow morning. There won't be anyone there, then. Bring it with you."

"But Signore—" The phone clicked in my ear. I had found the conversation more than a little annoying. I was going to have to get up awfully early the next morning to head out to find something called a *tanella*, in a town I'd never been to before, with absolutely no instructions on how to find it, or even what it was. I thought the word meant *den*, but that left me no wiser.

"How's the wine?" I asked, trying to sound normal.

"Really lovely," she said. "You are so kind."

"This looks nice," I said, admiring the way she'd arranged the food on paper plates on the tiny table by the window.

"Not much of a view, is it?" she said, pulling the curtain against the dull grayness outside. "My room's across the hall, but the view is much the same. No fire escape, perhaps, but another blank stone wall on the building next door. Shouldn't complain, though. The price is right. So tell me about your antique shop," she said, as we clinked glasses and sipped the wine.

I told her all about it, how I'd started the business, married Clive and then divorced him, losing the shop when I had to sell it to give him half as part of the divorce settlement. Then, how I'd bought back in, and now Clive and I were back in business together. I told her that my best friend, Moira, and Clive were now partners, a confession that made her raise her eyebrows theatrically. I told her just about everything, chattering away nervously, while I kept glancing at the chimera hydria, despite every effort not to, and starting whenever she looked at it.

"Your turn," I said finally, as I poured more wine. "What have you been doing for the last several years?" We both laughed.

"I was a secretary for many years, over twenty, actually. I suppose now one says something fancy like admin assistant, but still, I was secretary to the president of a manufacturing company. We made auto parts. I started as the receptionist and worked my way up from the typing pool."

"Good for you," I said.

"I suppose," she said. "I married very young, you see, and when it didn't work out the way it was supposed to, and I was on my own, I had to get a decent job. But it didn't turn out very well."

"How so?" My mind was racing, trying to figure out how to first of all put the chimera hydria away somewhere so neither she nor I could see it, and then to turn the conversation around to some subject that would permit me to ask directions to the Tanella in Cortona.

"Here I am, broke, and relying on the kindness of strangers. Not that you feel like a stranger, but you know what I mean. I wouldn't be drinking Rosso de Montalcino and eating prosciutto if it weren't for you."

"So what happened? Did the company go bankrupt or something?"

"No. In fact it was very, very successful. I got fired when the president died suddenly. Heart attack. His son took over, and poof, I was gone."

"That's not fair," I said.

"I suppose it sounds that way, but I got what I deserved," she said.

"Why on earth would you think you deserved that?"

She was silent for a minute. "Because," she said, "I behaved very badly. For several years that I worked for him, we were lovers. His wife was a good friend, too. Oh, I can't believe I'm telling you this," she said, putting her hand up to her mouth. "It must be the wine. You are going to think so badly of me."

"You're hardly the first secretary to find herself in that position," I shrugged. "And who's to say, anyway? Why would I judge you for that?"

"You're very generous," she said. "In more ways than one. I think my behavior was reprehensible, even if I was wildly in love with him. I feel terribly guilty about it still. Getting fired was a relief. His son called me in the first day, said he needed someone more in tune with the times to assist him, and handed me a check. I suppose his mother must have known all along. How awful for her."

"I hope you got a decent settlement, whether the son and his mother knew or not. After all, you'd worked there a long time. Over twenty years, didn't you say?"

"I gave most of it to charity," she said. "Part of my penance, I suppose."

"Isn't that rather—I don't know—Calvinist, of you?" I said.

"Calvinist." She laughed. "That's an interesting way of putting it. There are days I wish I were Catholic. Confession might help. I can't even bring myself to go to any place of worship, though. I haven't since I took up with George. That was his name: George. It seemed rather hypocritical to pray to God when I was acting the way I was."

"So how have you managed to get by, then?" I said. "Did you get another job?"

"I took a few temporary assignments. I was too old to get another permanent position."

"So how did you get from temp assignments to look-ing for what's his name's tomb?"

"Lars Porsena. One day, after a particularly trying assignment, I ran into an old acquaintance of mine. We were reminiscing about the summer we'd spent in Italy many years ago, working on an archaeology project at Murlo, Poggio Civitate, a great site south of Siena. We'd both signed up as volunteers on a dig being conducted by Bryn Mawr. It was the most wonderful summer of my life, I have to tell you, and suddenly I just decided to come back to Tuscany. I have some savings, and I think my Italian is good enough that I may be able to do some secretarial work from time to time. Finding the tomb of Lars Porsena was as good an excuse as any."

"And are you glad you did it?"

"You know, I am. I still get mad when I think about those louts, both of them, father and son, but when I'm out in the countryside poking around, I feel quite at peace. Telling you about it is making me angry again, though, so let's talk about something else."

"That's a remarkable story," I said. "But if you want to change the subject, I have a question for you. I've been thinking of doing some sightseeing tomorrow in Cortona. Is there anything you'd recommend I see while I'm there?"

"Yes, indeed. There's a nice museum, not huge, but a lovely collection. It has a fabulous Etruscan bronze lamp."

"I was thinking more outdoors." I don't know what made me think a tanella was outdoors, but given that I was reasonably sure that the word meant den, it made sense to me that it would be.

"Cortona itself is quite wonderful. Medieval hill town. It's certainly worth many hours of wandering.

I'm into Etruscan stuff, of course, so I'm slightly bi-
ased in what I'd recommend. As is the case with most
of the old Etruscan city sites, there's not much Etruscan left to be seen. There are a couple of places,
though, that are quite worth seeing: I'd be sure to go
to see the Meloni and the Tanella di Pitagora."

"What's that?"

"The Meloni are tombs, melon-shaped, as the name
implies."

"And the Tanella?"

"It's wonderful," she said. "It's an Etruscan tomb as
well, but very unusual. It's barrel-shaped and sits on a
very large stone base. The roof is supported—I'm telling you more than you care to know, I'm sure."

"It sounds very interesting," I said. "Where would I
find it?"

"It's not difficult to find. You take the Arezzo-
Perugia road toward Cortona. It's about two kilometers
from the highway, on the main road into Cortona. You
just follow the signs for archaeological sites. The tanella is well marked. It's partway up the hill on the
way to the old town. You can just park on the side of
the road and walk up. It's not far. You're supposed to
make an appointment at the museum to see it, but don't
worry about that. Just follow the fence around, and
you'll find a place you can crawl under without too
much effort."

"I'll do that," I said, picking up the wine bottle.
"There's still some wine left. I vote we finish it."

Her reply was interrupted by loud banging on a door
down the hall. "What is that?" I said.

"Signora Leonard, open the door," a voice said. I
turned and looked at Lola. Her face was white as a

sheet, and her hands were shaking. "No, please," she said. The banging continued for a minute or so, and doors opened and slammed down the corridor, as other guests presumably looked into the hall to see what was going on. There was a pause, finally, and the sound of a door opening, then a few seconds later closing, and then footsteps in the hall, heading in our direction. Soon there was a sharp knock on my door. We both stood motionless, hoping it would go away, but then I heard the clink of keys. It was obvious if I didn't answer, they'd come in anyway. "Who's there?" I said, grabbing my bathrobe.

"*Polizia,*" the voice replied.

"One minute, please," I said, quickly pulling off my blouse and pants and putting on the robe. I motioned Lola to get into the bathroom. She just stood there as if rooted to the ground. I scooped up the hydria from the bed and handed it to her, gave her a push, which got her going, and slowly opened the door a crack, as the bathroom door clicked shut.

"What is it?" I said. Two police officers stood at the door, one tall and thin with a rather dashing mustache, the other short and rather plump. They did not introduce themselves. Behind them, looking nervous, was the young man from the front desk.

"We are sorry to disturb you, Signora," the short one said, looking at my bathrobe and almost leering. "We're looking for Signora Leonora Leonard."

"I'm afraid you have the wrong room," I said, pulling the robe tight around me. "I believe she is staying down the hall."

"She's not there," the tall police officer said.

"Looks as if she took off without paying," the young

man from the front desk said. "Clothes gone and everything." The taller man glared at the kid, who blushed.

"She was here," I said, "For a drink. But she left." I knew the kid had seen me talking to Lola and might even have heard me invite her up to the room, so denying it would be a very bad idea. Lola had, however, neglected to mention the fact that she was no longer a resident of this hotel.

"Do you mind if we have a look?" the tall one said. I opened the door and stood in front of them, but they pushed past me.

"You didn't finish your wine," the tall one said, looking at the table. Two half-full glasses of wine sat there, along with the remains of our picnic.

"No," I said. "We'd had enough."

"Good wine," he said, picking up the bottle and peering at the label. "I wouldn't waste it, if I were you. Did she mention where she was going? Signora Leonard, that is?"

"No," I said. "I'm afraid not. I just assumed she was going back to her room. I wasn't aware she'd left the hotel, and she didn't mention it. I don't really know her very well, of course. We just met this morning."

The short policeman peered into the closet, then walked over to the bathroom door and pushed it open. He looked in but didn't actually walk into the room.

"Sorry to bother you," he said at last, and the three of them left. I half expected one of them to ask me to get in touch with them if I saw her, but they didn't. I closed the door and waited as their footsteps receded down the hallway. After opening the door a crack, just to make sure they were gone, and then securely locking the door, I leaned into the bathroom.

"It's okay, Lola," I said quietly. "They've left." Silence greeted my words. I pushed back the shower curtain. No Lola. I checked behind the door. It took me a minute to realize that the window was unlatched, although it was pushed closed. I opened it and looked out onto the fire escape. No Lola there, either. I couldn't see anyone down in the alleyway below, and there was no sound except the drip of the rain and the sound of cars out on the street to the left. "If it's a money problem," I called down as quietly as I could. "I could lend you some cash to pay your hotel bill." Still no answer. I could only assume that Lola was gone. It took another minute or so to realize that the chimera hydria had gone with her.

AT SOME POINT IN OUR WINE-FUELED EX-change of confidences, Lola had told me that Cortona was the site of a major battle between two implacable enemies, the legions of Rome and the Carthaginian general Hannibal, who, seeking to avenge his family's earlier defeat, had done the impossible and marched on Rome from the north by crossing the Alps in the dead of winter.

Ever the clever strategist, Hannibal ambushed the Roman army, under Flaminius, in the early morning, when, as is often the case, a thick mist covered the low-lying areas at the foot of the hill on which Cortona stood. The Romans, lost in the fog, panicked, some of them to be cut down by Hannibal's troops and the Etruscans of Cortona, who came down upon them from the hilltop. Others, disoriented, fled, only to plunge into nearby Lake Trasimeno and drown.

I know exactly how the Romans felt. It was pitch dark as I left the hotel and negotiated the road between Arezzo and Cortona. A thick fog covered the road that morning, too, and from time to time headlights of oncoming cars would appear out of the haze, startling me. I missed the turnoff for the town and had to do a U-turn, a hazardous undertaking at the best of times, and almost suicidal under the circumstances, narrowly missing a collision with a red sports car heading the other way.

The mist thinned only slightly as I started up the hill toward the town. I almost passed the sign for the Tanella di Pitagora but caught sight of it just in time. Cautious now, and a little frightened by the isolation of the place, I drove around the next switchback before pulling the car over to the side.

I walked back to the sign for the archaeological site and followed a path up the side of the hill, moving as quietly and carefully as I could. It was still dark, just before dawn, but the sky was lightening. The Tanella, a rather odd-shaped, arched stone structure on a large stone pad, sat perched on the side of the hill, surrounded by cypresses, in a enclosure of chain-link fence. There was a gate, locked, and a bell to summon the custodian, but no one was there.

I circled the enclosure on the uphill slope so that I could see someone coming from the road below. Sure enough, as Lola had predicted, there was a place on the downhill side of the site where the fence had been pulled up, and where someone with a reasonable degree of agility could climb under and up a slight rise to the tomb.

I was several minutes early, deliberately so, and

found myself a position, a rather damp one, where I could watch the site without, I hoped, being seen, and settled down to wait. I tried not to think too much about my circumstances. I'd had pretty much the whole night to think about Lola and the vase, and what exactly it was I was going to say to Lake when he asked to see it. 'Where is it?' would be only one of the many questions for which I had no answers. For instance, how had the vase gotten in my room in the first place? Had it been delivered to the hotel and placed in my room by the staff? I went down to the desk after Lola's disappearance, but the day porter had gone home and wouldn't be back for a couple of days. Antonio himself? But why? And how had he gotten in, in the first place? The last person who had it was the unpleasant Pierre Leclerc or whatever his name was. If Lake wanted it, and Antonio had it, why didn't he just give it to him? And what about Lola in all of this? Had she just seen an opportunity and taken it, knowing, given her interest in the Etruscans, that it was real, despite my ridiculous story about the art student, or was she more actively involved in this mess?

Seven o'clock came and went with no sign of Lake, and soon a slight breeze caused the mist to swirl. Rather than thinning, it became thicker, as the valley mists started to lift with the sunrise. Soon I could see no more than a few feet around me. Olive trees that had been quite distinct a few minutes earlier became ghostlike wraiths that hovered about me. Sounds became muffled, and I couldn't discern the direction they were coming from.

I had a sense of unreality, of being in some netherworld where alien beings, malignant in intent, lurked.

I thought I heard footsteps, but then I wasn't sure. Next I thought I heard voices, whispers almost, but it could have been the wind in the cypresses or early morning birdcalls.

A minute or two later, I was certain there was someone nearby. A foot slid in the mud, and a slight cough pierced the silence.

"She's not here," a voice said. I think that's what I heard.

"She'll be here," another voice said.

"Then we wait," said the first. Utter silence followed. I sat on the wet ground, wondering whether to announce myself or wait until the mist rose and I could see who was there.

All of a sudden, there was a great flapping of wings and a shriek. Was it a bird? A person crying out in terror? I didn't know.

I simply could not sit there another minute. I got up, and without worrying about how much noise I was making, tried to make my way back to the road. I could just see a few feet in front of me and had only a vague sense of whether I was heading up the hill or down. I kept telling myself that, because of the switchbacks, I had to come out to the road at some point. Just when I thought I should have reached safety, I found myself back at the Tanella. Mist swirled about the stones, and what just a few minutes before had been an interesting architectural novelty was now cold and menacing. For just a second, I could have sworn I saw a man on the downside of the hill, his back to me, but then he disappeared, if he existed at all, into the fog.

The Tanella had given me my bearings, so I went uphill, away from the man I might or might not have seen. There was a path of sorts, and I took it, keeping my eye on the ground ahead of me. A bump appeared on the path. It took only a second or two to ascertain that the bump was a man, that man was Pierre Leclerc, and that Pierre Leclerc was dead, garrotted. The wire was still around his throat. I stumbled the remaining few yards to the road and, scratched and frightened, got into my car and fled.

As I headed back down the slope, a police car, blue light flashing, came up the road from below. In my agitated state, I debated about flagging them down and telling them about Leclerc. Fortunately, I didn't have to. As I rounded the next turn, I saw the car pull over at the bottom of the path that led to the Tanella, and two carabinieri get out and head up the hill.

I went back to the hotel, packed, and checked out, and moved again, this time to a hotel in Cortona. I left only my cell phone number on Antonio's voice mail.

EIGHT

CORTONA

THE DARK FIGURE, FACE HOODED against the rain, stared for a moment at the osteria's window display, then walked past it and turned the corner down a tight little cobblestoned street. A few yards along the way, a door was checked, then the end of the street surveyed. As I watched, the figure turned right, then right again, and went into a church, reappearing a minute or two later, finally retracing the route back to the osteria.

"Hello, Lola," I said. "You have something of mine that I would like back, please."

She started and turned as if to flee, but I had blocked her escape route.

"You have no business with something like that," she said, obviously deciding that the best defense was a strong offense. "I may not know antiquities the way you do, but I bet that hydria is real. I have no idea how you got it, and I'll give you the benefit of the doubt that you think it's legal, even though you made up that ridiculous story about an art student. I saw the way you looked at it, and kept looking at it. It's Etruscan, and it should be in a museum, not in the hands of a collector!"

"Lola," I said. "Believe me, you do not want to have that hydria. It could be dangerous. If you would give me a—"

"People blame the *tombaroli*," she said. "But they are usually just poor farmers. If there wasn't a market for what they loot, they wouldn't do it. Who said that collectors are the real looters?"

"Ricardo Elia," I said. "But Lola—"

"I'd say he would have been more accurate if he'd said collectors and dealers like you! People who buy the treasures, or even steal them, then smuggle them out of the country—"

"Lola!" I exclaimed. "Shut up for a minute." She was waving her arms about, and speaking louder and louder, and people were beginning to stare at us. "I am not planning to smuggle the vase out of the country," I whispered. "I smuggled it in."

"Oh, right," she said. "What kind of idiot do you take me for? Smuggling an Italian treasure into Italy!"

"Well, it's true," I said. "I have a client who wants to return it to the museum it was stolen from. Now, where is it?"

"Why should I believe you?" she said.

"That's a very good question, Lola. I don't know quite what to believe about you, either. Why should I be standing here in the rain trying to reason with some-

one who leaves hotels without paying, thereby attract-
ing the attention of the *polizia*, and who steals
something from someone she's been sharing a picnic
dinner with only moments earlier? Answer that one for
me, will you?"

"Because I have something you want?" she said.

We stood glaring at each other, rain dripping off our
noses. My jeans were wet up to the knees, my shoes
soaked through to my socks. "Let's go in and get
something to eat and discuss this somewhere dry," I
said at last.

"I'm not hungry," she said.

"Yes, you are. I saw you doing your little match girl
impersonation at all the food store windows, and just
now you were checking out an escape route, weren't
you? You chose this restaurant because it's on a corner,
and has a back door. You were planning to eat and
run, weren't you? Maybe duck into the church and hide
in the confession box?"

She didn't answer, but she couldn't meet my gaze.
I suddenly felt very sorry for her. "You won't have to,
because lunch is my treat."

"I don't need charity," she sniffed. I couldn't tell if
it was the rain or tears on her face.

"You can buy next time," I said. "Now, let's eat." I
took her by the elbow and led her into the restaurant.
It was a tiny little place, with a rather gruff proprietor,
but it was warm and dry, the food was delicious, and
the house wine just fine. For awhile, we stuck to neutral subjects: the weather, the relative merits of Cortona
versus Arezzo, her ongoing search for Lars Porsena's
tomb.

"It was nice of you to offer to lend me the money

to pay my hotel bill," she said suddenly. "I did hear you, down in the lane, but I didn't say anything. I will pay it off, you know. I have found myself some work, a little freelance bookkeeping for a lawyer. I start next week, just a few hours a week, but I sent the hotel all the money I have and told them the rest would come as soon as I was able to send more. I hope that takes care of the *polizia* thing. I'd have paid off the restaurant with my first paycheck, too, if you hadn't come along."

"The offer still stands, Lola," I said, thinking that there were still a few dollars left in my now rather emaciated Swiss bank account. "But we need to talk about the hydria."

"You're not going to tell me again that you smuggled it into Italy, are you?"

"Yes. I found it in France," I said. That was true. I wasn't going to tell her I found it in the trunk of my car in France. That would be too much for just about anybody. "I have, as I said, a client—I'm not at liberty to reveal his name—who wants to return it to the museum it was stolen from."

"Where might that be?" she said.

"Vulci," I said.

"That makes sense," she said. "Vulci, or Velc, was a center for the production of Etruscan pottery. Some of the greatest Etruscan artists, like the Micali painter, were based in Vulci. It looks like the Micali painter, by the way, or one of his followers. Did you know that?"

"I thought it might be, but it would take an expert to ascertain that," I said. It was Micali school, the Interpol database said as much. I was afraid if she knew that, she'd never take a chance on returning it to me.

"You do know what you've got here, don't you?" she said. "Or at least what I . . . we've got."

"I think so," I said. I assumed she was talking about Micali. I liked the idea of *we*, though. It sounded promising in terms of my getting it back.

"Would I recognize the name of this client of yours? Given that you can't reveal it?"

"Probably," I said. "Where's the hydria?"

"It's safe," she said. "You have to tell me the name of the client."

"I really can't."

"Then you'll not get the hydria back."

That was progress of a sort. At least she was considering returning it to me.

"You'll have to promise not to tell," I said. There seemed no way around this, despite Lake's requirement for anonymity.

"I promise," she said. I looked at her carefully. "Cross my heart and hope to die," she said.

"You haven't got your fingers crossed behind your back, or anything, have you?" I said.

She grimaced, placed both hands on the table, and said, "I promise."

"Crawford Lake," I said.

"*The* Crawford Lake?" she said. I nodded. "Wow," she said. "Have you met him?" I nodded again. "In person?"

"Yes," I said.

"Where?"

"In his apartment in Rome. Why does this matter?"

"I'm not sure I believe you. I've heard no one gets to see him."

A cell phone was ringing somewhere in the osteria. It took me a minute to realize it was mine.

"Hello," I said.

"What happened?" Lake said.

"Why don't you tell me?" I replied.

"I'm told there were other people there. Did you bring them with you?"

"I did not. What do you mean by 'I'm told'? Were you there?"

"Of course not," he said. "I sent one of my people. Did you tell anyone about this meeting?"

"No!" I said. "Did you?"

"Where are you staying?" he asked, ignoring my question. "I called your hotel, and they said you'd checked out. You know you are supposed to let me know where you are at all times. Why didn't you tell me you'd moved?"

"I'm in the general area," I said cautiously. "And I left a message for Antonio, telling him I was on the move and letting him know you or he should call me on my cell phone, which is what you're doing."

He sighed loudly.

"And about Leclerc?" I said, waiting for his reaction.

"Leclerc who?" he said. "What are you talking about?" I said nothing. There had been nary a word in the papers or anywhere that I could find about a body found near the Tanella. I was beginning to think I'd been hallucinating in that fog.

"Where are you staying?" he said. "I'll contact you there later and set up a rendezvous place and time."

"Why don't we set it up right now?" I said. The man was beginning to annoy me.

"Today, then. I must have that vase," he said.

"Fine. Just tell me where and when. Please make it somewhere I can see you; that is, not in a fog bank, and not at night. Right out in the open. And come yourself this time."

"The Melone di Sodo," he said.

"Just a minute," I said. I put him on hold. "Do you know a Melone di Sodo?"

"Sure," Lola said. "Melon-shaped tombs here in Cortona. Is it him?"

"Yes."

"Ask him which one."

"Which one?" I said to Lake.

"The big one. Melone two."

"Melone two," I said, so that Lola could hear. She nodded.

"Five o'clock. Melone two. It's Sunday, so there'll be no one working there. It will be private. Bring the vase."

"Okay, Lola," I said, putting away my cell phone. "Here's the deal. You come to that Melone tomb at five this afternoon. With the hydria. I introduce you to my client. If you believe him and me, you hand it over."

"Okay," she said. "I guess that's fair. Do you want directions to the Melone? It's actually just across the Arezzo-Cortona road from where you turned up toward the town to get to the Tanella."

"Yes. Do you want me to pick you up and take you there?"

"No," she said. "I'd like to meet Lake. I'll be there."

I hope you will, I thought.

"Here," I said, handing her a hundred thousand lira

note. "A loan to tide you over. You can take a taxi from town if you want."

She looked at it for a minute. "Is it a loan or a bribe?"

"It's a loan," I said firmly. After a moment's hesitation, she took it.

"Thank you," she said. "I'll pay it back."

At four o'clock, I was at the Melone. It was a huge mound, melon-shaped as could be predicted from its name, surrounded by fencing. It was under excavation, and on the eastern side, below ground level, there was a large staircase, ceremonial in nature, that had been uncovered. Around the back, to the west, were two very long and narrow shafts, which I presumed were tombs of some sort.

I carefully scouted the site, not wanting a repeat of my awful experience at the Tanella. Lake had acceded to my wishes for a more open spot. The main road was clearly visible from the site. To the south of the mound was a slight incline, and beyond that, a narrow road, then a grassy area. I found a spot where I could see, but once again, hopefully not be seen until I was ready to be. It had stopped raining, and the sun was low in the sky, so I was careful to have my back to it. I'd brought a sheet of plastic to sit on this time, so I settled down reasonably comfortably to wait.

At about quarter to five, I heard a motor scooter approaching, and a man clad in jeans, tan jacket, and a helmet, appeared. I was worried it was someone checking the site, and that we might be interrupted, but when he took off the helmet, I saw, with some surprise, that it was not Lake, as might be expected, but Antonio. I was about to stand up and wave to him when he wheeled his motor scooter, a rather dashing purple number, around the corner where it couldn't be seen by anyone approaching from the highway. Then he, too, hid from view. It seemed a little peculiar, so I decided to remain hidden.

About five minutes later, Lola hove into view, walking along the edge of the highway and turning down the dirt and gravel lane that led to the site. She was walking rather slowly, indeed limping a little, and she looked vulnerable and tired. She must have walked a fair distance carrying a large wicker picnic basket, not by the handle, but in her arms as if it was a baby, or, given current circumstances, a priceless treasure. I hardly dared hope. As she came nearer, I could see the corner of a bright pink blanket protruding from the basket. *Thank you, Lola,* I thought.

I was just about to stand up when, from out of nowhere, three police cars appeared, blue lights flashing, sirens screaming, streaking down the hill from the town across the main road. They crossed it and bounced down the dirt road toward us. Lola stumbled and started to run, but she was immediately surrounded by six carabinieri, guns drawn. One of them grabbed the basket, opened it, and with a triumphant gesture held the hydria aloft so that the others could see it. Lola stood there, completely stunned, her mouth moving, but no sound that I could hear coming from her. In a matter of seconds, she was handcuffed, roughly pushed into the backseat of one of the police cars, and the three backed up the road to the highway, then sped away.

I sat there, absolutely aghast, until the cough of a motor scooter springing to life brought me back to my senses. It was too late. As I stood up, Antonio roared away and soon was a mere speck on the horizon. I sat on the plastic sheet, watching the sun set, until my cell phone rang.

"Something very bad has happened," Antonio said. He was not bothering to practice his English anymore, and was speaking so rapidly in Italian I was having trouble understanding him. "It is fortunate that you were not at the Melone. I believe you're in danger. We both are. Get away from here. Go home. Don't tell anyone about this."

"I know what happened," I said.

"How could you know? Are you, too, part of this?"

"Part of what?" He didn't say anything, but I could practically hear his brain working. "I was hiding out the same way you were."

"I don't believe you," he said.

"Nice scooter," I said. "Lovely plum color."

"If you saw, then you must understand it is necessary for you to go away."

"I can't," I said.

"What's to stop you?"

"Leonora Leonard. Better known as Lola," I said.

"Who is Lola?"

"Lola is the woman we both watched being ambushed by the police and carted away in handcuffs, probably because she hasn't paid her hotel bill, but now probably because she has been found in possession of an Etruscan hydria. A stolen Etruscan hydria to be precise. The same stolen hydria you placed in my hotel room in Arezzo. She had it in safekeeping." That was something of a lie of omission, but in a way, true. "She was bringing it to me so I could give it to your employer, so he could be a hero. I think that pretty much obliges both him and me to try to help her."

"I didn't do that," he said.

"What?" I said. "You didn't do what?"

"Put the pot in your hotel room."

"I saw you near my hotel," I said.

"Yes, but I didn't put it there."

"Who did?"

"I can't tell you."

"Antonio!" I exclaimed in exasperation. "Tell me right now!"

"You don't understand," he said. "I don't know who it was. It wasn't supposed to be like this. There is nothing I can do to help your friend."

"Yes, there is. You can talk to Mr. Lake and tell him he must come here to straighten this all out. Or better still, you can take me to him, and I'll talk to him about it. One word from him, and all would be well."

"No," he said. "That is a very bad idea."

"Then I'll have to find him myself."

"No!" he repeated. "It won't do any good. Hold on, don't go away." There was a pause. "I had to put more coins in the phone."

"Why won't it?"

"Why won't what?"

"Please don't be evasive, Antonio. Why won't it do any good to go to Mr. Lake?"

"I can't tell you."

"Then I'm going to the police."

"Don't you understand? I think that's what you're supposed to do."

"I guess I don't understand, Antonio. Why don't you explain it all to me?"

"You, I, that woman, what's her name, are all pawns."

"Of Lake?"

"Sort of," he said.

"I'm going to the police," I repeated. "Your name is certain to come up in the conversation. Your lovely Teresa isn't going to see you for a long, long time."

"No, please. We must discuss this. Not by telephone. I will try to explain everything. Now I'm running out of coins. There's a little town called Scrofiano south and west of here. Near Sinalunga. There's a house a mile or so outside the town." He gave directions rapidly. "Tonight."

"Not tonight," I said. There was no way I was wandering around in the dark under the circumstances.

"Tomorrow morning then. Early."

"Not until the fog has lifted," I said. "Noon."

"Noon might be too late," he said. "Make it ten."

"Noon. Will the carabinieri be there, too?" I asked. "They do seem to have a way of turning up whenever I'm supposed to meet Mr. Lake. Maybe it will be the same when I'm supposed to meet you."

"No," he said. "This is worse for me even than for you. Make it noon, then. Just be there, please. And be—" The call ended. I guess he ran out of coins in midsentence.

It took me all that evening and much of the next morning to find where they were holding Lola, in a cell in the carabinieri station in Arezzo. She looked old all of a sudden: pale, wan, and with a listlessness about her that made me really concerned for her welfare. She looked both surprised and pleased to see me.

"I didn't think you'd come," she said.

"Of course I came," I exclaimed. "Why wouldn't I?"

"Because," she said, but didn't finish.

"Because you thought I set you up?"

"Maybe. I don't know what to think."

"If I wanted the hydria for myself, letting the police get it wouldn't be a very good idea would it? And if I really intended to give it to Lake, then it wouldn't be a good idea in that case, either."

"No," she said. "I really didn't think you'd set me up. It didn't make any sense. One thing I do know is that I wish I'd never seen that hydria. If I hadn't taken it, then—"

"Then I'd be in here," I said. "I'm going to tell you something. I didn't purchase the hydria. I saw it in a chateau near Vichy and tried to buy it, but the owner wouldn't sell."

"Not the man who fell into his tomb?" she said. "Did he have it?"

"Yes. It was gone when I went back to try again to purchase it. Maybe it was stolen, maybe he decided he would sell it, and someone else got it. All I know is that it wasn't there. Then it turned up in the trunk of my car in France. I got it across the border because I didn't know what else to do. I didn't know it had been stolen at the time, but I found out later when I checked the Interpol database of stolen antiquities. In any event, when I got it here, Volterra actually, the carabinieri arrived at the hotel I was staying in and started going through the trunks of cars. Then I did something really awful. I put it into a car belonging to a French dealer that I thought had been the one to put it in my car in the first place."

"Why would he do that?"

"He was annoyed I wouldn't cut him in on the purchase of an antiquity."

"But you got it back," she said.

"Yes. It showed up on the bed in my room in Arezzo. I have no idea how it got there, and I was as surprised to see it as you were when we came through the door. I was supposed to take it to the Tanella, but of course I couldn't, because you had it."

She grimaced. "You seem to have found yourself in the middle of something. We both have."

"Yes, but what? The carabinieri showed up at the Tanella, too, but by then I was on my way back to the hotel. So that's three times when I had, or at least was supposed to have, the hydria with me, that they showed up. But it would have to be a coincidence, wouldn't it? They also showed up at the door of my hotel room while the hydria was lying on the bed, but it was you they were looking for that time."

"It was," she agreed. "Can you imagine a hotel calling the carabinieri just because someone leaves without paying their bill? It was only a few dollars. A couple of hundred. Maybe three. I suppose that's why they caught me with the hydria. They were after me, anyway, and just lucked out on the antiquity. It makes me mad, though, after I went to the hotel, in person, and paid off a big chunk of what I owed them, and promised the rest of it within a month. They agreed to my terms, too. Maybe I should give them the benefit of the doubt and say they just forgot to inform the police that we had reached an accommodation, but I think it's a bummer. You're probably thinking this serves me right."

"No," I said. "I'm not."

"Thank you. I suppose I should try to look on the bright side," she said. "They do feed you here. Nothing like the lovely meal you treated me to yesterday. Was it only yesterday?"

"Lola, everything is going to be okay."

"Yes. Before I forget, would you mind phoning Signore Vitali, the lawyer I'm supposed to be helping with his bookkeeping, and tell him I won't be showing up for work? Have you got a piece of paper? I memorized the number. They took my purse. He's a nice man; at least, he seemed to be. I feel bad letting him down like this."

"I'll take care of it," I said, writing down the number.

"He's semiretired. Just keeps a few clients now. He's interested in Lars Porsena, just like me. He's researched the area. We thought of combining forces to try to find the tomb. I don't know what he'll think when he hears I'm in jail. He's a lawyer. I don't expect he'd be too keen on an employee, even a contract one, who has been in jail. Too bad, really. I really liked him, and I thought maybe he liked me, too. No doubt he'd been even less keen on having a lady friend who'd been in jail."

"You don't know that," I said.

"Yes, I do. Didn't you tell me your partner is a Mountie? How thrilled would he be if he found out you were in jail?"

"Not very," I said. That was an understatement. I hoped I never had to find out how "not very" it would be.

"Maybe you could tell Salvatore—that's his name—that I've come down with laryngitis, or something, and can't talk, and don't want to infect him, but that I'll call him soon. I hope I'll be out of here in a few days. Do you think so?"

"Lola, listen to me. Everything is going to be okay. I'm meeting a colleague of Lake's later today, and I'm going to make him come in and explain everything."

"He'd be willing to do that?"

"I'm sure he would." *He will when I'm finished with him,* I thought. I was in no mood for Lake's delicate sensibilities about appearing in public. "You'll be out of here by the end of the day, or tomorrow at the latest. I promise I won't leave you here."

"Lots of people have made promises to me over the years," she said. "Few have kept them."

"I will," I said.

"I don't know. Sometimes you get what you deserve, and maybe this is it for me."

"Don't be silly, Lola. Sneaking out of a hotel without paying shouldn't get you in jail for possessing illegal antiquities."

"You don't know what I've done," she said. "I wouldn't blame you if you just went home."

"I'll be back," I said.

"I hope so," she said, as they led her away. I winced as the cell door clanged shut behind her.

I picked up the Autostrada del Sole at the Arezzo exit and headed south, pulling off at the turnoff for Sinalunga. From there, I picked up the *raccordo*, or trunk road, heading in the direction of Siena, staying on it until just past Sinalunga, at a turnoff for Scrofiano. The road climbed rather sharply and turned into the town, a pretty place with very steep and narrow cobbled streets, flowerpots in every window and doorway, and not much more in the way of public buildings than a church and a general store. I stopped at the store to buy water and to check my directions.

"Ah, that's Signore Mauro's house you're looking for," one of the customers in the store said. "You are perhaps interested in buying it?"

"Yes, I am," I said. *Why not?* One takes these opportunities when one can. I wondered if Signore Mauro was a name Lake used for purposes of anonymity, or whether he was just borrowing the place for the occasion. "Actually I was wondering if it is available for rent, rather than purchase. It is still available, is it? Or am I too late?"

"I don't think he's sold it yet, although from what I hear, he'd like to sell it rather than rent."

"I'm sure I couldn't afford that," I said. "Although it would be wonderful to have a place here. Quite expensive, I'm sure. Is Signore Mauro here, do you think?"

"Haven't seen him around here lately. As for expensive, the place is less than it would have been even six months ago. There are those who say he has to sell, a bad marriage, according to some. Others that he's fallen on bad times."

"Then perhaps I stand a chance," I said. He came outside with me and gave me directions. The road out of town quickly turned to gravel. To either side were vineyards, the grapes still on the vines, and fields already plowed under, the soil a raw ochre. By a white stone fence, I turned left onto a bumpy road, which I followed past several houses, and many dogs, all of whom raced my car from behind wire fences. The road came to an end at a row of cypresses, beyond which sat a lovely genuine old Tuscan stone farmhouse, two storys high. Home at one time, no doubt, to *contadini*, farmers, before it had been acquired by the likes of Signore Mauro, whoever he was, it was the last house on a ridge, blessed by a spectacular view across the valley to Cortona perched on its hill, and sweeping vistas of olive groves and vineyards the other way, with the dark outline of misty hills farther south.

The shutters on the house were closed up tight. I knocked on the door but heard nothing. I walked around the house to find a small but charming vine-covered terrace, with a small table and two chairs set out there. A jacket hung over the back of one chair.

"Antonio?" I called out. "Where are you? You don't have to hide. It's only me."

There was no answer. Not a sound, even, except the wind stirring the silvery leaves of the olive trees. I pulled out the other chair and sat down. Beside the terrace, a rosemary bush and sage gave off a wonderful scent. Somewhere in the distance, a dog barked. A little closer, came the squawk of a small animal or bird. Something creaked nearby, then banged, a shutter perhaps. For the first time since I arrived, I looked up.

The house had been outfitted with a pulley arrangement in the peak of the roof on this side of the house, presumably to pull large pieces of furniture, like the family's baby grand, up to the second floor. It was now serving a new purpose, supporting Antonio, a noose tight around his neck. He'd been strung up, perhaps still alive and fighting for his life, given that the fingers of one hand were caught between the noose and his neck, as if he'd struggled to keep it from strangling him. The rope that held him aloft had then been neatly

NINE

ROME

THE NEXT DAY BROUGHT ITS OWN SET of unpleasant surprises.

"Now, let's go over this one more time," Massimo Lucca said. He was a tall, thin man, with reddish hair and a dashing mustache. He was pleasant enough, polite, quiet spoken. He was also a police officer.

"What you're telling me is that you found the chimera vase, hydria, or whatever it is called—you corrected me on that score already—in France, and that you brought it back into Italy."

"That's right," I said.

"And your intention was to return this hydria to the museum in Vulci from which it was stolen many years ago."

"That's also correct."

"And Signora Leonard?"

"She was assisting me. She had the hydria in safe-keeping and brought it there to give to me. You arrested her before she was able to do that. Once the transfer was complete, Signora Leonard would most certainly have paid off her hotel bill."

"What hotel bill?"

"Her hotel bill in Arezzo," I said, heart sinking at the thought that I might have made Lola's situation even worse. "That's what you arrested her for, is it not? She already reached an arrangement with them. Go ask them."

He made a note on the pad in front of him. "No," he said. "We were not chasing down someone who didn't pay a bill. We were looking for the antiquity."

Somewhere in the back of my mind, I had already reached that conclusion, even if I'd refused to admit it to myself until now. "How would you know she was going to be there with the hydria?" I said.

"I'm not going to tell you that."

"Oh come on," I said. "It will all have to come out at her trial, won't it? You'll have to tell her lawyer." I had no idea whether or not this was true, given that I had no previous requirement to learn the intricacies of the Italian justice system, but it sounded good and did the trick. Furthermore, it had given me an idea.

"We were acting on a tip from a concerned member of the public," he said.

"Who?"

"You know I can't reveal that," he said irritably. "Anyway, I don't know. It was an anonymous tip, a phone call, which we are trying to track down."

"I don't suppose this was the first such anonymous tip on this subject you'd received, was it?" I said, as

the events of the past few days started to come together.

"No, it was the second. We were told a woman
would be at the Tanella di Pitagora with it a couple of
days earlier, but nothing came of it. We almost didn't
go to the Melone, thinking it was a prank, but my
supervisor, a very meticulous man, made us go. You
will understand, I hope, that I have more important
things to do than go dashing about the countryside
looking for pots."

"I don't suppose you could check whether there was
a similar call in Volterra," I said.

"I could, but why would I?"

"Doesn't it strike you as a little unusual, all these
anonymous calls?"

"A little," he admitted. "But there are people who
value Italian heritage and are less than sympathetic to
those who traffic in illegal antiquities."

"But we were planning to return it to its rightful
place in the museum."

"Here we are back at that story again," he said. "I
don't understand why you are doing this. Signora
Leonard has already said that she didn't realize that the
pot was an antiquity. That, I gather, will be her defense. Your story would appear to contradict what she
is saying, and if you think you're helping her by being
here telling me this preposterous tale, then perhaps you
should think again. I'm tempted to record this conversation to use in court ourselves, but I'm going to do
you a big favor and ignore everything you said to me
on the basis that you are trying to help a friend. If you
persist—" The phone at his elbow rang, and a young

woman knocked quickly and poked her head around the door.

"The call you've been waiting for, sir," she said. "Signore Palladini."

Palladini, I thought. *Familiar name. Where?* Then I had it. Vittorio Palladini was the fellow who'd got Boucher to put me in touch with Robert Godard in Vichy. It was a common enough Italian name, of course, but still.

"Grazie," he said, picking it up. "Yes," he said, and after a few moments, "I'm afraid so." Another pause. "It's being checked out right now."

He grimaced slightly. "You know that is not possible. There is nothing we can do now that it is here. Regrettable, I know. Perhaps next year. We'll speak again soon." He hung up and looked at me. I opened my mouth to speak, but the door opened again, and a rather pleasant-looking man poked his head around the door. He was dressed in jeans and a turtleneck and expensive-looking jacket and was carrying a small duffel bag of the sports variety, as if he was off to his gym any moment. He certainly looked as if he worked out regularly.

"All done," he said. "Oops, sorry to interrupt."

"No problem," Lucca said. "Everyone else is. Is it what we think it is?"

"Most certainly," the man said.

"Well, there you are," Lucca sighed.

"Indeed," the man said. "I'll be off now."

"Tell the others, will you?" Lucca said.

"I will," the man said.

"Could we talk a little more about my friend Lola?" I said.

The young policewoman interrupted us again. "Sorry, sir," she said. "Can I speak with you for a minute?"

"Not right now," he said.

"But sir, we have a problem."

"We always have problems," he said, irritably. "In a minute."

"A body, sir. Near the Tanella in Cortona," she said. I gasped quite audibly at her words.

"Don't say that kind of thing in front of visitors," Lucca said. "You've upset Signora McClintoch." The young woman rolled her eyes. In truth, I didn't know whether to be upset or just relieved I hadn't been losing my mind in the fog.

"As you can see," he said, turning to me, "I have more urgent matters to attend to. This may be a blessing for you, because I think you've said enough, don't you? I can sympathize with your wanting to help your friend, but that is enough. Signora Leonard has already told us you had nothing to do with this. If you persist in this fabrication, I'm afraid I will have to charge you with mischief, and you will get to spend more time with your friend, in circumstances you might not like. Now, I'm going to do you a favor, and terminate this interview. Thank you for coming in to assist us with our investigation, signora." He rose from his chair and extended his hand, then walked to the door of his office and opened it, ushering me through. "See that Signora McClintoch finds her way out," he said to the young policewoman. There seemed nothing else to be done, at least nothing in Arezzo.

But I wasn't giving up. First I went to get myself some traveling money. I was going to find Crawford

Lake and make him come forward to clear Lola's name, and I was going to use his money to do it. I went back to my hotel, got out my laptop, and logged on to the Internet. I went to Marzocco Financial Online and entered my account number, 14M24S, and then my password, Chimera.

"Access denied," the screen said. "Either the user ID or the password is incorrect. Please try again." I tried again. Same response. I tried a third time, and got booted right out of the web site. It seemed pretty clear that Lake was distancing himself as far as he could from this fiasco.

Furious, I stomped out of the hotel. I'd think about this later. In the meantime, I had things to do. First, I drove back to Cortona and paid a visit to Signore Salvatore Vitali, Lola's lawyer. I wanted to meet him in person, rather than simply phoning, to decide what to do.

A very pleasant-looking man opened the door. He was in his midsixties maybe, about Lola's age or a little older, dressed in nicely tailored pants and a lovely sweater. He had a shock of white hair, which he kept brushing back off his face when he spoke. When I told him I was a friend of Lola's, he welcomed me in and insisted on making me an espresso on a rather formidable machine he kept in a little kitchenette off the main room.

"Such a genteel lady," he said, when I told him Lola had laryngitis and was unable to call him. "I am so sorry to hear of her illness. Will you please assure her for me that she can start here whenever she feels well enough. She is not to worry."

"Thank you. I'll tell her." We sat sizing each other

up for a few minutes, commenting on the weather, and sipping our espressos.

"She has seen a doctor, I hope," he said.

"Yes," I lied.

"You will forgive me for asking. . . . Would you like a biscuit? No? Another espresso? I am not, as you can see, a very accomplished host. I have been living alone for too long."

"Another espresso would be great," I said.

He got up, and soon the machine in his kitchen was wheezing away. He returned soon enough, and we went back to contemplating each other.

"There, you see, I am putting off asking you a question," he said at last. "An important one, which I found myself unable to ask Signora Leonard. There was no reason at all to ask her under the circumstances, which is to say we were discussing a position in my office. As you can see, I am somewhat reluctant, actually quite nervous, to ask you. Something, though, is compelling me to do so."

"Yes?" I said.

"Is she married?"

"No," I said.

"I thought not. There was no ring. But she is attached?"

"No, I don't think so. As far as I know, she's free as a bird."

He positively beamed. "I confess that is the answer I was hoping for."

"She likes you, too," I said. "Please don't tell her I told you."

"Of course not," he said gravely. "Nor, please, will

you tell her I asked you that question. She is very in-terested in Lars Porsena."

"She certainly is," I said.

"I am as well. It seemed to me to be fate that brought us together."

"Actually, Signore Vitali," I said, "fate is keeping the two of you apart right this minute. I've been sitting here debating whether to tell you this, and I'm taking a big chance doing so, but Lola needs help, and even if she never forgives me for telling you, I'm deter-mined to get it for her. Lola, Signora Leonard, I mean, is in jail. She has been quite wrongly accused of pos-sessing a stolen Etruscan hydria. In fact, I was the one who had the hydria. She was keeping it for me and was bringing it so that I could give it to someone who was going to give it back to the museum, when she was caught with it, apparently because of an anon-ymous tip from a member of the public. The police do not believe her, nor do they believe me. She needs a lawyer, and she can't afford one. I am prepared to pay you to represent her." I had to stop to catch my breath.

"And this person who was going to return the hy-dria?" he said, waving away my attempt to get money out of my wallet.

"I can't tell you who he is," I said. "But I'm going to find him and make him come forward in person."

He raised bushy white eyebrows. "I see. You think he will corroborate this story?"

"I hope so," I said. "He likes his privacy, and not only that, but he seems to have closed a bank account that was supposed to cover my expenses. Needless to say, I'm going to try to get him to change his mind."

"Where is she?" he said, getting out of his chair and taking a jacket off a hook by the door.

"The carabinieri station in Arezzo," I said.

"I will go there now," he said. "Will you come with me?"

"No," I said. "I can't right now. But I'll be working to get Lola out of this mess, too." I meant it, too. Lola was big on getting what one deserved. Right now, she was getting what I deserved. I wasn't going to spend a lot of time beating myself up about why I was in the situation in the first place. But I was going to fix it somehow.

I hit the Autostrada del Sole once again and headed south to Rome. The next morning found me sitting under a market umbrella in a café in the Piazza della Rotunda, a lively spot, drinking coffee and reading the paper. Antonio had gotten his wish to be famous, unfortunately. There was a lurid account, as only the Italian papers can provide, of the man found hanging from the roof of a farmhouse in Tuscany. The man had been identified as an out-of-work actor by the name of Antonio Balducci. There was speculation it might be a mob hit of some kind, although the police were quoted as saying he'd hung himself. I kept thinking about the body, wondering how he would have done that. The owner of the farmhouse, Gino Mauro, who had, it was said, an ironclad alibi, given that he and his family were in New York at the time, was also said to be horrified at what had happened at his place. Mauro, reached by the intrepid reporter by telephone, said he did not know the dead man nor what he would be doing there.

I, too, was famous. A shopkeeper in Scrofiano had

told police that a woman, English or American—there are some advantages to being an anonymous Canadian—had asked directions to the house the day before Antonio's body had been found. Police said yet another anonymous call had led them to the body, and police were looking not only for me but for whoever it was had telephoned. The call had been traced to a pay phone.

Lola, too, made the news. There was a page-three article that said that the carabinieri had been successful in tracking down a stolen Etruscan antiquity. They had someone in custody, the article said, and were now proceeding with an investigation into its disappearance. Further charges were expected to be laid. I hoped that didn't mean me.

I sat for awhile, thinking about all this: about Lola in jail, but particularly Antonio, swinging from a rope. At the same time, I was contemplating the edifice that dominated the piazza where I was sitting. Variously known as the Pantheon, the Church of Santa Maria dei Martiri, and the Rotunda, it is one hundred forty-two feet wide, and the same high, with twenty-five-foot walls, and an oculus, or opening, in the top of eighteen feet, and it is truly an impressive sight. Built originally in 27 B.C.E. by Marcus Agrippa, then rebuilt in the early second century by Hadrian, it is considered one of the architectural marvels of the world, and as I sat there, drinking my cappuccino, tourists by the hundreds were pouring through its doors. The only feature that interested me at that moment, however, was the inscription etched over the entranceway. M. AGRIPPA L.F.COS.TERTIUM. FECIT, it said, and FECIT was

what I'd been able to see from Crawford Lake's bathroom window.

From my vantage place in the square, there seemed
to be only one street that could be the location of
Lake's apartment. Given the narrowness of the street,
a lane really, I couldn't get back far enough to see
clearly. But there was one building that looked to have
a roof garden—there were vines hanging over a railing
at the top—and I headed for that. There was an Apartment for Sale sign on the front of the building, and the
door was locked. I went and got myself a bag of groceries, making sure a nice Italian loaf and some carrot
tops were plainly evident, and then waited until someone came along and unlocked the door.

I made it before the door closed. The person, an
elderly woman, looked at me suspiciously, but I smiled
pleasantly and wished her a good day. She glanced at
my bag of groceries and decided I was all right. I took
the elevator to the top floor. I was wondering how I'd
know which apartment on that floor I'd been to, but I
figured it would have to be the front, for me to have
seen the inscription. It didn't matter. On the top floor
there was only one apartment, something I should have
suspected, given Lake's means.

I knocked at the door, but there was no answer. At
that point, the elevator sprang to life, and before I
could get away, a man stepped out. He looked surprised and not altogether pleased to see me. "There's
no one there," he said. "You have to make an appointment."

"How would I do that?" I said.

"The number on the sign," he said. I must have
looked baffled, because he added, "The For Sale sign

on the building. You have to make an appointment with the real estate agency." He waited until I left the building.

I called the agency and was put through to a woman by the name of Laura Ferrari. I told her I was only in Rome for a few days, was interested in purchasing an apartment, and was specifically interested in the one on the Via della Rosa.

"Who told you about the unit?" she said.

"Signore Palladini," I said. It was the first thing that came into my head, the name I'd heard at the carabinieri station, but it had the most wondrous effect on Ms. Ferrari.

"Ah," she said. "The owner. Then you have some idea of the price." She told me what it was. Needless to say, I couldn't afford it. Not even close, in fact. Knowing what I did about doing business in Italy, I had to assume it was probably even higher than the price she'd quoted me, given the Italians' propensity to avoid paying taxes at all costs. What was most interesting, however, was the fact that Signore Palladini—quite possibly the same Palladini who'd called Massimo Lucca while I was sitting there, and who could have been the same Palladini that had arranged for me to meet Godard—was the owner of the apartment. A coincidence? It was difficult to think that was all it was. It also begged the question as to whether or not Lake had a place in Rome or simply borrowed Palladini's place when he was in town. Surely Lake could afford a pied-à-terre of his own. Or—and this had a nice conspiracy ring to it—were Palladini and Lake the same person, a pseudonym Lake used for convenience?

Laura Ferrari and I arranged to meet at the building

an hour later. A dusty smell washed over me as we went in, and I had to stifle a sneeze. It was the same apartment, all right. The layout was the one I remembered, the painting over the mantel that Lake had claimed to be an original was there, as was the wall fresco. But everything else, all the furniture and the ceramics and books, all the collectibles, was covered in sheets. I got to see into the rooms where the doors had been closed shut on my first visit, but there, too, all was covered. No Anna. No lovely lemon cake. No sign of Lake.

"It would be better," Laura fussed, "to see the place without everything covered up, but I hope you can imagine what a wonderful apartment this is. I have a little surprise for you, signora," she added, beckoning to a door upstairs. *"Ecco!"* she said, with a flourish. "Magnificent, isn't it?"

I found myself in the roof garden, complete with a statue of David. "See," she said, pointing. "You can just see the Pantheon. The location here is marvelous. You could not ask for a better place for your stays in Rome. How is it you know Signore Palladini?"

"It's my husband who knows him, actually," I said.

"Then your husband is in insurance, too? Or is it law?"

"My husband's a lawyer. He argues cases before the World Court, so we're in Europe a great deal. They were at law school together." My, how the lies just rolled off my tongue. "I don't suppose Signore Palladini ever rents it out, does he, for short stays? I was thinking perhaps we could just try it out for a few days. I suppose we might ask him."

"I don't think so," she said. "I think he very much wants to sell it. Are you interested?"

"My husband will have to see it before we make a final decision," I said, edging toward the door. "I will speak with him this evening—he's in Brussels right now—and will get back to you as soon as I can. But I do think it's just perfect, exactly what I imagined our apartment in Rome should be.

"It is a gem," she said. "I look forward to showing it to your husband. You would have to be approved by the other residents," she added, "but I'm sure, for any friend of Vittorio Palladini, that would not be a problem."

I'd almost made it out of the place—we were standing in the entranceway—when a key turned in the lock, and the door began to open. Laura looked surprised. My heart was in my throat. A rather tall, slim, casually dressed man in jeans and a turtleneck came through the door. He started when he saw us.

"Signora Ferrari!" he exclaimed. "I'm sorry. You startled me. I didn't know you were showing the place right now. I was just checking it."

"Signore Palladini!" Laura said. "I did leave you a message I'd be showing it, but we just made the appointment an hour or so ago. You know Signora McClintoch, I think," she said.

"Do I?" the man said, shaking my hand.

"We haven't met," I said.

"That's right," Laura said. "It's her husband that you know. You were at law school together."

"McClintoch . . ." he said, stroking his mustache with a perplexed expression.

"That's my name, not his," I said. "His is Rosati."

It was the only name I could come up with, that of the nice man I'd stood up in Volterra. I hoped he wouldn't mind.

"Rosati," he said, slowly. "Yes, I think I recall him. How nice to meet you. I hope you like the apartment."

"It's lovely," I said. "You must hate to part with it."

"I'm finding it a bit cramped," he said. "I'm looking for something a little larger." So Palladini was moving up, not down.

"But Signora McClintoch and her husband are looking for a small *pied-à-terre*, are you not?" she said, clearly worried her client was talking her out of a sale.

"I am a little concerned about the size," I said. Most of us could have managed to squeeze ourselves into it, given that it was well over two thousand square feet. "But it is really attractive."

"And the location," Laura said. "You could not do better."

"Do you let it out on a short-term lease at all? Rent it for a week or two, for example?" I said.

"No," he said. "I have too many treasures here. You can't see them with the sheets over everything, but I collect. No, I'm only interested in selling it outright."

Well, somebody got to use it, somehow, I thought, looking from Palladini to Laura Ferrari and wondering. "You live outside Rome now, do you?" I asked him.

"No. I rent an apartment not far from here that I plan to buy, once this is sold."

"Ah. Then, I'll let you know," I said. "And now I must run. I'll tell my husband I ran into you."

"Please do that," he said. "Give him my regards."

I went to the little hotel I'd booked myself into the evening before, a very disappointed and confused person. Disappointed, but not defeated. I didn't know what Palladini and Rosati had to do with it, although I'd certainly eliminated the possibility that Palladini and Lake were one and the same. There was no denying that the same names kept cropping up in my life. Regardless, I knew Crawford Lake was responsible, whether knowingly or not, and in some way I couldn't yet define, for Antonio's death and Lola's incarceration, and perhaps even—and this was the first time it had occurred to me—for the death of Robert Godard in Vichy. I didn't care how much money the creep had, I was going to find some way to make him pay. There had to be someone who knew where he was.

TEN

INISHMORE

I MAY NOT HAVE KNOWN WHERE LAKE was, but I certainly knew what he was up to, as did anyone who read the financial pages of any of the major newspapers. Lake was on the move, it seemed, inexorably swallowing up his rivals. Right now he had two opponents in his sights, a small Internet trading company that had started out as a sort of electronic-age version of the family business, two brothers in their early twenties who'd had a good idea and had, with some fanfare, gone public a few months earlier. Now the young men were pictured on the front page of the business section of the *International Herald Tribune*, both of them with deer-caught-in-headlights expressions on their faces, as they recommended to shareholders not to accept the offer

of Marzocco Financial Online. I figured it was hopeless.

Hank Mariani, the Texas businessman who had outbid Lake for the Etruscan bronze statue of Apollo, was
also in trouble. His photo showed a man in his early
fifties, I'd say, and rather than the startled expression
of the two brothers, he had a world-weary look to him
as he sat, his company's logo behind him, his elbow
on the desk and his hand over his mouth, as if holding
back a scream. He'd tried to find another buyer for his
company when Lake tried to take control. The courts
had ruled in Lake's favor, and Mariani was about to
be looking for another job. In neither case, of course,
was there a picture of Lake, but it was clear he was
making good on the pledge he'd made to me when I'd
met him: to deal with Mariani.

Neither of these stories was going to get me in to
see Lake, however, so I kept on looking. It took me
the better part of the next day to find a link, however
tenuous, to Lake. I started with the only person I had
any connection with who was associated with Lake in
some way, an English art consultant and dealer by the
name of Alfred Mondragon, who, as I'd indicated to
Lake in Rome, I knew often handled Lake's art purchases.

I'd only met Mondragon once, but that didn't stop
me from calling him. Although we were rivals, I suppose, for Lake's business, I was counting on a guarded
collegiality among those of us in the same trade to
carry the day.

"I don't suppose you remember me," I said to him.
"We met at an auction at Burlington House a couple
of years ago." I certainly remembered him. He was a

large man who wore velvet smoking jackets any time of day and any place, and who favored expensive and particularly malodorous cigars.

"Did you buy anything?" he said.

"Yes, I did. Two large David Roberts drawings. I have a client who collects Roberts."

"I seem to recall it," he said. "One was *Kom Ombo* and the other . . ."

"*Edfu,*" I said.

"*Edfu,*" he agreed. "Yes, I remember you now. I'm not good at names, but I do recall objects rather well, and then sometimes the people who come with them. Reddish blond hair, reasonably attractive woman of about forty? Am I correct?"

"Yes, thank you."

"You were with a set of bone-handled steak knives. He paid too much for them."

"My business partner, Clive Swain," I said. "He did pay too much. That's why I do most of the buying for the store. You purchased a Carlevaris," I said, not to be outdone. "Architectural drawing. Venice, of course. It was gorgeous, and way, way, beyond my means. I was quite envious."

"Quite right," he said.

"You were with Derby biscuit porcelain," I added. "He overpaid for it, too."

"My life partner, Ryan. I adore him. He can buy whatever he likes," he chuckled. "Now that we've established beyond any reasonable doubt that we are birds of a feather, what can I do for you?"

"I need to get in touch with Crawford Lake."

"You and everybody else," he said. "I can't help you."

"I really need to get in touch with him. A friend of mine is in an Italian jail. You can imagine how awful that is. It is not her fault. The only person who can get her out is Crawford Lake."

"That is most unfortunate, but I really can't help you."

"Can't or won't?"

"Can't. That's not the way it works with Lake, you see. He calls you, not the other way around. He wants something, he tells you. You go and get it. I have no idea how to get in touch with him."

"But what if you found something that he didn't ask you to get, but you knew he'd want?"

"Doesn't matter. Right now, for example, I have a rather handsome piece of Egyptian statuary I know he'd like, but I have no way of doing anything about it."

"Have you ever met him?"

"Once."

"And?"

"Pleasant enough chap."

"Good-looking?"

"I suppose so, but not my way inclined, if you catch my drift."

"Where did you meet him?"

"Here in London. Look, I'd help you if I could, but I really can't. If he happens to call me in the next while, I'll tell him you're looking for him. Give me a number where you can be reached. I'm afraid that's the best I can do."

"Thanks," I said. "You can't think of any other connection I could pursue?"

"I'm afraid not. I'm sorry I can't help your friend."

"Me, too." He had no idea how sorry I was.

Next I combed the Internet, checking newspaper archives where I could, and anything else that came up when I keyed Lake's name in. There was a lot of stuff about him.

The bare facts were these: Lake was born in 1945 in Johannesburg, South Africa, to Jack, some kind of industrialist with links to the diamond trade, and Frances O'Reilly, an Irish model and socialite, who was better known as Fairy, if you can believe it. Crawford had an older brother, Rhys, and a younger sister Barbara. Carrying on the family's naming tradition, Barbara was always called Brandy. If Jack, Rhys, or Crawford had pet names, they were mercifully not mentioned.

Both parents and Rhys were killed in a plane crash when Crawford was about twenty-five and Brandy, sixteen. The two of them inherited fair amounts of cash. Even though Rhys had clearly been the designated heir where the family business was concerned, Lake proved himself adept at it, using it to build an even larger fortune and ultimately to become the billionaire that he was.

Brandy, on the other hand, spent lavishly. By the time she was eighteen, she was already a fixture on the social scene in Europe and in the U.S. I say "the social scene," but really it was the club milieu where she regularly had her picture taken with what I took to be signature items. She always had a white rose in her lapel or pinned to her clothing, and she always wore sunglasses, even though it was dark. Unlike the rest of the set she ran with, she was never photographed skiing in Gstaad or aboard somebody's yacht. She was obviously a person of the night, the last to leave the party. I learned a surprising amount about her. She was, at one time, the kind of person who gets in all the gossip columns. Her favorite drink was a mimosa, her favorite flower the white rose she always wore.

If her brother had an opinion of this lifestyle, he said nothing publicly about it, not, that is, until she took up with a young man by the name of Anastasios Kara-giannis, a Greek playboy, there is no other word for it. Brandy and Taso, as he was generally referred to— perhaps in those circles it's *de rigueur* to have a nick-name; I wouldn't know—were pictured together danc-ing at Regine's, or enjoying some revelry in Paris, and so on.

The trouble with Taso, in addition to the fact that he had no visible means of support, was that he was se-riously into the drug scene, and he drank way too much. It was at that point that Crawford came on the scene, and there was one archival photo in which someone, with head averted, was pulling Brandy out the door of a hotel somewhere. The caption said the person doing the dragging was Crawford Lake, al-though it could have been anyone.

Undeterred, Brandy and Taso announced their en-gagement and set the date for the wedding. Two days before the event, which was to take place somewhere tacky, one of those clubs with bare-breasted dancers, Taso died, killed in an absolutely horrendous car crash. The car, a snazzy little sports job that Brandy had given him as a wedding present, had spun out of control on a hilly road, and Taso had plunged to his death in a fiery tumble down the side of the hill. The car was checked over, what was left of it, and nothing mechanical was found that would explain the crash. Taso's blood-alcohol reading, however, was over the top. The medical report also said he'd burned to death, which must be a truly horrible way to go.

Brandy placed dozens and dozens of white roses on Taso's casket, and then, like her brother, disappeared from public view. Unlike her brother, however, her whereabouts were known to anyone who was prepared to do some digging: her mother's family home on In-ishmore, one of the Aran Islands off Ireland's west coast. I tried calling, but there was no listed number for Brandy Lake, nor for the O'Reilly family, at least not the one I wanted. I booked a flight for Shannon.

Before I went, though, I called Salvatore Vitali, Lola's lawyer friend. "How's she doing?" I said.

"Not well," he replied. "She's refusing to eat. She's such a tiny woman. . . ."

"I'm working on this," I said. "Try to get her to eat."

ACCORDING TO THE TIMETABLE I PICKED UP AT the airport, I'd missed the last ferry from Dolin. In yet another rental car, I headed up the coast for Galway, stopping only once, at a florist shop, and then on to Rossaveal. I caught the last ferry with only minutes to spare. The sea was rough and the air chilly as the boat plowed doggedly toward the island, about six or seven miles offshore.

At Kilronan, where the ferry berthed, I got a horse-drawn carriage and asked the driver to take me to a nice bed-and-breakfast inn. There was a light drizzle falling, and storm clouds hung low to the horizon. The island was rather bleak, small patches of grass surrounded by low stone walls the most prominent feature. Some might find it romantic, a windswept and rocky island, but in my present state of mind, I found it merely depressing.

The climate may have been unpleasant, but the welcome wasn't. The driver dropped me at a pleasant inn, and I was ushered to a cheerful spot by a warm fire, where I enjoyed a very nice glass of wine or two, a surprisingly fine dinner, and a very comfortable bed.

The next morning, the sun was shining brightly, and I felt I was in a different place and that I was a new person. I asked directions to the O'Reilly house and was delighted to find it was close enough to get there on foot. "Funny one, that," the innkeeper said. "Brandy Lake. Never goes out. She has help, of course. A maid she brought with her. Name's Maire. But herself hasn't been out in years. Too bad. I remember when she was young. She came here summers with her family, the grandparents, the O'Reillys. Lovely little thing. Always laughing and running about. Can't bear to think what happened to her to make her such a recluse now."

"Do people visit her?"

"People came a lot when she was first here, but not anymore. In the early days, those reporter types showed up, but we always said we didn't know anybody by that name. You're not a reporter, are you?" she said, suddenly suspicious.

"Absolutely not," I said. "I have a message from her brother."

"Crawford? He's not been seen around here since she first came. A serious young lad, he was. Doing rather well for himself, I'm told. It will be nice for her to hear from him, even if he won't come in person."

The road rose and fell gently, and there was a wonderful view across the water to the mountains of Connemara on the mainland, purple against the bright sky, and up ahead on a high promontory, the ruins of the fort of Dun Aengus. I found myself feeling much more optimistic, that I'd found a real link to Lake, that I was about to learn something that would make my path clear. Surely, if I could persuade her to get in touch with her brother, he'd have to listen.

The Lake—or rather I should say the O'Reilly—house was one of the largest on the island, but not in any way palatial. It was stone, two stories, with a large front yard. For some distance before I got there, a border collie ran alongside me in the fields, taking the stone fences easily, and barking in a not unfriendly fashion. He followed me right into the yard and up the stone walk to the door, his barking getting more intense the closer we got. I rang the doorbell.

I heard footsteps inside, and a voice called through the door. "Just leave it on the step."

"Hello?" I said.

The door opened a crack, and the dog, all excited now, started jumping up and down and putting dirty paws on my coat. "Who are you?" the voice inside said.

"My name is Lara McClintoch. I'd like to talk to Ms. Lake," I said over the din created by the dog.

"Hush, Sandy," the voice said. "Down. Don't bother the lady." Sandy ignored her. Finally, the door opened wider. "You'd better come in or you'll be a mess from that dog," the woman said.

"Many thanks," I said, brushing doggie prints off my coat and pant legs.

"She doesn't have many visitors here," the woman said. "Not many come to visit. I was expecting a delivery of some milk."

"Are you Maire?" The woman, a rather solid woman in her forties, I'd say, who'd worked hard all her life, nodded. "Would you ask Ms. Lake if she would talk to me?"

"She won't," the woman said. "Why are you here?"

I'd thought a lot about this question, given that it was an inevitable one. I'd thought I could say I was a friend of her brother's, or that I knew someone she did, although who that would be I couldn't imagine. In the end, standing there, I opted for the truth.

"I have a friend who is in an Italian jail for something she didn't do. The only person who can help her is Crawford Lake, but he won't see me, so I'm trying to find a connection to him, some way of getting in touch with him, so that I can help my friend."

"I'm sorry," Maire said. "But she still won't talk to you."

"But won't you ask her?"

"It won't do any good."

"Please. I'm throwing myself on your mercy, here. I'm getting pretty desperate. I mean, an Italian jail!"

"It won't do any good, I tell you. No."

I decided retreat, at least for the moment, was the only option. "Will you at least give her these?" I said, handing over a package that I'd babied all the way from Galway. The woman peered in the top.

"White roses," she said, wistfully. "She'll like these. I'm sorry we can't help you."

"Me, too," I said. "I'm staying at the inn outside Kilmurvey," I said, "in case she changes her mind." I walked away from the house. The dog was nowhere to be seen. At the gate, I turned back. In the upstairs window, a lace curtain moved slightly, and I caught a glimpse of a face, probably Maire's. I trudged back to the inn.

I was sitting in front of the fireplace, feeling sorry for myself, and for Lola, when the phone rang at the desk. "Miss McClintoch," the innkeeper called to me. "Maire just called. You can go back to the Lake house."

Maire was waiting for me, the front door slightly ajar. The house was still rather dark, with heavy blue velvet curtains pulled against the light. The house was center-hall plan, with two pleasant rooms on either side of the entranceway, one filled with books, a desk, and sofa and chairs, the other with leather furniture and a television set. It was, however, all very gloomy.

Maire led me up dark stairs. "Are you sure you want to see her?" she said at the top. "You may regret it."

"That may be," I said, "but it's the only route open to me at the present time."

The woman shrugged her shoulders. "Well, then, come in."

The room she led me into was so dark, it took me a minute to adjust to the light. It was rather chilly, too.

"Are you the one who brought me the roses?" a voice said, and I peered into the gloom to see a woman in a rather pretty blue dress and pink fuzzy bedroom slippers sitting in a chair in the darkest part of the room. She was wearing sunglasses. The roses were in a crystal vase on a small table beside her.

"Yes," I said. "I hope you like them."

"They are my favorites," she said. "Do I know you?"

"No," I said. "I'm rather desperately trying to get in touch with your brother."

"Rhys?" she said.

"No, Crawford." Rhys was dead, didn't she know that? My heart sank.

She arched her head back in a grimace. She had bad teeth, discolored, and an eyetooth was missing. I was horrifed. Was she being kept prisoner here against her will, suffering pain from her teeth? What was going on here?

"He killed him," she said. I was about to say who killed whom, but I suddenly knew the answer.

"Taso," I said. "You think Crawford killed Taso."

"I don't think, I know. I just don't know how he did it. Perhaps you could find that out for me."

"Now, Brandy," Maire said. "You shouldn't talk like that about your brother. You know he's very generous, sending money every month."

"He's buying my silence. Crawford can't stand not to get his own way. He was always like that, even when we were little," she said. "If someone crosses him, he gets rid of them. He was such a beautiful boy. They wouldn't let me see him. I expect they thought I wasn't strong enough. But I am strong," she said. "Look at me. I would have to be, wouldn't I? I think Crawford forbade them to let me see him."

"Do you know where Crawford is?"

"No, do you?" she said. "I wish I knew where he was. It's nice to have a visitor. Would you like some tea?"

"No, thank you," I said. The place was giving me the creeps.

"I'd like some," she said. "Would you get me some, Maire?"

Maire looked at me for a moment and then nodded. "I'll be right back," she said. I couldn't decide whether her comment was reassurance for Brandy or for me.

"Now she's gone," Brandy whispered. "I think you can help me."

"What would you like me to do?" I whispered back.

"I've been watching that fly on the ceiling," she said, pointing upward. It was too dark for me to see if there was a fly there or not. I wasn't even sure there were flies on the Aran Islands. "And I think I know how it's done."

"How what's done?"

"Walking upside down on the ceiling, of course."

"Oh," I said. "I see."

"Yes," she said. "Now, if you'll help me to get up there—you could give me a boost up on to the dresser or perhaps even the top of the cupboard door—I think I could do it. Will you help?"

"Uh . . ." I heard Maire's steps on the stairs.

"Shush." Brandy said. "Don't tell her, will you? You come back sometime when she's not here. She shops every Monday morning. Come back then."

"Okay."

"Do you think I'm pretty?" Brandy said, as Maire pushed open the door and set down a silver tea service, which she placed on a table near Brandy.

"Now, dear," Maire said. "Of course she thinks you're pretty. Here's your tea. I've brought you some nice biscuits to have with it. Are you cool enough?"

Cool enough? I was getting the shivers. I didn't

know whether it was the room temperature or the general atmosphere.

"Are you the one who brought me the flowers?" Brandy said again, cupping her hands around one of the blooms.

"Yes," I said. "I hope you like them."

"Perhaps you should leave," Maire said.

"Yes," I said.

"Can we go out today, Maire?" Brandy said.

"No, dear," Maire said. "The sun is shining."

"Oh well," Brandy said, in a philosophical tone. "Perhaps it will be foggy tomorrow."

"I'm sure it will," Maire said. "We'll go for a little walk tonight, maybe. I'm going to show this nice lady out, all right?"

"All right," she said.

"Do you know where her brother is?" I asked as we descended the stairs.

"No," Maire said.

"But he sends money every month."

"Yes. Bank transfer from Switzerland. It doesn't help you. I'm sorry. It's part of the arrangement, you see. Her brother is very generous in his support, but that is all. I don't know where he is. I should never have let you come. I felt perhaps I'd been too abrupt with you, when you came here this morning and were so evidently distressed. And she seemed better earlier. She was so excited about the roses."

"What's the matter with her?" I asked.

Maire looked at me for a minute. "Porphyria," she said at last.

"Isn't that . . . ?" I bit my tongue.

"Vampire's disease? Is that what you were going to say?"

"Yes. I'm sorry." That explained, though, the sunglasses all those years, and the bad teeth. People with the disease often had a terrible sensitivity to light.

"Promise you won't tell anyone. If you tell people, they'll harass her. It's a horrible disease, and people do not understand it. It frightens them. They think they'll catch it, or worse, that she's out at night sinking her fangs into animals or people. They always tried to keep it a secret. Their father had it, too. It's like a terrible curse on the family. This is one of the few places she can be comfortable. It's cool most of the year, and it rains a lot. If we had to leave, I don't know where we'd go."

"I promise you I won't tell anyone. Is that what has affected her mind?"

"Perhaps," she said. "It could. I've always rather thought it was the death of her lover, though. She was wild about him."

"It can't be much of a life for you, either," I said. "Do you ever get away from the house?"

"Her brother pays me well, although," she said looking across the bleak landscape, "there's nothing much here to spend it on. If rocks were worth something, we'd be the richest people in the world, wouldn't we? Anyway, you've seen her, the state she's in. How could I leave her when she's like that? My mother worked for the family, the O'Reillys. We're joined somehow, my family and hers. And do I get away sometimes? I do. A friend comes to visit from time to time to give me a bit of a holiday, when she can get out. It's just she does it less and less. So I'll say good-bye. It's been grand having a bit of company, but I don't think there's any point in your coming back here, do you?"

"No," I said. "But thank you."

"I hope your friend comes through all right."

I turned to go, but then thought of one more question. "It's hereditary, isn't it? Porphyria? Does her brother have it, too?"

"Yes," she said. "I'm afraid he does."

I thought of the man I knew as Crawford Lake, that first and only time I'd seen him in person, tanned and standing in a beam of sunlight in the apartment in Rome. *Oh shit,* I thought.

ELEVEN

ROME

So the man I knew as Crawford Lake, wasn't. There was no other possible interpretation of what I had learned. To say that one fact put a different spin on the situation was merely facile. It was much more fundamental than that. Three people were dead, two of them, at least, at the hands of someone else. Another innocent was in jail.

It was a very long trip back to Italy, not just in the hours spent traveling but in the mental ground I had to cover. The most generous interpretation of what had happened was that Lake, given his medical condition, had asked someone to stand in for him in his discussions with me. In this rather halcyon version of events, Lake really had chosen me to find him the Bellerophon, the whole affair was perfectly legitimate, and the deaths a horrible coincidence. It was a scenario I found

I could not cling to for long, and I soon sank into gloomy self-pity and blame. Why had I ever thought that someone like Crawford Lake would ask me to do anything? I wouldn't get to carry out the garbage of someone like that, let alone buy him a bronze horse. Was it vanity that had made me so vulnerable? I didn't play in Crawford Lake's league. I just liked to think I could.

Still, I'd been skeptical, hadn't I? I'd asked him why he'd called on me. His reply had been that he had been looking for someone no one had ever heard of. Surely that was not an appeal to my vanity. On the other hand, he'd praised my ability to do research and get things done. Was that so terrible?

The point was that it didn't matter why I'd done it, why I'd believed him. What counted was that it happened at all. Was it a hoax, a practical joke gone terribly wrong? Then who was the joker? I couldn't think of anyone who'd do anything that elaborate, nor could I think of anyone who'd stoop to murder to protect the hoax.

Was it worse than a joke? Was it a deliberate attempt to discredit me in some way? Why bother? I co-owned a nice little shop in Toronto, had my regular customers, got occasional mention in the design and antique magazines. Why did that make me a target? Thinking that someone would go to such trouble for poor little me was perhaps even more vain than I'd been in the first instance, when I'd accepted the assignment.

So, what to do? The sensible choice would be to simply go home. I hadn't been accused of anything, no one knew, really, about my involvement in the sorry affair. I could get on a plane at any time, be in my usual spot in the little office off the main showroom in the shop within twenty-four hours. I would feel chastened for awhile, but I'd get over it. Life would go on.

But pictures kept floating across my consciousness: Antonio rescuing me from robbers in Paris and then practicing his English over a bottle of wine, Lola sitting on the edge of my bed eating cheese and telling me about her love life and her search for Lars Porsena's tomb. And then, more sadly, Lola in prison and Antonio, his lovely smile stilled for all time, swaying ever so slightly in the breeze.

Suddenly, I was no longer feeling sorry for myself. I was really, really angry. Someone had made a fool out of me, but much worse, had used me in a horrible plot. And I was damned if I was going to slink home, tail between my legs, leaving Lola starving to death in prison and Antonio swinging, figuratively now, from a hook on a Tuscan farmhouse, no matter how lovely the view! To be a friend was a joy, but it was also a responsibility, Antonio had said. He was right.

Yes, I would have to be careful. I would have to get used to the idea that any event, no matter how innocuous it seemed, carried the potential for menace. And I was going to have to go back over a lot of ground. I would reinterpret every event since the first moment I walked into that apartment in Rome from this different vantage point, hoping a pattern would emerge. I would have to try to reconnect with all the people I'd come in contact with, however peripherally, in the last several days, to try to find out how it all fit together: Boucher and Leclerc; Dottie and Kyle; Signore Mauro, the owner of the farmhouse; Palladini, the owner of the apartment; Cesar Rosati, the nice man at the restaurant in Volterra, just because he was there. But first and foremost, I could somehow track down the man who had passed himself off as Crawford Lake and force him to tell me who'd talked him into doing it. I had no idea how I was going to find him, of course, but I was just going to have to do it.

Finding Dottie, however, was easy. Or to be more accurate, she found me. "Lara!" she trilled, and I turned to see her ensconced at a table in the café in the piazza near my hotel. "Over here! Isn't this just amazing, the way we keep running into each other?" It certainly was, just way too amazing, despite the fact I'd known her for years, and it is, as they say, a small world. She got up and hugged me, holding me for a second or two longer than really necessary, as if she really was glad to see me. "Here," she said, pushing some newspapers aside. "Come and sit with me. This is Angelo, by the way. My new beau."

Angelo was almost as good-looking as Kyle and, if anything, even younger. "Why don't you go and buy yourself that lovely suit you liked, sweetheart," she added, getting some rather large bills out of her wallet. "So Lara and I can have a little gab, just us two girls." Angelo pouted, as if he couldn't bear to be away from her for even a few minutes, but then got up and swaggered off.

"I'm so happy to see you," she said. "And glad you're okay."

"Why wouldn't I be, Dottie?" I said, looking at her suspiciously.

"Oh, I don't know," she said. "The last time I saw you, you'd just found that poor man Godard. You didn't look too good that night." There was no arguing with that, but taking a closer look at Dottie now, on this occasion, she was the one who didn't look so hot. She had lost weight, and there were dark circles under her eyes that her makeup, which looked as if it had been applied with a trowel, couldn't hide.

"What happened to Kyle?" I said.

"I got bored with him and sent him packing," she said. "Anyway, when in Rome, take up with a Roman, isn't that what they say? Angelo is such a darling," she rattled on. "I can't tell you how much I'm enjoying Italy. I'm really glad you mentioned it when we saw you in Nice. I don't think I would have come here, otherwise. Now I'm wondering why I spent all those years just going to France. My business, of course. I'm thinking of adding some Italian antiques. Just try out a few, and see how it goes. Where have you been since I saw you last?"

"I've been a few places," I said, with what I thought was considerable understatement. "Tuscany, primarily, as I told you." Maybe she knew exactly where I'd been. That was the trouble now. Everyone was a suspect in my mind.

"Isn't Tuscany wonderful? Florence: absolutely fabulous. Siena: if anything, even lovelier. Now Rome. I thought I was just going to hate it. I'd heard it was so noisy and dirty and that the Roman men were all old lechers. Instead, I just adore it. I've already extended my European trip by a couple of weeks, and I may keep right on going. Until I get tired of Angelo, anyway. He's an actor," she added.

"Where do you find all these younger men?" I said. I was just making conversation and didn't expect an answer, but I got one anyway.

"An escort agency," she replied. "They call it an agency for actors. I know that's not a good idea, but I was kind of lonely after Kyle and I busted up, and I didn't feel like going home just yet, so I called one of those places. I really just wanted someone to have dinner with, but it has kind of worked out, if you know what I mean."

I suddenly felt grateful to Dottie because she had given me an idea. Antonio had told me he was an actor, at least a wannabe, and he'd mentioned an agency. If Antonio had been hired from this agency, then why not the other one, the Lake impersonator, too?

I was quite pleased with myself for having thought of that, until I caught a glimpse of a headline on the newspaper on the table.

"Would you mind if I had a look at that newspaper?" I asked.

"Go ahead. I can't read it. It's in Italian. Angelo got it."

"I haven't seen an Italian newspaper for a few days," I said. "I'm feeling a little out of touch."

"Feel free," she said. "It's pleasant just to sit here and read, isn't it? You read that, I'll look at Italian *Vogue*. I can't read a word of it either, but the photos are spectacular."

The article I was interested in was right on the front page and was written by a reporter by the name of Gianni Veri, a name I thought I'd heard before, although I couldn't imagine where. It had caught my eye because of a rather nice photograph of an Etruscan hydria, almost certainly the same one, in fact, that I'd had in my possession more than once. Veri was on something of a rampage, journalistically speaking.

NATIONAL DISGRACE!
AUTHORITIES FIDDLE WHILE
ITALIAN PATRIMONY LOOTED.

Members of the Commando Carabinieri Tutela
Patrimono Artistico are sitting idly by as hundreds if not thousands of Etruscan artifacts are
stolen, looted, and then smuggled out of the
country. This reporter has seen with his own eyes
the exquisite Etruscan hydria pictured here, a hydria touched by the hands of none other than the
Micali painter from ancient Vulci, and knows for
a fact that it was on its way to Switzerland when
the local police force apprehended an American
woman who had it in her possession. The woman
is part of a smuggling ring, headed by a foreign
businessman, that systematically moves priceless
pieces of our Italian heritage to foreign countries
where they are sold illegally to collectors worldwide, where they are destined to remain hidden
in the private collections of those with no scru-
ples, never to be seen by Italian eyes again.
While the woman remains in police custody, the
ringleader moves about the country, indeed the
world, without fear of prosecution. One has to
ask whether it is incompetence on the part of
Italian officials that permits this to happen, or
worse yet, complicity. Or, perhaps worst of all,
that the police are being directed by the most
corrupt of politicians.

The article went on to talk about how the Etruscans,
as all Italian schoolchildren knew, were the true an-

cestors of the Italian people, a fact that would no doubt be proven when the results of DNA testing became known, and that all Italians should be enraged by the fact that evil foreigners were allowed to go free. It was all rather overwrought, if not inflammatory, and a little light on both details and accuracy as far as I could see, but it was really depressing when one thought of Lola in jail. It was definitely not looking good for her. The article ended by asking Italians to express their views by E-mailing the reporter at Veii at an Italian ISP address.

I looked up to find Dottie watching me over the top of her reading glasses. "Anything interesting?" she said.

"I was just reading about some stolen antiquities," I said. "Apparently someone is smuggling Etruscan artifacts out of Italy. I suppose people like you and me have to be careful when we're buying."

She looked startled. "We certainly do," she said after a moment's pause.

"Speaking of buying," I said. "I'd better be on my way. I can't be idling away the hours here, no matter how pleasant it is, when there's work to be done. It was nice to see you again, Dottie. Perhaps our paths will cross again."

"Why don't we get together for dinner?" she said. "Angelo knows some fabulous places."

"That's very kind of you," I said. "But really—"

"You have to eat sometime. We'll come and pick you up at your hotel around eight. Where are you staying?"

I gave her the name of the hotel. There didn't seem any way around it. She wrote down the name and the street address. I kept thinking she must know, somehow, where I was staying, because here she was in the square just a few yards away. But there was absolutely nothing in her manner that would lead me to believe that. I decided I was being paranoid and that I should just get on with finding the fake Crawford Lake.

"See you this evening," she said. "Maybe I could ask Angelo to bring one of his young friends for you."

"No, thanks, Dottie," I said. The idea of spending an evening in Rome with a young man from a modeling agency just depressed me.

I went to check telephone listings. My memory was a little fuzzy on the subject, but for some reason, I recalled that the agency name Antonio had told me about with evident pride had made me think of an Italian classical composer. I looked at the listings again. Arcangelo Corelli, seventeenth-century Italian composer, pioneer of the concerto grosso form. Corelli Ponte, actors' agency. That was it.

I telephoned Corelli Ponte for an appointment. I spoke only in English and told them I was an advance scout for a small but particularly highly thought of film company. I told them I was looking for actors who looked good in suits and could pass for successful businessmen. I also told them my name was Janet Swain, and while I knew I was being completely unreasonable, hoped they'd be able to accommodate me that very day. There was a little protestation about such short notice, but in the end, they suggested I come in and look at some photos that afternoon.

It was a small office in a very old building but in a good location off the Via Veneto. I rang at the street door and was buzzed in, then entered the office, which was on the main floor. A young woman took my jacket, motioned me into the first of a series of rooms that led off a central hallway, and then took her seat at a desk. The walls were covered in photos of very beautiful people, male and female. Two particularly large photos, one a man, the other a woman, were front and center behind the reception desk. The woman looked very familiar, one of their star models perhaps. The young woman at the desk asked for my business card. I made a show of rummaging about in my bag and then shrugged my shoulders. "Sorry," I said. "I must have left them at the hotel. The Hassler," I added, naming one of the more expensive hotels in town, and one, now that Lake's money had been cut off, way beyond my means. The receptionist, however, did not look impressed.

"You'll be seeing Signora Ponte," she said in a low voice. "I would ask that you not mention the incident. She has just returned to work this week."

"The incident?" I said.

The young woman looked about to ask me if I were new to the planet. "Her husband," she whispered. "Killed himself." She may not have wanted me to mention the incident, but she was obviously rather keen on discussing it with me herself.

"Of course," I said, suddenly putting the face and the name together with the news reports. "Dreadful. He threw himself off the *balze* in Volterra, didn't he?"

"Yes," she said. "Can you imagine? Just left his office without saying anything, drove all the way to Volterra, and then threw himself off. They say the place is haunted, you know."

"So I've heard," I whispered back. "Why do you think he did it?"

"You just never know, do you? He . . . shhh," she said. I could hear footsteps in the hall, and the woman whose glorious face, albeit a few years earlier, was on the poster behind the desk, entered the room.

"Eugenia Ponte," she said, extending her hand. "How may we be of service?"

She was a very attractive woman of about forty, shoulder-length hair bleached reddish blond in the style that Italian women of a certain social status seem to favor in Rome and Milan. She looked casually elegant in very slim black pants and a white silk shirt, black flats, and some simple but expensive looking gold jewelry, a bracelet, necklace, and a pair of large, round earrings. If she was grieving her late husband, she didn't show it. Her manner was completely professional.

"I'm looking for actors who appear well-to-do, professional businessmen," I said. "They have to be able to act. It's not good enough they just stand there. They have to present themselves well verbally, too. Smart enough to learn their lines. Very presentable."

She asked a couple of questions about age, height, and so on, and then led me into a small conference room. "I'll have some photos and résumés sent in to you right away. I'm sure you will be able to find what you want here," she said. "Just make yourself comfortable. I'll have Angela bring you a coffee. Will an espresso do?"

"Thank you," I said.

"When you've made your selection, bring the albums to my office. It's the last one on the right," she said, gesturing down the hallway.

The men were in alphabetical order, and given I didn't have a name, I had to start at the beginning. I found Antonio right away, Antonio Balducci. He looked so nice, with such a lovely smile, I just had to stop for a minute, a lump in my throat, and pull myself together. Angelo was next, Angelo Ciccolini. He looked rather fetching, too. It took me almost half an hour, but finally, there he was, Crawford Lake smiling out at me, only his name was Mario Romano.

I was a little surprised by Mario's credentials. He'd actually appeared in a rather impressive number of films, and not always in small roles. He wasn't the male equivalent of Sophia Loren in terms of name rec-ognition or anything, but he wasn't doing badly at all. I couldn't imagine why he'd bother to accept a small part playing a mysterious billionaire, a role in which, as far as I knew, he'd never be seen by anyone but me.

I took the photos of Romano and Antonio to Eugenia Ponte's office, as directed. It was much larger than the other offices, befitting her status, and had glass doors that led out to a courtyard garden. Everything was very high style, great Italian design, elegant and contem-porary.

"Lovely office," I said, trying to establish some rap-port.

"Thank you," she said. "I like it, too. Now, what have you found?"

"I'm interested in these two," I said, handing her the photos and watching her reaction.

She fiddled with one of her earrings, but other than that, showed no emotion.

"Can you tell me about them?"

"Excellent choices," she said. "Two of our very best actors. I'm sure you'd be happy with both of them. However," she said, and this time, she chewed her lip. "Only one of them is available. This one is available," she said, pointing. "Mario Romano. Unfortunately Antonio Balducci is . . ." she paused for a moment.

Deceased? I thought.

"Unable to accept assignments," she said, finally. "I suppose we should remove him from the catalog."

"In that case, how about Romano's availability?" I said. "We'll be shooting in the next couple of weeks."

"Mario is extremely busy. You've seen his résumé," she said. "But I'm sure we'll be able to work something out."

"Would it be possible for me to interview him in person? It's rather difficult to tell from a photograph if he will suit our purposes. I'd have to hear his voice. It is just a small part in a commercial, but my director believes that all the details must be perfect. I'm sure you know the type of person I'm talking about."

"Indeed I do," she said. "Difficult, of course, but attention to detail always shows, doesn't it? I can assure you Mario is utterly professional, so he will understand."

"Could you tell me where I could get in touch with him?"

"We will arrange for you to meet him here," she said.

"Great," I said. "Could that be later today or tomorrow morning? Deadlines, you know."

"I think so," she said. "But let me call Angela and ask her to see what she can set up." Removing one

earring so that she could use the telephone more comfortably, she dialed an extension. I could hear the
phone ringing down the hall.

"Where is that girl?" she said with more than a touch
of impatience. "Give me a minute, please."She got up
and I listened to her footsteps recede down the hall. In
a flash I stood up, reached over to the file folders,
opened Romano's, and found the address. As I did so,
I inadvertently knocked her earring on the floor. I could
hear footsteps coming my way. In a panic, I whipped
around the desk, found it and was about to set it back
in its place, when I noticed something that gave me
pause. The earring was gold, heavy, and obviously
good quality. On it was embossed a scene of some
kind. I took a closer look. It was a chimera, with Bellerophon poised for the kill above.

Seeing it stopped me dead in my tracks. I just stood
there, holding it and staring at it, thinking that the earring reminded me of something else, although what, I
just couldn't recall, and wondering what it all meant.
Almost too late I remembered the footsteps in the hall.
I set the earring in its place and, given I was on the
wrong side of the desk and she was nanoseconds from
coming through the door, turned quickly and stared out
the doors.

"Gorgeous garden," I said. "It makes such a difference, doesn't it? To have something beautiful to look
at, I mean."

She looked suspiciously at me but then, checking her
desk and seeing nothing out of order, agreed. "Angela
says you're staying at the Hassler," she said, reaching
for her earring and putting it on. "Lovely hotel. We
will set up an appointment for you with Romano and

leave a message for you there. I know that time is of the essence, so we'll try to set up something for later this afternoon or first thing tomorrow."

"Many thanks," I said. "I'm glad we'll be doing business."

"I am as well. How did you hear about us?" she asked.

Good question. I thought of the photo of Angelo Ciccolini. "Dorothea Beach," I said. "She's an antique dealer in New Orleans. She recommended you highly."

"Ah, Signora Beach. Of course. We deal with her whenever she's in Rome. I must be sure to tell her we appreciate her recommendation," Eugenia said.

I turned to go but then had another thought. "Do you have any older women actors? Say about sixty. The kind who could play the part of somebody's mother, for example, or perhaps an older maid?"

"Not many," she said. "But you're welcome to look at more photos if you wish."

"Thank you," I said.

In the older woman category, the pickings were pretty slim, a comment, I suppose on how society treats women actors over the age of about thirty. After only a few minutes of leafing through photos, I was interrupted by Signora Ponte, who had slipped a rather smashing black cashmere shawl over her shoulders. "I'm afraid I'm going to have to leave you," she said. "I have a luncheon appointment. But if you see anyone you're interested in, Angela will make the appointment, and you can see her at the same time you see the others. It's been a pleasure meeting you."

"For me, as well," I said. "I look forward to seeing you when I come to meet the actor." I had no intention

of returning, of course, something they'd figure out
when they tried to leave a message for Janet Swain at
the Hassler. It took me only a few more minutes to
check the rest of the photographs. No sign of Anna,
she of the lemon cake and tea. I went outside and
hailed a taxi.

Mario Romano, aka Crawford Lake, lived across the
Tiber in Trastevere, a neighborhood known for good
food, night life, and a place for artists, and I suppose,
reasonably successful actors, to live.

Romano, according to the names on the mailboxes,
was on the top floor. A little girl sat outside the first-
floor apartment, and after some smiling and waving on
my part, she opened the door and followed me up to
the first floor before giving up and going back to sit
outside her door.

A rather pretty young woman of about eighteen or
twenty, close to Jennifer Luczka's age by my estimate,
opened the door a crack. She was dressed very casually
in jeans and a white T-shirt, her long, dark hair pulled
back and tied with a black ribbon. She looked as if she
had a bad cold, with her red nose and eyes. "I'm looking for Mario Romano," I said.

"He's not here right now," she said.

"Can you tell me when he'll be back?"

"Soon," she said, but I wasn't sure she was telling
the truth for some reason, a certain look about her eyes.
It occurred to me she was alone and possibly a little
nervous about strangers appearing at the door.

"I'm a friend of Antonio Balducci's," I said.

"Oh," she said, opening the door. "Come in. Isn't
that the most awful thing? I can't believe Antonio
would do that. Oh," she said, bringing her hand up to

her mouth. "You do know that he's dead, don't you? I hope I'm not giving you a terrible shock."

"I heard," I said. "So you're . . ."

"Silvia," she said. "Mario's my dad."

"Of course!" I said. I could see the resemblance now that she'd told me. "I've heard about you. I'm Lara. I'm just in Rome for a few days, and I saw the newspaper story about Antonio," I said. Silvia gestured toward the sofa, and I sat down. The newspaper article I'd just referred to was faceup on the coffee table.

"Is there going to be a funeral?"

"It's today," she said, glancing at her watch. "I'm terribly sorry, but you've missed it. You could never get there in time. Antonio lived in Rome, of course, but his family wants him buried in his village down south. That's where my dad is now. It's going to start in about an hour."

"I'm sorry," I said. "I would have liked to have gone." That was true, actually. "I didn't see anything in the paper about the funeral."

"No," she said. "It took a long time for the carabinieri to release the body so Antonio could have a proper funeral. But given what happened, the suicide and everything, it's just family and really close friends. I can't believe he did that, can you? I wouldn't have thought suicide is something Antonio would even think about. Do you think it had something to do with Teresa? He was so afraid she'd take up with someone else."

"Yes, he was," I said. "He told me about Teresa and how all the other men were like bees around a lovely flower."

She smiled a little. "That sounds like Antonio. I was,

still am, a little bit in love with him. You won't tell my dad, will you? I've had a crush on Antonio for at least three years. I've just been sitting here having a bit of a cry about it. Dad wouldn't take me along, unfortunately, because he's going somewhere else directly after. Look, I'm being terribly inhospitable here," she said. "I haven't even asked you if you'd like a drink or something."

"I'm fine, thanks. But tell me how your dad is doing."

"He's okay," she said. "I suppose you heard he and my mother have split."

"No," I said.

"Well, they have. I'm supposed to be at my mother's right now, so please don't tell my dad if you happen to run into him. I like staying here better." She waved her hand about the room. I could see why she'd like the place. It was a cozy apartment by North American standards, but probably sizable enough for Rome. The walls were covered in art and framed posters, a couple of them for exhibits of Etruscan art, and one whole wall was devoted to bookshelves. The furniture was large and comfortable, and the place had a nice, casual feel to it.

"Dad's taken a few months off to get his life back together again. But his agency called a few minutes ago with something for him, so maybe he'll get back to it. He's with the Corelli Ponte agency. They're huge," she said. "The people wanted to see him today or tomorrow, though, so maybe it will be too late when he gets back."

"Is your dad coming back tomorrow, after the funeral?" I said. "I'm only here for a day or two, so I'd like to get in touch with him if I could."

"I'm afraid not," she said. "He's taking a holiday weekend in the country. He won't be back until Monday. I'm glad for him. I hope it means he's getting over the split with Mum. I'd like him to find a new girlfriend. Hey!" she said, brightening. "You're about the right age. Are you available?"

"No," I said, laughing. "I'm spoken for. But thanks for asking."

"Too bad," she said. "He really needs something or someone to cheer him up. The business with him and my mother was bad enough, and now he's just devastated over what happened to Antonio. They were like brothers. Dad even called Antonio his little brother. He was always trying to help Antonio find work. He kept telling Antonio he'd make it. Antonio had the looks for it, that's for sure."

"He did," I said. "And he was also really kind."

"Yes," she said, and a tear rolled down her cheek. "And funny."

I gave her hand a rather awkward pat.

"When did you see him last?" she said. I told her, omitting several details, of course, about how he'd saved me from the Gypsies, and how we'd shared a bottle of French wine on the Left Bank in Paris, and Antonio had practiced his English. It wasn't the last time I'd seen him, of course, but it was the time I wanted to remember forever. We both snuffled a little.

"I can't figure out how he would have even managed it," she said. "I know the papers said it was a mob hit or something, but Antonio never had anything to do with the mob. Dad says Antonio killed himself. But how would he get himself up there in the first place? My dad says the carabinieri claim he got into the house somehow—there was one window that wasn't properly fastened—attached the rope lower down, went upstairs, and threw it over the metal pole on the peak of the roof from a second-floor window, put the noose around his neck, and then jumped out of the same window. It seems like such a lot of trouble to go to. I don't know . . ."

In my mind I heard again the banging of the upstairs shutters that had made me look up. It was possible, I supposed, when I thought about it, but she was right. It was a whole lot of trouble to go to.

"You have to wonder why he'd even know about that farmhouse, let alone use it," I said.

"Dad knows the owner, Gino Mauro."

"He does?"

"Yes," she said. "I'm not sure how, but he does. He talked to him when it happened. Mauro lives in New York but is coming over in the next day or two. Dad is expecting to get together with him at some point."

"Look," I said after a few more minutes of conversation. "I'd better be going. I have work to do. It was really nice to meet you."

"I'll tell Dad you were here," she said. "If he calls. He won't, of course, because he thinks I'm at Mum's, and he doesn't like to call there unless he's sure I'll be the one to answer the phone. But I'll tell him you were here."

I gave her my card and wrote my hotel number on the back. "I know you opened the door for me," I said. "But really, you shouldn't have. Don't answer it unless it's someone you know and you're expecting them." I was suddenly frightened for this sweet young woman and also for her dad. Antonio was involved in the same hoax Mario was, and Antonio was dead. "Promise me you won't open the door," I said. "In fact, I'd be a lot happier if you went to stay with your mother."

"Okay," she said. "I will, as soon as I pull myself together. You'd be perfect for Dad. You're both fuss-pots."

"Thank you," I said. She actually gave me a hug. I felt like a jerk. I waited outside the door until I heard the bolt click.

I went downstairs and walked along the street, look-ing for a taxi. As it turned out, I didn't need one. I'd gone only a few yards when a limousine pulled up beside me. I ignored it at first. It couldn't have any-thing to do with me. But after a cyclist went by and rounded the corner, and I was the only one on the street, a very large man got out and grabbed me. I tried kicking and scratching, but I was no match for him. I was pushed into the backseat of the car. The last thing I saw, through the rear window, was the little girl from the first floor in the doorway, watching, as we pulled away.

The limo came to a stop some time later, maybe twenty minutes, although I wasn't sure. I was pulled rather roughly out of the car and found myself standing in a garage of some sort. There was another limo there, and a scooter, and an air-conditioning unit was blasting away. The man who'd abducted me punched a code, and the door swung open. I was led up a flight of concrete stairs and then pushed down a hall and into a dark room. The door closed behind me, and I was alone.

At least I thought I was alone, until a voice emanated from a very dark corner of the room. "I understand you've been looking for me," a voice said out of the darkness.

"Mr. Lake?" I said, peering in the direction of the voice.

"I don't like extortionists," the voice said. My eyes were adjusting to the light, and I could make out a man in dark glasses and a dark suit sitting in the gloomiest corner of the room.

"Nor do I, Mr. Lake," I said. "It is Mr. Lake, is it not? If you're calling me an extortionist, then you're wrong."

"Then perhaps you will explain why you visited my sister in Ireland. Bribed her with roses, didn't you? White ones? It shows some inventiveness, I'll grant you. What do you want?"

I told him about how I'd met this actor who was impersonating him, who'd asked me to get Bellerophon, about everything that had happened since.

A long silence greeted my account. "Then I'm afraid you've been made the goat, haven't you, Ms. McClintoch?" he said at last. "You've been played for a fool."

"I'd have to agree with you," I said. "Are you telling me you know nothing about any of this?"

"That is exactly what I'm saying," he said. "I would go even further and say your troubles have absolutely nothing to do with me."

"But they just have to, Mr. Lake," I said. "In some fashion or another, they just have to. If you could just look into this for me—"

"Do you have any idea," he said suddenly, "what I

would give to be able to stand on a lovely beach with the wind from the sea in my hair, the sand shimmering from the hot sun and the heat, without feeling as if maggots were crawling through every blood vessel in my body?"

"I'm sorry," I said.

"Good day, Ms. McClintoch," he said. "Kindly refrain from invoking my name in this matter. If you do not, I will have to resort to legal action. Indeed, if you so much as mention this meeting, or your discussions with my sister, or anything at all you have learned about either of us, I can assure you, you will very much regret it. You will not have a friend left nor a dime to your name when I'm finished with you. I hope I'm making myself perfectly clear."

He was perfectly clear, all right. Really pleasant fellow, Crawford Lake. When it came right down to it, I preferred the fake one. I could have clawed the real one's eyes out in frustration. I went back to my hotel, packed, and checked out, leaving a note for my dear friend Dottie Beach.

TWELVE

DOTTIE BEACH OPENED THE ENVELOPE I'd left for her and frowned. In it I apologized profusely for standing her up, citing the excuse—entirely fictional, given I was standing a few feet from her but hidden from view—that I'd been called away to Geneva to check out a silver collection a client wanted. I told her I'd tried to reach her at the Hassler to let her know but hadn't been able to leave a message for her for some reason. She'd know perfectly well what that reason was, given that I had indeed tried to call her there, only to discover that Dottie wasn't staying where she said she was. More and more about Dottie seemed false.

She crumpled the paper with some force and then turned to leave the hotel, pulling her cell phone from her bag. Once outside, she placed a call, at the same time signaling to Angelo, who was parked nearby in a lovely silver Mercedes convertible, top down. In a minute, I was in a taxi following them. Angelo dropped Dottie at the eastern entrance to the Piazza Navona. After taking my time paying the taxi driver, to give Angelo time to pull away, I followed her into the square.

The piazza was packed with tourists and locals, and I almost lost her, but I caught a glimpse of her taking her seat at one of the outdoor cafés. I, too, found myself a seat across the wide expanse of the square from her and on a slight angle. I'd bought opera glasses for the occasion, and ordered a Campari and soda, which I was determined to make last as long as necessary.

Angelo joined her shortly. They were seated at a table set for three, and the waiter cleared the third place. Soon they were sipping cocktails interspersed with a kiss or two. I waited for about thirty minutes, with my waiter hovering about hoping I'd order at least another drink. I did, a San Pellegrino, which wasn't what he had in mind, despite the fact the place was charging about three times more than it should for Italian designer water.

Across the piazza, the waiter brought Angelo and Dottie dinner menus, and they proceeded to order. It all looked absolutely legitimate. They'd made a reservation for three, just as they said they would. They were having dinner. What was sinister in that? My only reason for suspecting her was that she turned up once or twice too often in my life, and now that I knew Crawford Lake was actually Mario Romano, I had to look back on every single event in the last several days with a jaundiced eye.

It was difficult not to be suspicious. The carabinieri had turned up three times when I was supposed to have the chimera hydria in my possession. The fact that I didn't on two of those occasions was something known only to Lola and to me. That seemed to be at least three times too many that my path and that of the carabinieri had almost crossed.

The question was, who had known where I was going to be on each of those occasions? Antonio had been able to pick up my trail in Paris very easily, because I'd left a message for him, giving my hotel number in case there was a problem with my cell phone. He'd shown up in Vichy, too, although I had not seen him following me there from Paris. Yves Boucher knew I was going to Vichy, as did Pierre Leclerc. I'd met Dottie for the first time that trip in Vichy, and both she and Leclerc had presumably been out to the chateau before I was, the morning Robert Godard took a header into his tomb.

Mario Romano had known where I was staying in Nice and in Volterra. Indeed, he'd recommended the hotels and arranged to have a reservation made for me. Dottie turned up in Nice but not in Volterra. In fact, she'd vanished for a few days, not reappearing until Rome. Leclerc was in Volterra; I saw him, and I saw his car in Nice. It was in Nice that the hydria had miraculously made its way into the trunk of my rental car. Somehow he'd managed to get the chimera hydria out of his trunk before the carabinieri got to it, because it had turned up in my hotel room in Arezzo, and he ended up dead in Cortona.

Both Antonio and Romano knew that I'd moved to Arezzo but hadn't known about my consequent change to Cortona. I'd seen Antonio near my hotel in Arezzo, just before the hydria had turned up in my room.

Romano and Antonio had also known about my early morning visit to the Tanella di Pitagora in the fog, but Romano had said something about leaving Antonio out of it when he told me to go to the Melone di Sodo. Antonio had shown up, though, and hidden in the bushes the same way I had. He obviously knew that something was wrong, or he wouldn't have done that. Was that the reason Antonio had died?

After about an hour of watching Dottie and Angelo nuzzle each other between bites of their dinner and sips of their wine, I decided I might as well give up and go back to my hotel. The thought of spending another evening alone in a small room with a television the size of a toaster was terribly depressing. Several people were hanging about, waiting for a table, however, and the waiter clearly wanted me to leave. I signaled for the bill and started to gather up my belongings.

"This is probably rude of me," a man's voice said, "but you look as if you're leaving. Would you mind if I sat here so I could lay claim to this table?"

I looked up to see an attractive man in dark turtleneck and slacks and a nice tan suede jacket, wearing lovely Italian leather loafers with socks. I like men to wear socks with their loafers. "Please," I said. "Help yourself. I'm just leaving. I'll pay my bill and be out of your way in a minute or two."

"Thanks," he said, pulling out the chair opposite mine and sitting down. "Rather difficult to get a table in the Piazza Navona this time of the evening. Have we met? You look familiar to me," he said.

Oh right, I thought. *The universal come-on.* And when it came right down to it, too many strangers had been asking to sit with me since I'd arrived in Italy.

But when I looked at him more carefully, I realized he looked familiar to me, too. It took a second or two before I placed him.

"I don't think we were formally introduced," I said. "But our paths crossed in the carabinieri station in Arezzo."

"Yes," he said after a pause. "That's right. You were with that fellow—what's his name?—Lucca. Massimo Lucca. I hope it wasn't anything serious."

"No, it wasn't." *Merely a friend in jail,* I thought. "And you? I hope it wasn't serious for you, either."

"No," he said. He wasn't being any more forthcoming on the subject than I was, which was fine with me.

"It was nice to meet you," I said, handing the waiter some money.

"Please," he said. "Permit me to buy you a drink."

"I don't think so," I said. "But thank you."

"How can I persuade you?" he said. "I really dislike drinking alone."

I stood up and was about to decline a second time, when I saw someone come over to Dottie's table across the way. I sat down again. "Well maybe just one," I said. The man at Dottie's table sat down, too. Dottie had phoned someone as she left my hotel. Was that someone there now?

"Terrific," my new companion said, signaling the waiter again.

"A glass of white wine would be lovely," I said. Across the way, Angelo stood up and looked as if he was going to punch the newcomer out. In a split second, the stranger was behind Angelo and had pulled the young man's arm up behind his back in what I've been assured, by people who know these kinds of things, is called a chicken wing hammerlock. Within seconds, Angelo was out in the square. The man came back and sat down.

"So," my new companion said. "Is this your first visit to Rome?"

"No," I said. Dottie dug a handkerchief out of her bag and blew her nose. I couldn't see the tears from this distance, but I was sure there were some.

"Of course it isn't," he said. "Your Italian is too good. It was a stupid question, a rather prosaic opening line. You'll no doubt have noticed I'm a little rusty when it comes to meeting attractive women. I'm Nicola Marzolini, by the way."

"That's okay," I said. "I'm a little rusty at opening lines myself. I'm Lara McClintoch. And thanks for the compliment." The stranger at Dottie's table poured himself a glass of wine and chugged it down. The one at mine went on talking.

"You're welcome. I believe then, that the next conversational gambit is yours, signora."

"Okay," I said. "So what was your business in the police station?"

He burst out laughing. "You American women are so direct. I like that. I like you."

"But you didn't answer the question."

"It's no secret," he said, smiling. He had a really lovely smile, not as beautiful as Antonio's perhaps, but still, rather attractive. "I act as a consultant to the police on some matters. Now you will no doubt ask me which matters these might be, so I'll tell you. They ask for my professional expertise in the field of antiquities. I'm a curator for hire, as it were. I assist museums on a contract basis, and I work with the police, as a public-minded citizen. Now, of course, it's your turn. What do you do? Why are you here? And what were you doing in the police station?"

Warning bells were clanging away in my head at the mention of antiquities, but he looked perfectly innocent. "I'm an antique dealer from Toronto. I'm here on a buying trip for my shop."

"Interesting. What kinds of things are you shopping for?"

"Mainly I've been shopping in Tuscany. The Tuscan farmhouse look is very hot right now."

"So I understand. You're not into antiquities, I hope."

"Not if I can avoid it," I said.

"Good," he said. "I will then be able to spare you my lecture on how the antiquities trade is destroying culture."

"Sorry I have to miss that one," I said.

He laughed again. He had a really nice laugh, spontaneous and genuine. He was, when it came right down to it, a very attractive man.

"I don't suppose I could talk you into having dinner with me. I hate eating alone even more than I hate drinking alone. There I go again," he said. "Another horrible line, rife with implied insult. What I'm trying to say is I'd be delighted if you would have dinner with me."

Before answering, I checked out Dottie's table again. They were both still there.

"Thank you," I said. "I'd like to have dinner with you."

"Shall I pick the restaurant?" he said.

"What's wrong with right here?" I said.

"I know a much better place near the Campo dei Fiori. We can walk."

I was about to protest, but then Dottie and her new dinner companion got up and started to leave. There didn't seem to be any point in hanging around the piazza anymore. Nicola tossed a bill onto the table, took my arm, and we were off. Using Nicola as a shield of sorts, I had a quick look at the mystery man of Dottie's as they left the square. I didn't recognize him, but he and Dottie seemed to be close. He handed her his handkerchief as they went by, and she blotted her eyes.

Nicola chose a pleasant restaurant where he seemed to be well-known, and where, despite the lineup outside, we were seated at the bar immediately and at a table a few minutes later.

"How did you manage that?" I said.

"I eat here a lot," he said. "It's not far from my place. The maître d' is a cousin, which doesn't hurt. The gnocchi are wonderful, by the way, and I'd recommend the steak or any of the seafood."

We spent a very pleasant evening together. We talked about art, music, theater, all the subjects I love to talk about. He told me he painted for relaxation. I told him I had no hobbies except my store. He flirted a little. I flirted back, just a little. It was altogether a rather wonderful evening.

"Can I interest you in a nightcap?" he said. "At my place?"

I smiled. "Thank you, but I think I have to say no."

"You're spoken for, aren't you?" he said.

"Yes, I am," I said.

"I thought so," he said. "I don't know why. No ring, but I just thought you were."

"I hope you don't think I've been unfair here. I've had a wonderful evening."

"I have, too, and I don't want it to end just yet," he said. "So please, come and have a nightcap. Despite what you have heard about Italian men, I promise to behave myself. What does this partner of yours do?"

"He's a sergeant in the Royal Canadian Mounted Police."

"Really?" he said. "A Mountie? Then I really must behave myself. How daring of you. Or is it public spirited?"

I laughed. "He's a really fine person," I said. "I grow fonder of him all the time."

"Fond," he said. "Interesting word, but I think I won't probe. Speaking of police," he said, "I don't believe you ever answered my question about why you were in the Arezzo carabinieri station."

"I was checking on an antiquity," I said. "As you know, you can't be too careful."

"Very wise," he said. "There was a beautiful one there, by the way. I was called in to have a look at it. They caught some woman red-handed with it. An Etruscan hydria. You know what I mean by hydria, don't you? Water jug with three handles? Yes? Stunning."

"And was it authentic?" I said in my most neutral tone of voice.

"Almost certainly," he said. "A really fine example, in perfect condition. Now, let's go see my place."

The building was rather unprepossessing, and the elevator more than a little rickety. I took a quick look behind us as I entered the place, but I couldn't see anyone I knew. To my surprise, Nicola's place was a stunner. It was a very large room on the top floor, loft-style we'd call it, with a glass wall on one end, and a fabulous view over the rooftops. There was a small kitchen on the wall opposite the window, a partitioned-off area for the bed, which I stayed away from, and decorated with a few pieces of very modern, beauti-fully designed, Italian furniture. While I'd been rather careful not to ask him about his personal life, it was so obviously a bachelor's place, I knew I didn't need to probe. The walls were covered in art, some of it really quite good.

"Can I take your coat?" he said.

"Sure," I said. "But just toss it somewhere."

He took it and, despite what I'd said, he carefully put it on a hanger and placed it in a closet near the door. He then took off his jacket, folded it very care-fully, looked about to put it on the back of a chair, but then hung it up as well.

"I'm surprised we've had such a pleasant evening," I said with a smile. "I'm rather untidy, you see. I call it creative clutter." *We'd end up killing each other,* I thought.

He smiled, too. "You've noticed I am somewhat compulsively neat," he said. "Sorry, does it bother you?"

"Of course not. I'm just jealous," I said. "I'd love a modern home like this. It's just that modern is mini-malist, and as certain friends have pointed out on more than one occasion, I don't do minimalist. Mine is rather more, shall we say, eclectic in taste. Modern, primitive, whatever catches my eye, and lots of things do."

"Seriously," he said. "Do you like the place?"

"It's fabulous. I'm surprised, for some reason. I'd

have thought a curator would have, I don't know. . . ."

"Less modern furniture and art?" he said. "It's not as strange as you think. I've found I enjoy good design, regardless of era. But more to the point, I can't own antiquities, now, can I? And once you've seen the real thing, reproductions don't work, at least not for me. This furniture is the genuine article. I've collected some of the best examples of what I think is called midcentury modern where you come from. I work with thousands-of-years-old artifacts during the day, which have a beauty all their own, and then I come home to a different kind of world, a different kind of beauty, I suppose you might say."

"I can tell you picked each of these pieces, the furniture, the area rugs, the glass vase here, the paintings, individually. I know I'm not expressing this properly, but some people just buy stuff, they don't choose it with real care. They buy sets, or something. Or is that a North American phenomenon?"

"I'm not sure," he said. "But you are rather perceptive. I did pick each piece individually. I'm a collector at heart, I guess."

"But a very selective one," I said.

"Perfection is an important concept for me," he said. "In people, too, I'm afraid. It no doubt explains why at forty-six years of age, I still live alone. That and the fact I'm compulsively neat."

"You paint, obviously," I said, gesturing toward an easel by the window. "Are any of these paintings your own work?" I felt we were entering dangerous territory here, conversationally speaking, and I thought I'd just change the subject.

"No," he said. "I'm afraid mine are considerably less

exuberant than these abstract paintings. I'm a detail person. You have to be to do the kind of work I do. So when I paint, I'm afraid that love of detail comes out, despite persistent efforts on my part to break free. I could show you some of my work, if you promise not to judge me against these other paintings."

"I'd love to see it," I said.

"There's one piece on the easel," he said. "And I'll bring a few more out." He went out into the hallway, and I started to follow him. "Just wait there," he said. "I have a little work space just down the hall, where I keep my work. It's a glorified bathroom really, just some extra storage space and a worktable when I bring stuff home from the office. Don't come, though." He laughed. "It's almost untidy." I followed him anyway. The room was filled with books, most of them on antiquities, and there was a worktable covered in shards of ceramics, and a kiln in the corner. It was messier than his living quarters but still awfully well organized. "I do some of my research here, as you can see," he said. "It's not a very sophisticated setup, but I can test a few hypotheses from time to time."

I pulled one of the books from the shelf. It was a well-thumbed tome on Etruscan art. After idly flipping through it while Nicola looked through drawers, I put it back. As I turned away, I caught him pushing the spine of the book I'd just replaced, so that it lined up perfectly with the others.

Despite his modesty on the subject and his compulsive tidiness, Nicola's painting was quite exceptional. It was, as he said, rather detailed, small works on canvas, some as small as six or eight inches square, that drew heavily, to my eye, anyway, on ancient designs.

The brushwork was confident and the overall impression very pleasing. "I love these," I said, as I sipped a limoncello. "In many ways, perhaps because of the work I do, I feel more of an affinity to yours than some of these others. It's the ancient quality to it, I think, that appeals to me."

"You are very kind," he said. "I don't show my work to many people. It's a little like baring your soul, isn't it? Thank you for being so gentle with it."

He was standing so close, our shoulders were touching, and I knew it was time to go home.

"I'd better go," I said.

"I'll take you back to your hotel," he said.

"No," I said. "You don't need to do that. If you'll just find me a cab?"

As I left, he kissed my hand. "Here," he said. "For you." It was a small painting. "I think this was your favorite?"

"You mustn't," I said.

"Please, I want you to have it."

"Thank you," I said. "I'll think of you every time I look at it."

"If you're ever back in Rome," he said, handing me his card. "Or if you grow less fond of the policeman, I hope you will think of me."

The streets were almost empty when I left. I looked back through the rear window of the taxi and saw him standing, framed in the light, watching me leave.

For some reason, the way the light hit the glass, perhaps, or the way the windows were framed, he looked to me as if he were imprisoned. Which maybe he was, with his immaculate clothes and his perfect furniture, carefully placed, and not so much as a crumb to be seen. For me, it was a stab to the heart.

THIRTEEN

AREZZO

I SPENT MOST OF THE NEXT DAY IN BED, in a funk so black I could hardly lift my head from the pillow. I snapped at the chambermaid, ordered food but couldn't eat it, opting instead to drink cup after cup of coffee, until my nerves were so frayed my eyeballs hurt. Then I checked my E-mail, thinking it would make me feel better, but it made me feel even worse.

"*Hi Lara,*" the message said. "*Hope you're enjoying France, Italy, or wherever it is you are. The operation I'm involved in is taking a little longer than expected, but everything is fine. In fact, the assignment, as usual, is rather boring. I'll be back home soon. Hope you will be, too. I love you, Rob.*"

I hit Reply. "*Hi Rob,*" I typed. "*Italy is fine. I just have a couple of things left to get under control here,*"

*and then I'll be home. I'll see you soon. Love you, too.
Lara"*

I hit Send, then just stared at the screen for awhile.
Rob had never actually said to my face that he loved
me, although I suppose I knew that he did, in some
fashion at least. Had he had to do it the day after I'd
had dinner with a handsome Italian? Come to think of
it, I'd never told him I loved him, either. I wondered
what it was that had made him say it now, even if it
was only electronically. I hoped his brief and cheery
message wasn't covering up the kind of situation that
mine was, both in terms of the mess I was in or the
evening I'd had the night before. If it was, he'd be as
suspicious of my message as I was of his. My mood
grew even blacker.

At about nine at night, I realized I had two choices:
I could sit in the hotel room, staring out at a bleak
interior courtyard as the rain dripped on the pavement
below and the smells of the kitchen permeated the
room, until I rotted, or I could face the music, as it
were, and do what I'd been putting off for about three
days.

By ten o'clock, I'd showered and was in the car and
back on the road. It occurred to me that, at that point
of time, my personal version of purgatory was driving
up and down the misnamed, at that moment at least,
Autostrada del Sole, as the windshield wipers flapped
and the rain poured down.

"Come in, come in," Lola's friend Salvatore said.

"I'm sorry to show up so late," I said. "But I need
a place to stay. Can I crash on your living room sofa,
or the floor, or something?"

"Most certainly not," he said. "I have a guest room.

I don't have much company, but I believe the bed is reasonably comfortable, and the room is yours. I'm so happy to see you. Please tell me you've come with good news. Tell me you've found the businessman who was going to return the hydria and that he'll come forward and my Lola will soon be free."

"Unfortunately not," I said, and his face fell. "I found him, but he wasn't who I thought he was."

"You must tell me everything," he said. "Come, sit down and tell me." So I did.

"Do you think if I told this story to the police, to that Massimo Lucca fellow, that he'd believe me?"

"No," he said.

"Well then, I'm just going to have to tell him the hydria was mine. There's nothing else for it. I don't know why Lola doesn't tell them herself, but I gather she hasn't."

"I don't think that will help," he said.

"You know, last night at this time," I said, checking my watch, "I was having a very pleasant evening with a man I just met. I went to his apartment, and he gave me a piece of his art."

"So?" Salvatore said.

"So, I'm in a relationship," I said. "My partner is a policeman, and right now he's on an assignment of some sort, which I can't know about, and which I'm sure is dangerous."

"And did you violate the terms of that relationship?"

"I didn't stay there, if that's what you mean."

"And how would you feel if this partner of yours, the policeman on a dangerous mission, spent an evening with someone he met, and then left."

"I don't know how I'd feel about it, but I know what

the really terrible part of it is," I said. He waited. "I was traipsing about in Rome, eating a good meal, drinking fine wine, and flirting with a stranger, while Rob may have been in danger and Lola is fading away in jail."

"Perhaps that's your way of dealing with difficult situations."

"Perhaps it is. You know, for the last few years, I've felt reasonably comfortable about who I am and how I react to things. I'm not perfect, I know, but I've learned to deal with it all. Now, for some reason, I feel like the most awful person in the world.

"I don't know what to do now," I said. "I feel so tired, so terrible. I don't even know whether to be angry or depressed."

"If you have a choice, then be angry. It is so much healthier."

"Then angry at whom? Myself? The reason that Lola is in this mess is that I was stupid enough to believe that someone as important as Crawford Lake not only knew who I was but wanted to do business with me. I mean, how stupid can I get? As for helping either Lola or myself, I simply have no idea how to proceed from here."

He looked at me for a moment. "I know what you need," he said, rising from his chair at the kitchen table. "First: grappa," he said, taking a bottle down off a shelf and pouring a small tumblerful. "Drink," he said. "You're shivering.

"Second," he said, taking a large pot and filling it with water before setting it on the stove and turning on the flame. "Pasta. You haven't eaten much today, have you." It was a statement, not a question, and he was right. "*Pasta con aglio e olio,* garlic and oil," he said, setting a skillet on a second burner and reaching for the olive oil. "And perhaps to fortify you, *peperoncini,* hot peppers. That should do the trick. Why don't you cut yourself a slice or two of bread to go with it.

"And third," he said, walking over to a small CD player on a table by the window. "Music. Opera, of course. One is tempted, on these occasions, to move outside Italy, Mozart perhaps, or Wagner. Big music, even bigger emotions. *Tannhauser* or *Don Giovanni.* But no. Verdi. *Otello,*" he said as the first jarring chord washed over us. "No matter what else there is for us to learn from *Otello,* it is about finding out the hard way whom to trust.

"And now, while I cook," he said, handing me a pen and a large pad of paper, "you will write down the names of the people you have come in contact with, even in the most peripheral way, since this whole Crawford Lake affair began. Everyone, you understand? And if you can, put them in the order in which you came in contact with them. You must take action, not sit here feeling sorry for yourself."

"Okay," I said and wrote for a minute or two.

"Let me see," he said, taking the list in one hand, as he stirred with the other. "Antonio Balducci, the young man who followed you everywhere. Mario Romano, that's the fake Crawford Lake, no?"

I nodded.

"So you went to this apartment and only Lake or Romano and Balducci were there?"

"Yes. I mean no. There was a maid by the name of Anna."

"Just Anna? No surname?"

"Just Anna, I'm afraid."

"So then you went to Paris, and Antonio followed you. There you met . . . ?"

"Yves Boucher," I said.

"And you were put in touch with him by Lake, Romano, I mean."

"Not exactly. The person who set it up, according to Boucher, was Vittorio Palladini, who just happens to own the apartment in Rome."

Vitali handed me the paper again. "Is his name here? Yes? Now, who is next? Pierre Leclerc, wasn't it? Or Le Conte with a question mark," he said.

"He told me his name was Leclerc. Godard thought it was something else like Le Conte. Godard may simply have been mistaken."

"And he is the one who died at the Tanella. I read about that in the paper. They hadn't identified the body yet, but foul play is suspected."

"More than suspected, I'm sure," I said. "Didn't the paper say he was drugged first, then strangled?"

"Let's not dwell on that. Boucher took you to meet Robert Godard, is that right? But first you met Dottie Beach, yes, and Kyle. Who is Kyle? One name only?"

"I'm afraid so," I said. "He was always just Kyle. American, young, very attractive. But he's gone back home, according to Dottie."

"And this Dottie. You have known her for many years, you've told me?"

"Yes."

"You aren't competitors in business or even in love? She didn't fancy your ex-husband Clive many years ago?"

"No. I don't think so. Dottie was married to Hugh Halliday when I met her. They're divorced now. Anyway, when Clive fooled around, it was with younger women than Dottie, and Dottie likes younger men than Clive."

"Robert Godard, the man in the tomb. Do you think he fell?"

"Not really. I thought he was quite adept at getting himself down into the tomb. It's possible he fell, but given all that has happened since, I wouldn't want to bet on it."

"Eugenia Ponte I know, of course. Palladini owned the apartment, as you have already pointed out. He's in insurance in Rome? And Cesar Rosati? That name is familiar."

"I met him in Volterra. Other than that, I have nothing that links him to this. He owns something called the Rosati Gallery. I need to check that out."

"Perhaps I can help with that," he said. "But you don't have enough names here. You must try harder. Who would have told whoever is behind this that you were even in Italy? Who knew?"

"My shipper, Luigi D'Amato, but I've been dealing with him for years."

"Never mind. You told me you've known Dottie Beach for years also, and I think now you are not so certain about her. Signore D'Amato goes to the top of the list, given he is the first person in all this you dealt with. But he can't be the only person who knows you're in Italy. Your business partner?"

"Clive? I used to be married to him," I said.

"Bad marriages have been the cause of many a crime, I'm afraid," he said.

"I know, but Clive, for all his faults, wouldn't be involved in something like this. I suppose he might inadvertently have told someone where I was. In fact, he did, now that I think of it. He mentioned that someone by the name of Antonio phoned the shop asking what hotel I was staying in. Clive thought Antonio worked for D'Amato."

"And your partner in life, Rob his name is, I think you said."

"Rob knows where I am, but he's unavailable at the moment. His daughter Jennifer is well-trained and wouldn't tell anyone where I was unless she knew them really well. She'd E-mail me with their name and phone number, but she wouldn't give mine to them directly."

"But many people know you are in Italy now."

"Yes," I said. "I can see Lola's court case will be in good hands."

He smiled. "Am I interrogating you? Perhaps a little. But we must go on. Do you know who owned the house where Balducci was found?"

"Yes, it was in the newspapers. Mauro, Gino Mauro. And he knows Mario Romano. His daughter told me."

"His daughter? Put her on the list, too. Anyone else?" he said, setting a steaming bowl of pasta in front of me and pouring a grappa for himself and another one for me, "People who would know that you are looking for Lake. His sister."

"Brandy, yes. And Brandy's nurse and housekeeper, Maire. I don't know her last name, either. She told me that she couldn't get in touch with Lake, but someone did. He knew I'd been there and even that I'd taken white roses."

"We're speaking of the real Crawford Lake now, are we? Then we have twenty names. That's it? Twenty?"

"I forgot Angelo. Dottie's new boyfriend. Also young and cute, and she found him at Eugenia Ponte's agency."

"Angelo," he said. "Twenty-one."

"Angelo Cippolini," I added. "And Alfred Mondragon."

Salvatore looked at me. "I told you there were many people you were overlooking. Who is Mondragon?"

"I talked to him on the telephone. A British art dealer. He buys art for the real Crawford Lake, but he said he didn't know how to reach him, either. Maybe he did, maybe he didn't."

"So, twenty-two. Actually twenty-four."

"Twenty-four? Who are the other two?" I said.

"Lola and me," he said. "Life, as I've already mentioned, is about learning who to trust. Right now you should trust no one. You should make it twenty-four, despite what you think of your partner in life and his daughter and your business partner."

"Salvatore," I said. "I think we can narrow the list down just a little. I may have more enemies than I can ever know, but I do know who my friends are. Please delete you and Lola, Rob, Jennifer, Clive, and D'Amato. I'm godmother to one of D'Amato's kids, for heaven's sake. I had dinner at his home only a couple of weeks ago. Also delete Silvia. She's a lovely and innocent young woman, no matter what her father is up to. And I think we should eliminate Godard, because he's dead, Antonio and Pierre Leclerc for the same reason, and also Yves Boucher. That makes it thirteen, and that's more than enough."

"Why do you eliminate Boucher?"

"Because I talked to him at length, and he was just too out of it, too ineffectual to have anything to do with this. He was completely out of his depth. I'd like to take Brandy off the list, too, given she can't really leave her house, but I suppose she has the wherewithal to get the job done if she chose to do so. I'd also eliminate Kyle, and maybe even Angelo, although he worked for Eugenia Ponte."

"All right then. Tomorrow, we will begin. I will take this list of names, and I will learn what I can about every single one of them. There must be something here. We already know there is a connection between your friend—I use the term loosely—Dottie, and Eugenia Ponte's agency, and between Ponte and Romano and Balducci, and again between Romano and Mauro. Perhaps there are other connections as well. If there are, I am determined to discover them. But first I will tell Lola about the disappointment about Lake."

"No," I said. "I'll tell her. That's what I came up here to do."

"Are you sure?"

"Yes," I said.

"And after that?"

"I don't know. What do you suggest?"

"You have been the prey all along, have you not? Now I think you will have to become the hunter. These people who are always popping up in your life? Perhaps it is time you popped up in theirs. Tomorrow you are going back to Rome to pay them each a visit."

•   •   •

LOLA WIPED A SINGLE TEAR FROM HER EYE when I told her about Lake and the whole sorry mess. She looked thin, pale, and ill. "That's okay," she said.

"No, it's not, Lola. It's not okay at all. I was the one who was so proud of myself and what I do, that dishonest people were able to get the better of me. I'm the one who should be in here, not you."

"But that's not true!" she exclaimed. "This is about me. It's not about you."

"How do you figure that, Lola?" I said. "Where can you see any justice in this situation?"

She looked away from me for what seemed to be a long time, staring at a stain on the wall beside her. "You at least were trying to do the right thing," she said. "I wasn't. I don't think I can ever begin to describe my feelings when I saw that Etruscan hydria sitting on that awful pink blanket on your bed, but I want to try to explain it to you. It's important to me that you understand just what I did.

"I was sure, despite what you said, that it was the real thing. It almost seemed a sacrilege that it was in that kind of grotty hotel, with that lurid red bedspread and curtains, and that hideous wallpaper. It was so perfect: the workmanship, the shape, and most of all the decoration. It could only have been the Micali painter. It is, isn't it?"

"Yes," I said.

"It was absolutely gorgeous. I've never seen anything like it up that close. I wanted to touch it, try it out, run my hands over the surface." She laughed a little. "It sounds as if I'm describing a lover, doesn't it? And you know, it was love at first sight. Like a besotted lover, I had to possess the object of my love.

Or was it lust? I don't know. I've spent most of my life studying the Etruscans. People laugh when I tell them I'm looking for Lars Porsena's tomb, but it's out there somewhere, isn't it? And it would be a worthwhile thing to do, wouldn't it, to track it down?"

"Yes, it would. But—"

"I don't know why I picked the Etruscans, rather than the Romans, or the Maya, or North American Indians for that matter. Maybe it was opportunity, more than anything else. My class was going to Italy, so I went, too. I can remember going to Tarquinia that summer and making my way down into The Tomb of the Leopards, and just gaping at the sight of it. I've spent more hours than you can imagine studying them since then, standing in front of glass cases in museums, peering at Etruscan ceramics from every angle, tramping the countryside looking for Lars.

"And you know what else I've done? I've written letters to Italian authorities and UNESCO, decrying the trade in antiquities. I've penned articles for the local archaeological society newsletter, telling everyone not to purchase antiquities. I even picketed outside one of the large auction houses in New York, protesting their sale of an Etruscan bronze! You heard one of my declamations on the subject that first morning we met over breakfast. All rather holier than thou, wasn't I, lecturing you on the subject! I'm surprised you didn't toss a bun at me. Can you believe anybody could be that hypocritical? I keep thinking about those people, you know, policemen who go into schools warning students about the dangers of drugs, or psychologists and priests who counsel against extramarital sex, who succumb to the lure of the very evil they've been advocating against."

"Lola, please. Don't be so hard on yourself. You made a mistake."

"And then I see the hydria," she said, ignoring my protestations, "and every single thing I thought I believed in flew out the window. I had to have it. Not only that, I told myself it was already stolen goods, so I *could* have it. I was prepared to smuggle it back home and hide it somewhere. Even though I knew I could never show it to anyone, I wanted it. In the few seconds it took for you to open the hotel room door that evening, I was already plotting how to get it home, no matter what the risk. And then there you were, holding off the police at the door, and I was stealing it from you. You'd fed me, given me a ride in the rain. You even offered to help me with my hotel bill. I heard you, when you were out on the fire escape. I heard you say you'd pay my bill, and I just stood there clasping my beloved to my bosom and waited until you gave up and went in. You have no idea what I felt at that moment."

"In a way, I do, Lola," I said. "Lots of times I've seen rare artifacts I know I shouldn't buy, but that I really want, not for the store but for myself, and there's always a moment when I almost give in to the urge."

"But you don't," she said. "That's the difference between you and me. You tell me that you let yourself be duped by these people. Maybe you did. Maybe your pride got the better of you for awhile. But you never lost your moral center the way I did." She started to cry.

"That's ridiculous," I said. "You came to your

senses. You brought it back. You can't pay for a lifetime for one small slip, can you?"

"People pay for slight slips all the time, don't they?" she said. "A moment of inattention, and someone dies. Another plans a joke, perhaps, that goes terribly wrong. Someone makes one mistake, and a lifetime of hard work is like nothing. So you talk about justice? I'd say justice has been served."

PART III
THE SNAKE

*... the Etruscans were vicious. We know it, because
their enemies and exterminators said so.*

—D. H. LAWRENCE

FOURTEEN

ROME

DOTTIE BEACH MADE HER WAY SLOWLY down the Via Condotti, stopping often to look into the shopwindows, and from time to time entering one of the establishments, to emerge some time later with another parcel. After about an hour and a half of this, it was pretty clear to me that Dottie was merely shopping. Not just anywhere, mind you, but in some of the finest designer stores there are. I gave up on her, for the moment, and found myself a place where I could watch the door of the building where the Corelli Ponte agency did business.

While I waited, I called Clive. "Hi Clive," I said.

"Where are you?" he demanded.

"Rome."

"I hope you're calling to say you're on your way home. You've been away a long time, and it's tough running this place all by myself," he grumped.

"You're not all by yourself," I said. "Alex is with you, isn't he? Anyway, what was all that stuff about my having a nice holiday? You and Moira take several holidays a year."

"I suppose," he said. "Not as long as this, though."

"Guess who I've run into a couple of times?" I said, ignoring his ill humor.

"Who?"

"Dottie Beach. I've had dinner with her a couple of times in France, and I saw her again in Rome."

"What's she doing there?"

"Buying for her store, of course," I said.

"Boy, if you and I went bust, and then tried to turn right around and open another store right away, do you think they'd let us? Of course not. I don't know how some people do it!"

"What are you talking about Clive?"

"She went broke. Didn't I tell you?"

"No, Clive, you didn't."

"Sorry. I guess I forgot. It's not as if she's our best friend or anything."

"When did all this happen?"

"Just after the last New York winter antique fair," he said. "She was there, and pretty desperate, let me tell you. Looking for a partner for what she called her successful business, of course, but you know how gossipy it is in the trade. Everybody knew she was in trouble."

"I thought she was doing okay. What happened?"

"Her husband, Hugh what's his name, is divorcing her. I did tell you that, didn't I? Very messy divorce, too. Not civilized like ours. He's refusing to give her a dime. He says he set her up in that antique business, and paid for the whole thing for years, and if she couldn't make a go of it, now it's her problem, not his. Or words to that effect. She didn't last long after the show."

"She must be doing okay again, because she's out shopping in the designer stores on the Via Condotti," I said.

"Some people always land on their feet, don't they? Maybe they named the street after her. Dottie, Via Con-Dottie. Get it? Har har. Now, when are you coming home?"

"Soon," I said.

"Soon?" he wailed. "What does that mean?"

"I'm having trouble booking a flight," I lied. "Airline strike pending."

"Those Italians!" he said. "They're always striking about something."

"Does the name Pierre Leclerc mean anything to you, Clive?"

"Pierre Leclerc," he repeated slowly. "I don't think so. Should it? Who is he?"

"A rather sleazy art dealer in France," I said. "Would Pierre Le Conte ring a bell either?"

"Le Conte, Le Conte," he said. "No. But why don't you ask that Mondragon fellow we met at Burlington House? He seemed to know everybody. You're not dealing with this sleaze are you?"

"Trying not to. Mondragon is a good idea. See you soon."

"When's soon?" he said.

"Just soon," I said.

Around one, Eugenia Ponte left the building and

strode purposefully along the Via Veneto. Unlike Dottie, she ignored the shopwindows, but turned into one of the fancier hotels, crossing the lobby and entering the bar cum restaurant. A rather tall, slim, and handsome man rose from his seat as she arrived. I got a table behind a pillar.

After a few minutes of animated conversation, they ordered, and a bottle of champagne and two plates of raw oysters arrived, which should have given me a clue as to what was going to happen next. Their love food downed, the two of them walked out of the restaurant and headed directly for the elevators. I knew who the man was, given I'd met him already. But just in case he wasn't who he said he was, I waited until the maître d' had left his post at the entranceway and checked the book to see if there was a name I recognized. There was: a table for two at 1:15 for a Signore Palladini. Circles within circles: the man who owned the apartment with the woman who'd supplied the actors. I felt as if I was closing in on something, even if I didn't know what it was.

At three, as previously arranged, I called Salvatore. "What have you got?" I said.

"I began with those I could identify personally, and looked, as you suggested, for a link to Crawford Lake," Salvatore said. "Cesar Rosati was first, because I already knew something about him, and he is very easy to research. Rosati used to be a banker, quite a successful one. He started to dabble in Internet banking, and he got run out of business by Marzocco Financial Online, which as you know, is Crawford Lake's company. Rosati survived it somehow. He seems to have recovered rather nicely, although not in banking."

"He has a gallery, I think," I said. "His wife's family's collection, or something."

"Yes, indeed. Together they own a lot of Etruscan objects. He seems to have gotten around all the restrictions on ownership of such things by opening his wife's family home to the public, as a museum and gallery, getting special dispensation, as it were. It's called the Rosati Gallery, as you probably already know. The gallery admission is rather steep, so maybe that's what keeps him in style. Maybe he just married well, although I have always thought his wife's family was more style than substance, if you see what I'm saying.

"He's made a real name for himself in a very short period of time. One of the reasons he is so well-known is that he has an exceptional track record in finding and repatriating Italian antiquities. He recently, perhaps a year ago, found a beautiful Etruscan stone sphinx, carved of nenfro, which had purportedly been stolen from a tomb in Tarquinia. It is now on display at his gallery. A couple of years ago, he announced with something of a flourish that he'd found an Etruscan kylix, a water cup, decorated by the Bearded Sphinx painter, who, as I am sure you know is, like Micali, an identifiable and rather spectacular Etruscan painter. It, too, had been stolen many years ago, this time from a museum.

"Now you should know there are those among us who are skeptical, who think that Rosati was already in possession of these antiquities; which is to say, that he dealt in stolen goods and was now trying to legitimize the objects by pretending to have found them elsewhere. But Rosati says he and a group of donors bought the sphinx from a collector in Switzerland, the kylix in England, and brought both back to Italy, to cheers all round. One of the donors, by the way, was Gianpiero Ponte, Eugenia's late husband. I found a photograph in the newspaper archives here showing Ponte, Rosati, and Vittorio Palladini at the unveiling of the kylix."

"Eugenia Ponte is having an affair with Palladini," I said.

"Is that so?" Salvatore said. "This is most interesting. I checked out Ponte and could find no relationship to Lake. Ponte did, of course, commit suicide. Some said his business was falling apart, so thinking of Lake's rather predatory practices, I looked into that. I could find nothing in it. The rumors, according to some colleagues of mine, are that the problem was a marital one, and that the marriage has been something of a matter of convenience for some time now. You know Italy and divorces. Just not done. It would appear the stories are true. She's wrapping up her husband's company, and it looks to me as if she'll do reasonably well out of it. And she's always been quite successful. She was a model first, then a television star, although I never saw her show, and her agency always seems to have done well enough. I can't find any indication of legal or financial problems of any sort. The only negative is what you and I know, but no one else really does, and that is that both Antonio and Mario were on that agency's roster.

"Now, before I get on to Palladini and the others, let me finish with Rosati."

"That kylix you mentioned," I said. "I think he told me it was stolen."

"Correct. About two years ago, there was a break-in at Rosati's museum. The alarm system went off, but the police were not as fast as they might have been getting there, and when they did, they found the security guard bound and gagged in a closet, and the Etruscan kylix missing. At the time this happened, the museum from which the kylix had been stolen many years ago was demanding its return. I mention the break-in for a number of reasons: one, the obvious resemblance between the story of the kylix and your hydria, both stolen and found outside Italy in the hands of collectors, but also because the insurance company that had to pay up when the kylix was stolen was the one at which Vittorio Palladini is employed as head of their legal and claims department. The kylix was insured for a great deal of money, even more perhaps than one would think it was worth, if one can put a price on such objects. He must have been more than a little disappointed when it went missing."

"Could you find a link between Palladini and Lake?"

"None."

"But the Pontes and Palladini and Rosati are all linked, and Rosati knew Lake, or at least knew what doing business in competition with Lake was like."

"Yes," he said.

"And Palladini told Yves Boucher to put me in touch with Godard."

"Apparently," Salvatore replied.

"Is there more?"

"Gino Mauro. He's an American, actually, although when he's over here, he's more Italian than the Italians. He maintains he's descended from royalty or some such thing, but in fact, his parents emigrated to America from a dirt-poor village in Sicily."

"And made their fortune?"

"They didn't, but he did. He is, or was, a pugilist."

"A what?"

"A pugilist. Actually, a wrestler, or a former one. WWF, I think you call it. He fought under the name of Gino the Supremo." Salvatore paused. "Does that name work in English?"

"Sort of," I said. "And I'd be willing to bet I've seen him, in the Piazza Navona with Dottie Beach. The person I'm thinking of threw her young friend out of the place faster than you can almost imagine."

"I see," he said. "That sounds about right. As a pugilist, Mauro was moderately successful, knew when to retire, and got into fiber optics."

"Here comes Lake," I said.

"You are quite right. Lake tried to buy the business. Mauro refused to sell. Lake stole most of Mauro's customers."

"And now the farmhouse is for sale. Does he have links to anyone else in this group?"

"None that I was able find."

"Anything more on Palladini?"

"Just what I've told you. He is a corporate lawyer and works for the insurance company."

"He owns a rather lavish apartment in Rome. Do you make enough money as head of the legal and claims department of an insurance company to own that kind of place?"

"I don't know. I can tell you he bought it a couple of years ago and is already selling it. Maybe he got in over his head."

"I don't think so. He's looking for a bigger place. I suppose he could be lying about that. Anything else?"

"Not so far. I can find nothing on Yves Boucher nor Pierre Leclerc. Anna, I have nothing to go on. Maire, either. And you, what have you found? Other than that Eugenia and Palladini are close?"

"I discovered that Dottie Beach is broke but is still shopping the Via Condotti," I said. "I've also discovered that she has not been exactly forthcoming about her store. I'm wondering if she was lying about having a store in New Orleans? Or has she found another partner to replace her husband as the money supply?"

"Did you say New Orleans?" Salvatore said.

"Yes."

"Just a minute, please." I heard paper rustling, and then he came back on the line. "Gino Mauro has a winter home in New Orleans," he said. "His headquarters is New York, but yes, he has a place in New Orleans. Perhaps you are quite right about the fellow with Dottie Beach in the Piazza. And he is usually in Italy this time of year."

"Yes, Silvia said he was coming here. But he wasn't in Italy when Antonio died. At least that's what the papers say. Maybe I'll see if I can track down the reporter who wrote the piece on Antonio's death. I can't recall who it was, but it can't be too difficult to find out."

"I have the clipping here," Salvatore said. "After our discussion last night, I went through all the last few days' papers. Please stay on the line, and I'll get you the name of at least one of the reporters. Gianni Veri," he said after a minute.

"The same fellow who wrote the article on the hydria and Lola's arrest," I said.

"I believe you are correct," Salvatore said. "Already I do not like him."

It took me awhile to track Veri down. I went to the offices of the newspaper I thought he worked for and was told he was a freelancer. I told them I was very interested in finding him in order to commission an article, and after a few minutes of my being absolutely charming, at least trying to be, someone took pity on me, or possibly on Gianni, given what I was to discover, and gave me his phone number. From that I found his address.

Veri had an office about the size of a broom closet on the third floor of a walk-up in a rather insalubrious part of town. His name was in peeling gold letters on the door, and when I went in, he had to close the door in order for me to get around the desk and sit down. I told him I was an antique dealer, and that I had a newsletter, which regularly contained articles written by experts on subjects of interest to collectors, and having seen his article on the businessman who was smuggling antiquities right from under the noses of the police, I'd wanted to find him to commission an article. He looked rather pleased.

"I'm sorry to drop in unannounced like this," I said to him. "But I was very interested in your article. I thought it showed you really knew what you were talking about. I tried to E-mail you," I added. "Veri at something or other."

"That explains it," he said. "It's Veii, nor Veri. Silly of me to choose something so close to my own name.

It confuses everybody. Veii is the name of one of the Etruscan city states."

"Like Cisra," I said, recalling Godard, "or Velathri."

He looked startled. "Exactly," he said. "I see you are a student of the Etruscans. What did you say your name is?"

I told him, putting my card in front of him.

"Signora," he said, his mood changing abruptly. "I'm afraid this visit of yours is in vain. I am a serious journalist, not a hack. I do not write articles for commercial newsletters. Thanks for dropping by."

He rose from his desk and opened the door, which he could do without moving his feet. I tramped back down the stairs, got out my cell phone, and called Salvatore.

"Add Gianni Veri to the list," I said.

"I already did," Salvatore said. "As soon as you noticed he'd written both articles, I phoned a journalist friend right away. Veri was a real up and comer only two years ago. He was well on his way to becoming editor, according to a friend of mine. Then he wrote a piece attacking Lake. He brought up the rumor about Brandy and her fiancé. Lake's response was apparently immediate. Veri lost his job. Everyone thinks Lake had Veri silenced. Nobody else will touch Veri after that, they wouldn't dare, so now he's a freelancer. I'm not sure how well he's doing."

"Not well at all," I said. "Your mention of Brandy and Taso makes me think I should revisit all the files I looked at when I was looking at Lake to see if there's something I missed. I'll call you tomorrow morning as planned."

I had missed something. It was easy enough to do.

I'd been mesmerized by the pictures of Brandy and the dozens and dozens of white roses on Taso's coffin. There were three women around the coffin: Brandy, a woman wearing a veil who was described as Taso's mother, and a third, Taso's aunt. The aunt's name was Anna Karagiannis, and the last time I'd seen her in person, she was serving lemon cake in Crawford Lake's apartment.

I called England. "Is Alfred Mondragon there?" I asked.

"No, I'm sorry. Alfred is on vacation for a week. I'm his associate, Ryan Mcgillvray. Is there any chance I might help you?"

"I hope so, Ryan. I was talking to Alfred just the other day and was hoping to catch him again. Actually, I believe we met at an auction at Burlington House. I'm Lara McClintoch."

"Yes, I believe I remember you," he said.

"Ryan, I've been approached by an agent by the name of Pierre Le Conte or Leclerc. I may not have the name right. He has a painting I'm interested in. He gave Mr. Mondragon's name as a reference."

"Of all the cheek!" Ryan said. "Alfred will be furious. Don't deal with Leclerc or Le Conte or whatever he calls himself, please. It wouldn't surprise me if he had several names. He's a crook."

"I won't tell anyone, I promise," I said. "What do you mean by a crook?"

"I mean, he's absolutely horrible. He worked here, you know, for a few months. Alfred made a little mistake, and Le Conte . . . I get so annoyed just thinking about this."

"What do you mean by a little mistake?" I said.

"Alfred purchased a lovely Greek wine jug, thinking the paperwork was in order. But it wasn't. It had been smuggled out of Italy by the owner for sale in Britain. Poor Alfred was exhausted after doing three antique shows in a row and didn't check the paperwork the way he should have. It's as simple as that. It could happen to anyone. Le Conte comes and tells him it was smuggled and tries to extort money from Alfred. Alfred is not one to be blackmailed. He called the authorities, told them he had bought this in error, and returned it to Italy. Then he told Le Conte to get lost, fired him on the spot.

"In revenge, Le Conte then tried to set himself up with Crawford Lake. You know who I'm talking about, right? The billionaire nobody has seen for years? He's a client of ours from time to time, and Le Conte tried to steal him away from us. Lake figured the fellow out right away, of course. You don't get to be a billionaire by being gullible. Blew Le Conte off pretty fast. But still, it was a terrible situation."

"Terrible," I agreed. "I expect Lake is not the kind of client you'd want to annoy," I added. "I've been reading about his financial exploits. People have rather unpleasant things to say about him."

"We've always found Lake to be an honorable person," Ryan said. "He's fair about commissions and certainly not difficult to deal with from a personality perspective. I haven't met him, of course, but Alfred has, once anyway, and says he rather likes the man. I mean, what can you expect from Lake's enemies? They're bound to say bad things about him. All I can say is that we are glad to have him as a client."

"Thanks for letting me know, Ryan. I'm sure you've

saved me from making a dreadful mistake with Le Conte."

"I hope so," Ryan said. "The man is a pig."

I figured I had time for one more visit that day, to the Rosati Gallery, located in a huge old villa just off the Borghese Gardens. I paid a rather steep admission, as Salvatore had said I would, and went in. The museum was housed on the main floor of the house. It was small, as museums go, but the pieces in it were exceptional, particularly the Etruscan room. I found the nenfro sphinx that Salvatore had mentioned, and peered carefully at several displays of Etruscan ceramics. It was very quiet: I saw only a woman with a young child and a student sketching the sphinx. At the far end was a door marked Office of the Director. I went in. I was in a small reception area, with no receptionist, that led to only two offices. One said Director; the other had a temporary sign stuck on with tape.

That one said N. Marzolini.

Great, I said to myself. *Add another name to the list.*

I carefully tried Nicola's door. It was locked. I could hear voices in the director's office, however, and decided to wait to size up the situation before I barged right in. The conversation, in English and quiet at first, became progressively louder. I thought of leaving and coming back in a few minutes, until the words I heard began to make sense.

"Look, I'd like to help," the one voice said. I was pretty sure it was Rosati. "But the point is, you paid far too much for it, way over market. I hope you'll forgive me for saying so, but you let your wish to beat out Lake cloud your judgment. I told you what it was worth."

"So what would you pay for it?" the second voice, an American, said.

"I can't pay anything. I have no acquisitions budget to speak of, and frankly, this is not really a commercial venture. I get certain tax benefits out of it, which I could offer to help you with, if you have income in Italy and are prepared to donate it," the voice I took to be Rosati, said.

"Maybe the group would consider it."

"Perhaps. That's not up to me. You know, though, they couldn't come up with anything like what you paid for it."

"Okay," the second man said. "I'll think about the tax angle, and we'll talk some more."

Before I could duck out into the museum, the tiniest cowboy I have ever seen came out of the office. He was dressed in a gray suit that was perfectly tailored for him, with everything, even the buttons, scaled down in proportion to his height, a white shirt, and string tie. To complete the look, he wore rather elaborate black cowboy boots and a Stetson. Including the hat and boots, he wasn't as tall as I am. "Ma'am," he said, tipping his hat to me as he went out.

Rosati was a few steps behind him.

"Hi," I said.

"Well, hello again," he said, looking surprised. "Did you come to claim that dinner I promised you in Volterra? You stood me up."

"I'm sorry. I got called away on business. Did you not get my message?"

"No, I did not."

"I would have thought such a nice hotel would have better service. This is a wonderful place you have."

"Then you've come to take me up on my offer of a tour. I'm delighted."

"No. I came to talk to you about Crawford Lake," I said.

He looked mildly amused. "Why would you want to do that?"

"That's a very good question, and one for which frankly, I don't have a good answer, other than that I feel I've been duped by the man, and I wanted to talk to someone who knew him."

"I see. Sit down, please," he said. "We'll have that drink we missed the last time. Campari and soda, perhaps? It's late in the afternoon. I think I'll have one, if you will."

"Sure," I said. He poured the drinks, taking ice from a small refrigerator under the counter, and the soda and Campari from a credenza.

"Now," he said. "Crawford Lake. What do you want to know?"

"Just your involvement with him."

"He put me out of business, or rather he put the bank I worked for out of the Internet banking business for awhile, and me out of a job."

"So, did you ever meet him in person?"

"No. I think that was one of the most offensive parts of it. This person whose face I couldn't even picture made a mess of my life."

"Do you hate him?"

"I did for awhile. I got over it. I have a rather nice life now, as perhaps you can see. I love art and antiquities, and I have this wonderful place, as you put it. I have good people working for me now, so I don't even have to work that hard. I just get to come in here whenever I want and enjoy myself."

"By good people, you mean someone like Nicola Marzolini," I said. "I couldn't help noticing his name on the door."

"Yes, Nicola is one of the people I employ from time to time. Do you know him?"

I nodded.

"He's a consultant, not full time, but very good. He knows his stuff, and he pays attention to detail. Pleasant fellow as well, although if you've met him, you probably know he has a thing about neatness. He has a fit when one of the others doesn't keep the work area absolutely tidy. He's always making sure the books on the shelf here line up perfectly. As you can see," he said waving his hand toward the desk in the room behind, "I'm of the school that believes that a tidy desk is the sign of a diseased mind. I haven't seen the top of my desk in months. But to get to your point, I probably should thank Crawford Lake for what happened, although I don't think I've reached that stage quite yet. Does that answer your question?"

"It does," I said. I just really didn't know whether to believe him or not. "Would Hank Mariani feel the same way you do? That was Hank Mariani, was it not? The Texas oilman who outbid Crawford Lake for the Etruscan bronze Aplu?"

"How ever would you know that?" he asked.

I shrugged. "I saw his picture in the paper. Lake was making a hostile bid for Mariani's company, if I remember correctly. Has he reached the same Zen state you have on the subject of Lake?"

"He isn't too relaxed about it, no. To be fair, though, it was only a few days ago that he was asked to clear out of his large corner office, when Lake won the battle. It will take awhile for him to recover, I'm sure."

"Presumably he had shares to sell and doesn't have to worry," I said. "Financially, I mean."

"Oh, I think it was more than just his pride that was hurt," Rosati said. "He spends rather lavishly, I'm afraid, and he did some rather stupid things to try to stop Lake from getting the company. As a result, he wants me to buy the Aplu, but like all museums or galleries, I essentially have no budget for doing so. I'm sure he'll land on his feet, however, and I shouldn't be gossiping about him like this. Another Campari?" he asked.

"No, I better not. But thank you, both for the drink and your candor."

"I hope whatever Crawford Lake has done to you is not too serious. Whatever it is, my advice to you is just to get on with your life. There are always other opportunities."

"Thanks again," I said.

"You're welcome. Let me walk you to the door. I'm leaving, too. I'll show you a few of my favorite things as we go."

"Good-bye, signora," the security guard said. "Have a good holiday tomorrow, signore," he said to Rosati.

"I'm spending a day in the country," Rosati said as he shook my hand. "An annual get-together with friends. I'm rather looking forward to it."

Outside the museum, I tried to call Salvatore to get him to look into Nicola Marzolini, but there was no answer. I went back to the hotel.

"Signora McClintoch," the bell captain called to me. "A package was delivered for you. I have taken the liberty of having it sent up to your room."

"Thanks so much," I said. *What package?* I thought.

A reasonably large box well wrapped in brown kraft paper sat on the bureau in my room. I regarded it with deep suspicion. The sender's name and address were quite clear, however: Salvatore Vitali at his address in Cortona.

I opened the box. It contained a bubble-wrapped package protected by a rather large quantity of foam chips. Gathering that it must be something fragile, I unwrapped it carefully, and found myself staring, once again, at the chimera hydria.

At that very moment, the phone rang.

"Lara!" Salvatore exclaimed. "I'm so glad to have reached you. I have such good news. I can barely speak, I am so happy. We wanted to phone you right away."

I said nothing, just stared at the hydria.

"Are you there?" he said. "Lara?"

"Yes, I'm here," I said through clenched teeth. "What is your news?"

"My Lola is free!" he said. "She is right here with me."

"That's wonderful," I said. "Congratulations. How did you manage that?"

"But I did nothing," he said. "As much as I would like to claim credit, and so to win my Lola's heart, I cannot do so. The evidence, you see, has disappeared. Thieves broke into the police station three days ago and stole several articles, including the chimera hydria. Massimo Lucca, the policeman in charge of the investigation, called this morning. No vase, no case. Do you understand? Lucca said he could not hold Lola any longer under the circumstances. Isn't that wonderful news?"

"Wonderful," I said.

"We must celebrate before you return to America," he said. "A good meal at my favorite restaurant, a bottle or two of their best Barbaresco. Lola must eat. I'm going to make her some pasta right away."

"And the parcel you sent me?" I said.

"What parcel?" he said.

"You didn't send me a parcel?"

"No," he replied. "Now, can you come this evening to celebrate with us?"

"I don't think so," I said. "There are a couple of things I still have to take care of here." That was an understatement. His excitement sounded so genuine, I didn't know what to think.

"Then tomorrow," he said. "Promise you'll come."

I picked up the hydria carefully and just held it for a few minutes, feeling its heft, the balance, the smooth surface. I placed it on top of the bureau in my hotel room and just looked at it for a long, long time.

Then I picked up my list of possible suspects. *Pick one,* I told myself. *They can't all be guilty.* I made three columns, and tried to assign the people on the list to at least one of them.

The first group I called the charade, those people whom I knew or at least suspected to be part of the false Lake scenario: Romano, first and foremost, as the Lake impersonator; Antonio; Boucher; Palladini; Anna Karagiannis or Anna the maid; Eugenia Ponte, whose agency both Antonio and Romano had come from; and

Dottie, because she knew Eugenia, or at least Eugenia's agency.

The second list I called Lake's enemies: Rosati, despite what he said; Gino Mauro; Gianni Veri; and perhaps most of all, Brandy Lake; and Anna again, because of Brandy's fiancé and Anna's nephew, Taso; and Maire, Brandy's helper. Because Dottie could well have known Mauro—I was almost certain he was the mystery man in the Piazza Navona—she made the list, too. Leclerc, assuming Ryan's story about Leclerc getting fired by Mondragon after trying to deal direct with Lake was true, I also placed in that column.

The third list I called the hydria, those who could be associated in any way with the object, either through their work or simply because they had seen it: Dottie; Leclerc, despite the fact he was no longer with us; Godard, of course; Antonio and Romano, both of whom had known I had it; and Nicola Marzolini and Rosati, both on the list because of their occupations. I also put Alfred Mondragon on the list for that reason, and because he knew Lake.

I eliminated dead people, and others like Maire, who just seemed unlikely suspects. There was only one person on all three lists: Dottie Beach. I looked back at the hydria. Three groups, like the three heads of the chimera. All by itself, the hydria had changed everything.

FIFTEEN

ORVIETO

DOTTIE BEACH STOOD OUTSIDE THE Hassler, her arm through that of her mystery man, who I had decided, based on nothing more than his performance in the Piazza Navona, was Gino the Supremo, Gino Mauro. I'd thought Dottie was lying about staying at the Hassler, but she hadn't been. She had neglected to mention that she was staying in a room reserved in Gino Mauro's name, that's all. A few minutes after they came outside, a Jaguar pulled up beside them, Eugenia Ponte at the wheel and Vittorio Palladini in the passenger seat. Gino and Dottie got in, and they took off. I pulled in behind them.

Eugenia took the Autostrada del Sole at a leisurely pace before turning off at the exit for Orvieto. Rather than taking the road to the town, she skirted the hill on which Orvieto is perched, crossed the valley, and started up the slope on the other side. Cypress trees, caught in the late afternoon sun, cast long, shadowy fingers across the fields. The road climbed progressively higher through a series of switchbacks, with several side roads leading off the main one, and I was afraid I might lose them, but about five miles out of town, she turned off the road and through large, wrought-iron gates.

I waited a few minutes, then drove through the gates and up a long driveway, finding myself at a rather attractive stone home set in a grove of cypress trees and handsomely landscaped. There was a large parking area, where the Jaguar, now empty, sat, along with a Mercedes or two, a Jetta, a couple of Opels, a rented Fiat, and a red Lamborghini with a bright yellow umbrella visible through the back window, the sight of which took me back to Nice and Volterra.

I took the box out of the trunk of my car and walked up to the main door. I rang, then knocked, but there was no answer. I walked around the house and up a slight slope and found myself in a lovely back garden. To one side, at the top of a slight incline, there was a swimming pool, and across the valley, Orvieto sat on its lofty plateau, sunlight shimmering on the cathedral dome. There was absolutely no one there, despite all the cars in the parking area. Dottie and Gino, Eugenia and Vittorio had vanished into thin air.

I knocked on a back door. There was no answer there, either, but a long buffet table had been set up in the loggia. It was covered with a linen tablecloth; plates, napkins, and cutlery were artfully laid out at one end; there was a lovely flower arrangement in the middle; and several candles, unlit.

I peered in the windows: again, no sign of life. I scanned the back garden and saw a piece of red cloth tied to the branch of a tree at the far end of the property. It marked the start of a path into the woods that angled down at first, then back up through the trees. At the end of it was a long, stone-lined passageway, open to the air, cut into the side of a hill, which ended in a wooden door, propped open, which appeared to lead straight into the hill.

It was rather dark inside, and there was an acrid smell like rotting leaves and mold. I was at the top of a very old and broken stone staircase that led into the gloom. There was a dim glow at the bottom. I picked my way slowly and carefully down the steps, trying not to dislodge any pieces of stone that would reveal my presence. I reached the last step, took a deep breath, and stepped into the light.

I don't know what they saw in me, other than a woman in black loafers and pants and a white shirt, holding a large cardboard box. A nuisance that had to be disposed of? A teacher who'd found them doing something naughty in the schoolyard? Or even an avenging angel of some kind?

I know what I saw: twelve people, all of whom I recognized, some wary, some embarrassed and frightened, still others merely curious. But I saw something else, too. Perhaps because I was so frightened, the urge to flee almost unbearable, I had a sense of being able to penetrate the civilized veneer to the monster that lay beneath. It was a writhing mass of evil, created partly by a carelessness caused by oblivion to consequences and partly through calculated malice.

"I believe this is yours," I said, extending my arms with the box in them toward the group.

Dottie Beach burst into tears. "I didn't kill Robert Godard," she sobbed. "No matter what you've been told."

As she spoke, Nicola Marzolini stepped forward, took the box, lifted its precious contents, and set the hydria on a stone bench. We all stared at it for a moment. It looked perfectly at home, which it should have, given that most of these ceramics were made for the dead. We were in an Etruscan tomb, something I could thank Robert Godard for knowing.

I was in the entranceway to a chamber about twenty feet long and almost as wide, with a gabled roof painted red. Stone benches, on which pillows had been heaped, lined all four walls, breaking only at the entranceway where I stood, and at another door, to my right, that led to some darkness beyond. The wall paintings were almost gone, faded to the point where only a few details could be made out, pale blue and yellow swallows flitting across one wall, the shadow of a feast of some kind on another. There was a false door painted into the far wall, and over the door, faint but still distinguishable, was a chimera, drawn and painted by some ancient hand.

A table had been set up in front of the false door, covered in a cloth that matched the ceiling, and on it was set up a bar. Wine chilled in a large bucket of ice, a blue glass bottle of grappa stood open, there were bowls of olives and a cheese platter, and several candles on the table and scattered about the room provided the light, casting large shadows against the walls.

"There is an explanation for this," Cesar Rosati said.

"One I'm sure we'd all like to hear," a voice behind me said. My heart leapt into my mouth. If I'd thought I could stay in the doorway and make a fast exit if necessary, I'd obviously been wrong.

"What are you doing here?" a tall woman with long, gray hair, pulled loosely back into a chignon, said. She looked rather more patrician than she had when I first saw her, dressed as she had been in a maid's outfit.

I looked over my shoulder. A tall man dressed in a white suit, white hat, and dark sunglasses stood in the doorway. His tie was not the right width to be fashionable, nor were his lapels, but I suppose if you don't get out much, there isn't much point in buying a new suit every season.

"Hello, Mr. Lake," I said. What I didn't know was whether his arrival improved my odds, which had been twelve to one before he got there, or made them worse.

"Ms. McClintoch, Anna," he said nodding politely in our direction. "And you, Mondragon." Alfred Mondragon nodded curtly.

"Lake!" Gino said. "Are you serious? Is this really Crawford Lake?"

"How did you find us?" Hank demanded.

"I followed Ms. McClintoch. Just about everyone here was following somebody, so I thought I'd join in," he said dryly.

"This is by invitation only," Hank said.

"I've been musing what the invitation, had I received one, would say," Lake said. "Buffet supper at six. Cocktails at four in the tomb?"

"If this place is not to your liking, then you know what you can do," Hank said.

"On the contrary, this is exactly my kind of place,"

he said, carefully replacing his glasses with a pair of a lighter tint. "Now, I believe Ms. McClintoch was about to get an explanation. Perhaps we could start off with some introductions. I'd prefer not to shake hands, if you don't mind. I'm Crawford Lake, and this is Ms. Lara McClintoch. And you are?"

Anna Karagiannis, the aunt of Brandy Lake's dead fiancé, declined to introduce herself, but the rest of them did. Besides Anna; Dottie and Gino; Eugenia and Vittorio; there was Cesar Rosati, the man I'd stood up for dinner; Mario Romano, the fake Lake; the art dealer Mondragon; the journalist Gianni Veri; Hank Mariani, the tiny cowboy; Nicola Marzolini, my date a few evenings back; and the one person I hadn't been expecting, Massimo Lucca, the policeman from the carabinieri station in Arezzo. Hank Mariani was the last to introduce himself. He came up to me with his hand out.

"How do you do," he said. "I'm Pupluna."

"Pupluna?" Lake snorted.

"We call this group the Società della Chimera," Mario Romano said defensively. "We meet every year around this time. We call it our annual meeting, and we have it here because, as I'm sure you know, the Etruscan kings met in this area—at a place they called Velzna—to discuss matters of state, trade, defense, those kinds of things. Anna has this wonderful home here, complete with Etruscan tomb, so she has graciously offered to be our host every year.

"We limit our membership to thirteen, after the Etruscan city states, and we all take the name of one of those cities. That's what Harold here meant when he said he was Pupluna. I'm Velc, Anna is Velzna, Dottie here is Clevsi, Cesar, Rusellae, and so on." He paused for a moment. "It sounds rather foolish when you tell a stranger, I'm afraid." He suddenly seemed at a loss for words.

"Perhaps I should carry on, then, shall I?" Nicola said. "This group has been meeting for what? Almost ten years now?" Several of them nodded. "We're rather fanatical about all things Etruscan. We have a little Internet chat group, to share information and just talk about our passion. At some point—I think maybe four or five meetings ago, wasn't it?—we decided we needed a project. We were beginning to feel we couldn't always be a social club."

"Someone, I think it was Cesar," he said, "suggested repatriating an Etruscan antiquity every year. We initiated an annual assessment for membership and built up a nest egg to help with expenses, and purchase, where necessary. I searched the records for missing artifacts and came up with a list. Alfred Mondragon here, with his inestimable knowledge and connections in the art world, has been able to track down four of them so far, a lovely small bronze of a warrior, a very nice stone sphinx, both of which now rest in Cesar Rosati's collection, a kylix by the Bearded Sphinx painter, which unfortunately we no longer have, and now, the *pièce de résistance*, the chimera hydria, which like the others would be donated to the Rosati Gallery. It's very probably by the Micali painter, did you know that?" I nodded. "Perhaps you could take it from here, Alfred."

"The hydria resided with Robert Godard, Senior, in Vichy," Mondragon said, glancing carefully at Lake. "We found out that Godard was an Etruscophile like the rest of us, and so we offered him a position in the

Società. Godard died shortly after, which put a crimp in our plans, but we persevered and extended the same invitation to his son, also Robert. We thought we had convinced him to bring the hydria as a condition of his membership. Unfortunately, we didn't know that Robert Junior was disabled and would have real difficulty coming to Italy.

"For awhile we were still hopeful that Godard would bring it himself. He kept saying he would. But Nicola here, who went to see it and photographed it for us, thought it was pretty clear Godard was broke, ill, and wouldn't make it," Mondragon said. "At least not without help.

"And so," he said, pausing for a moment, "we had to come up with a different plan. Cesar, I think I'll turn it over to you at this point, as you were the one who came up with the idea."

Rosati cleared his throat. "A few of us got together, a committee I suppose you could call it, to figure out how to make this work. The simplest thing would have been to buy the hydria from Godard. However, we'd already told him not to sell the hydria, that it was his ticket into the Società. The alternative seemed to be to help him get here. That's when we looked around for someone who could get money to him in a way he would find acceptable, that is to buy something from him. It couldn't be one of us, because if he came here and saw us all, he'd know something was up, and he mightn't be too inclined to donate the hydria then. And maybe he couldn't afford to. That's when we came up with the, um, plan," Rosati said.

"This plan being the one in which you used my

name to trick Ms. McClintoch into assisting you with this," Lake said.

"I hope you will understand that our intentions were good," Eugenia said. "Once you've heard the story."

"Ah, intentions," Lake said. "We know all about those, don't we?"

"What I understand is that you thought ends justified means and were prepared to use someone unwitting, like me, to carry out your plans," I said.

"I take it you counted on the fact that no one would know what I looked like," Lake said. "Why did you choose Ms. McClintoch here?"

Dottie looked as if she was going to cry again. "I thought you'd be perfect for it," she said to me. "You have such an honest face, and of course you were here. I found that out easily enough. Now I feel really awful about it. I'm thinking you may never forgive me."

"I arranged for a fellow by the name of Yves Boucher to get Lara to Godard in Vichy," Vittorio Palladini said. "Actually, we'd already asked Boucher to try to buy it for us, or anything else Godard was prepared to sell, but he'd been singularly unsuccessful. Godard didn't take to him at all. We didn't think you knew much about Etruscan bronzes, Lara, so we concocted the idea of the Bellerophon, knowing—Nicola had checked the place out—that there was a large bronze that might pass as a Bellerophon."

"Unfortunately," Nicola said. "You seemed to know rather more than we thought you did—I hope you'll take this as a compliment—and you ascertained correctly, and immediately, that it was a fake."

"Then Godard had his unfortunate accident," Palladini said. "Dottie told us." I looked over at Dottie. She was biting her lip and wouldn't meet my gaze.

"There's this little ray of sunshine. Lara has the hydria. We don't know how she managed it, but she does," Hank said. "Not only that, but she gets it across the border. We figure all we have to do is get it from her, and we keep on trying, but it doesn't work out."

"But there's the final catastrophe," Palladini said, looking accusingly at Massimo Lucca. "The carabinieri got it."

"It wasn't my fault," Lucca said. "I didn't make the anonymous calls, and I didn't arrest that woman."

"And then, of course," Gino said. "It disappeared again."

"Unbelievable," Lucca said, "that it could be stolen right out of the carabinieri station. Heads will roll on this one, I can assure you. I just hope one of them isn't mine. And by the way, I'm not sure I can overlook the fact that you stole it, Ms. McClintoch."

"Oh, come now," Eugenia said. "After all, there was another good thing about its disappearance. We felt badly your friend was in prison," she said, turning to me. "We knew it wasn't her fault. So while we were very disappointed not to get the hydria, we were glad she was released."

"We'd pretty much given up on the whole idea," Hank said. "We figured we'd just get together for the social event this year, and decide what, if anything, we wanted to try to do next year. And then who shows up but you, little lady, with the hydria!"

"So there you have it," Mario said. "We are in your hands really, all of us. I hope you'll understand our intentions were good, if we were occasionally a little heavy-handed."

"Yes, you could lose several of us our jobs," Lucca said.

"She won't," Dottie said. "Will you, sweetie, please? We were planning to donate it. You have to believe us." They all looked at me.

I had felt myself getting more and more furious as these waves of self-serving rationalizations and downright lies washed over me. "Is that it?" I said. I was almost gritting my teeth as I spoke.

"What do you mean?" Eugenia said.

"I believe Ms. McClintoch is referring to the fact that there are *lacunae*, holes, in this story that even I, as a relative outsider, can see," Lake said.

"I suppose there are one or two details missing," Mauro said.

"We're not talking about one or two minor details," I said.

"We don't know how you got the hydria out of the carabinieri station, if that's what you mean," Lucca said. "As I believe I've already mentioned."

"That's not what I mean," I said. "Your version mentions only one of the three people involved in this farce who are dead, omitting the two that were almost certainly murdered."

"Murdered? What is she talking about?" Hank said. "Nobody was murdered."

"Antonio Balducci was," I said. "So was Pierre Leclerc. Robert Godard may have been."

"Oh no, not Robert Godard! He wasn't!" Dottie said.

"Balducci? He killed himself," Mauro said. "At my farmhouse. Why he would choose that moment and that place I will never know. But he did kill himself."

"No, he didn't," I said.

"He was my best friend," Romano said. "I'd never do anything to hurt him. This is outrageous."

"The papers didn't say anything about him being murdered," Eugenia said. "He killed himself. I must object to this as well. He was one of my actors."

"Please," Lake said. "Enough of these protestations. If, in fact, some of you think that this is impossible, then I'm afraid that makes you the goat. You may object to this term, you may prefer to use Cesar's word *committee*, but the analogy is yours. You are the ones who have adopted the chimera as your symbol, and quite frankly, you fit it better than you know."

Lucca, I saw, was looking at me with some interest. "I'd like to know who Pierre Leclerc is or was," he said.

"A sleazy art dealer," Mondragon said. "Lake knows him, too. But I didn't know he was dead of any cause, let alone murder."

"He's the man found out by the Tanella," I said to Lucca. "The one you haven't been able to identify yet."

"I've never heard of him," Eugenia said. "What has he got to do with any of this?"

"Perhaps we should begin again, and hear Ms. McClintoch's version of events," Lake said.

"Last night I made three lists, although I think I now prefer Mr. Lake's analogy," I said. "Three lists, three groups, three heads of the chimera. I called the first of mine the charade. This roughly corresponds to the plan you had to get me to Vichy with money for Godard, and yes, Mr. Lake is quite right. Those of you, assuming there are some, who believed this version of events, are indeed the goat. So let's start the story again. Dottie?"

"Oh," she said, putting her hand up to her mouth. "I don't think . . ." She took a deep breath, and straightened up. "Okay," she said.

"Don't!" Gino said.

"I've got to," she said. "I can't live with myself otherwise."

"We're all waiting, rather breathlessly, I must say," Lake said.

Dottie opened her mouth a couple of times, but no sound came out. "You went to the chateau in Vichy the morning Robert Godard died," I prompted her.

"That's right," she said at last. "My job was to keep an eye on things in Vichy, but I also wanted to buy a dining suite," she said. "I'm opening a new store in New Orleans soon, and I need inventory. Godard said he'd think about it, and that I should come back the next day. I went into the chateau without knocking. He didn't answer, you see. It would take him too long to get to the door. It was open, though, so I just went in. When I got to that room with all the antiquities, you know that awful one with the bare lightbulbs and the birds flying around," she said to me.

I nodded encouragingly.

"The cabinet with the hydria in it was open. I went over and decided I'd just try and buy the thing, or tell him I was a member of the Società and I'd take it to the group on his behalf or something. All this pretend stuff about Lake seemed silly once I was there.

"I took the hydria out of the case and carried it to Robert Godard's study," she said. "I didn't mean to frighten him. He was just attaching some ropes to a harness and there was a trapdoor open. He saw me standing there with the hydria and he must have thought I was planning to steal it from him, because he started yelling at me and then sort of lunged at it. He fell right into the hole. It was the most horrible sound when he hit the floor down there. There was this crack . . ."

"His skull, I expect," Lucca said. "Hitting stone."

"Don't, please," Dottie said. "I can't bear to think about it. He looked so horrible lying down there, with the blood oozing out of his head like that. I panicked."

"So where was the hydria then?" I asked her.

"I had it," she said. "I was halfway to town before I realized I was still holding onto it. I swear I didn't mean to take it. And I didn't kill Robert Godard. It was an accident. I didn't touch him. But I know it was my fault." She started to sob.

"If you had it, why didn't you just bring it?" Hank said. "I mean how did Lara get it?"

"When I got back to town, I tried to decide what to do," she said. "I knew I had to report Godard's death. I thought I'd do it anonymously, from a phone booth or something. But then that odious man found me."

"What odious man?" Eugenia said.

"Pierre Leclerc," she said. "He must have been at Godard's, he must have seen what happened, and followed me. He pretended he was being helpful, but I knew he wasn't. He was horrible. He said the police would think I'd pushed Godard into the basement and stolen the hydria, but he, of course, was sure I hadn't. I told him how we were a group of people trying to get the hydria back to Italy for the Rosati Collection. He pretended to be sympathetic. All I had to do was give him the hydria and twenty thousand dollars, and he'd take care of everything."

"Good lord," Hank said. "That's extortion!"

"You think?" Gino said.

"I didn't have twenty thousand dollars, so I called Gino for help," Dottie said. "He's wonderful. We're getting married."

I thought I heard a soft harumph from Lake.

"He told me I should just head for Italy."

"That's all there is," she said. "Gino said he'd look after it. I'm sorry to bring you into this, honey," she added, turning to him. "But neither of us did anything wrong, so I think we should just tell everybody what happened."

"What's to tell? I arranged to have the guy paid what he wanted, and that's the last I've heard of him," Mauro said.

"Gino!" Dottie said.

"Okay, okay. The deal was that Leclerc would get the twenty thousand bucks only if he delivered the hydria to Italy. I figured we might as well try to get something out of this fiasco. I arranged to have him paid ten thousand in France, with the second ten to be given to him once the hydria was safe in Italy and turned over to one of us."

"And was it?" Lucca said.

"Yes," he said. "Leclerc told me that Lara had it."

"And did you?" Lucca said.

"Yes," I said. "For awhile, anyway. Leclerc put it in my car in Nice."

"He gave it to you? Why would he want to do something like that?" Hank said.

"So Lara would get it across the border, of course," Lake said. "Leclerc may have been a bottom feeder, but he wasn't stupid. He wasn't going to risk getting stopped at the border with it. If Lara got caught, then he still had his ten thousand."

"I expect that's essentially correct," I said. "I did get it into Italy, so he called Gino and told him I had it, and once that was confirmed, Leclerc had twenty thousand. Not bad for a day's work."

"That man is a disgrace to our profession," Mondragon said. "An absolute brigand."

"I guess we know what happened after that," Hank said. "We tried to retrieve it, failed, and then it ended up in the carabinieri station."

"There were a few more 'incidents,' shall we say, in between," I said.

"The thing I can't figure out," Palladini said, interrupting me, "is why all those phone calls to the carabinieri? Was that Leclerc being cute?"

"I think, given the reports I've read, and if that body at the Tanella really is Leclerc, that he was dead at the time some of the calls were made," Lucca said.

"I believe that brings us to my second list," I said. "The lion, or what I called the anti-Lake group."

"I can hardly wait," Lake said. "Sorry to interrupt," he added.

"The lion head of the chimera wasn't nearly as keen on seeing that the hydria was returned to an Italian museum as some of the rest of you were."

"What were they keen on?" Palladini said.

"Discrediting Crawford Lake."

"I'm thinking of suing," Lake said.

"Be careful what you say, all of you," Palladini warned. "Remember, I'm a lawyer."

"I'm not afraid of saying what I think," Mariani said. "I don't intimidate that easily. You put me out of business, Lake, and not in an ethical way, either. Your business practices stink."

"I couldn't agree more," Gino Mauro said.

"Nonsense," Lake said. "Both of you. To carry the chimera metaphor a step further, your roar is a toothless one. You, Mariani, are a blowhard who knows what everything costs but the value of nothing. You paid too much for the Etruscan Aplu, and you paid too much for everything else. If I hadn't come along to take over your company, someone else would have.

"As for you Mr. Mauro, you've been too busy enjoying the trappings of wealth, or at least what you see to be the trappings. While you were spending time with your countless girlfriends, making promises you had no intention of keeping, your customers were leaving in droves."

"Did he say *countless* girlfriends?" Dottie said, looking at Gino.

"I regret to tell you, madame," Lake said, looking at Dottie, "That your boyfriend is still with his wife. And you, Rosati? Are you going to join in?"

"I'm not wild about you, Lake," Rosati said. "But when it comes right down to it, I don't much care, and I have absolutely no knowledge of what you call this lion plot."

"I think we are forgetting there are more important issues at stake here," Gianni Veri said. "Like freedom of the press. I am not afraid to speak out against censorship. I lost my job because I dared to print something negative about you, Lake. You had me fired. I was on the fast track to editor, and you ruined my career. As far as I'm concerned, your continued success is a slap in the face to freedom of speech everywhere."

"You lost your job at the newspaper," Lake responded, "not because you wrote about me. I have something written about me almost every day, and I assure you, I take little, if any, notice. No, you lost your job because, as you have just irrefutably demonstrated by being a part of this group, you have complete contempt for the truth. I had nothing to do with your dismissal, but I heartily endorsed it when it happened."

"And what are you going to say to me, Crawford?" Anna said.

"Careful, Anna," Eugenia said.

"I will not be careful," she said. "I accuse Crawford Lake of killing—murdering—my nephew, Anastasios Karagiannis. Taso was supposed to marry Crawford's sister, Brandy, but he died in a terrible car crash just before the wedding. Some people think Lake tampered with the brakes on Taso's car. I'm one of them. So sue me. I would relish the chance to have my say publicly."

Lake sighed deeply. "Of all those here, Anna, you are the only one with a legitimate reason for hating me. But I have to tell you, whether you believe me or not, that I did not kill your nephew Taso, at least not in the way you think. I rather liked the young man. What I did do was tell him something I believed he needed to know about the woman he was about to marry and her family. If he chose to drink himself into oblivion when he heard it, and then either accidentally or willfully drive his car off the road, then that is something I have to live with."

"I don't believe you," Anna said.

Lake turned to me. "I think you know what it is I

felt I had to tell Taso. Was I right to tell him when my sister absolutely refused to do so?"

I thought of life above the tomb, the sun shimmering on Orvieto, the clouds scuttling across the sky, the feel of the warm air on my face. And then I thought of Brandy Lake trapped in her upstairs room in the big old house in the Aran Islands, Maire's fears of the prejudice Brandy would encounter if anyone knew of her disease, of Crawford Lake unable to enjoy the fruits of his obviously brilliant mind and business acumen.

"Yes, you were," I said.

"What did he tell him?" Anna demanded.

"I believe I threatened you last time we met," Lake said before I could reply. "I regret that very much. I suppose so far from much human contact, I have become rather eccentric and suspicious of everyone. This is not something about myself that I like. I hope that you will hold what you know about me and my family confidential, but if you do not, if you have some reason, perhaps to help your friend, that you feel you must reveal it, then nothing will happen to you, I promise."

"So far no one here has done anything that would make me feel I wanted to share secrets with them," I said.

A slight smile crept across his face. "No, perhaps not. But you seem to be up to the challenge. Now, how was the toothless lion proposing to hurt me?"

"I was supposed to be caught red-handed with the hydria," I said. "Once the word got back here that I had the hydria, someone had what they thought was a brilliant idea. Getting the hydria for the Società would be nice. Getting you, Mr. Lake, would be even better. I was supposed to be apprehended with the hydria, at

which point I was expected to tell the police that Crawford Lake had asked me to get it for him. That would
be all it would take."

"I expect it was Gianni here who came up with the
idea," I said. "Although the others probably encour-
aged him. He wrote the articles. He'd even had the first
couple of them published already, hinting that he knew
who was responsible for the smuggling of Etruscan antiquities out of Italy. A successful foreign businessman,
wasn't it?"

"I remember them well," Lucca said. "Something,
too, about the carabinieri condoning such activities.
I've been meaning to discuss this with you, Gianni."

"So why didn't you tell the carabinieri that Lake had
sent you for the hydria?" Gianni said belligerently,
turning to me.

"Because I had given my word that I wouldn't tell
anyone, and, as foreign a concept as some of you may
find it, I believe in keeping my word. My plan was to
find Lake and get him to step forward," I said. "If he'd
refused, then I would. I found him. Or rather he found
me. Then I knew there was no point in telling the carabinieri that Mr. Lake had sent me, because it was
patently obvious he hadn't. So I had to look for another
explanation, didn't I?"

"Let me make sure I understand this," Lake said.
"While one group, the goat, was rather ineptly trying
to get the hydria into Italy, the other, the lion, was
plotting to. stop it, by telephoning the carabinieri and
reporting a stolen antiquity. Is that about right?"

I nodded.

"This is one of the dumbest ideas I have ever heard,
Gino," Dottie said.

"Why would I bother to sue?" Lake said. "No one would believe such bungling."

"So, it didn't happen," Mauro said. "You can't arrest us for evil thoughts. It was a bad idea, okay, but there's no harm done. Now let's just enjoy the party, and we'll give Nicola the hydria to take back with him at the end of the day."

"Not so fast," Lake said. "I believe, if I have followed you so far, Lara, that now we come to the snake."

"The snake," I agreed.

"This is preposterous," Nicola said. "You make it sound as if all of us are under suspicion."

"You are," Lake said. "Now what is this snake about?"

"It's about this," I said, walking over to the hydria. I picked it up, raised it straight in front of me at about shoulder height, and as they all watched me, I let it go. The chimera hydria dropped like a stone and smashed into hundreds of pieces on the stone floor.

It was bedlam. People were yelling, shaking their fists. Anna fell to her hands and knees and started grabbing at the pieces, pathetically trying to fit them together. Several others rushed to help her, then stopped, realizing it was hopeless.

"What have you done?" Dottie said.

"She's destroyed a priceless antiquity," Lucca said. "I cannot believe you have done this. I am placing you under arrest."

"Relax," I said, picking up a shard and looking at it closely, relieved to find I'd been right. "It's a fake."

"How can you be sure?" Anna said.

"The weight, the balance," I said. "The feel of the surface. It didn't feel like the real one."

"We went to all this trouble for a fake?" Romano said incredulously. "Didn't you say it was authentic?" he said, turning to Nicola.

"Well, yes," Nicola replied. "But of course I didn't have a chance to have a really close look at it. I would have needed my lab equipment . . ."

"What do you mean when you said it didn't feel like the real one?" Lucca said. "Was this theoretical or . . ."

"There have been two chimera hydrias being passed around," I said. "One genuine, the other, this fake. The balance in the real one was absolutely perfect. Despite its shape and size, it would pour like a dream. I know, because I held it. You cannot say the same thing for this one here.

"Until this was delivered to my hotel yesterday," I said, picking up a shard, "I thought that the deaths of Antonio and Leclerc were linked to the plot to discredit Lake. It seemed obvious at first, at least to me, that all of this had to have something to do with Lake. I just couldn't figure out what. I knew some of you were linked to Lake in a way that would make you suspect. Had it not been for the reappearance of the hydria last night, I would have stuck with that theory. But I would have been wrong." They all stood, silent for a change, watching me.

"What seeing this hydria told me is that this is not about revenge for wrongs, real or imagined, any more than it has to do with saving priceless antiquities. It's about greed, about people who are addicted to collecting, who have to possess things whether they are legal or not, and who have the financial wherewithal to do so. And it's about the shadowy dealers who feed their habit.

"The key to the murder was not Mr. Lake but the chimera hydria. At first, I could not figure out why it had been stolen from the police station and then sent to me. The only reason I could think of, at the end of the day, was that somebody wanted it to arrive at its destination, and for whatever reason, I was the one who had to get it there. So that's what I did.

"The piece of the puzzle that was missing, the one that would help make everything come together in my mind, was what Dottie told us about Leclerc. Leclerc got the hydria from Dottie—"

"Just a minute," Lucca said. "Was that the real one?"

"Yes," I said.

"And he put a fake one in your car, right?"

"No, he put the genuine hydria in my car, and I carried it across the border. Then I gave it back to him."

"Why on earth would you do that?" Hank said.

"Perhaps it was because she didn't know what the plan was," Lake said. "Given you never bothered to tell her."

"Yes. Given I was not party to the discussions about how all this was supposed to work, I did something, inadvertently, that led to Leclerc's death, and possibly, much as it gives me great pain to say so, Antonio's as well. I put the hydria into Leclerc's car in the parking lot at the hotel in Volterra. The carabinieri were searching cars, I saw him arrive, and, on the assumption, a correct one, I think, that he had put the hydria in my car in the first place, I put it back in his."

"Are you sure you put it in the right car?" Dottie said to me.

"Yes, but I left immediately after that. It is possible,

indeed probable, that someone else got their hands on
it in the meantime. Regardless, a day or two later, it
reappeared in my hotel room in Arezzo. I've thought
a lot about who sent it to my hotel. For awhile, my
choice was Antonio, who, I thought, was doing it in
an effort to help me. But he denied it vehemently, and
I believed him. Given that, I was then quite sure it was
Leclerc, but now I'm not so certain."

"Surely the real question is whether or not the hydria
delivered to your hotel was the real one or a fake,"
Lake said.

"I had the hydria for only a short time before Lola
took it from me. In fact, I never got a good look at it,
nor did I really have a chance to hold it, except for a
second or two. I'm going to hypothesize, however, that
it was a fake, and that at some point between the time
I put the real hydria in Leclerc's car and the time a
hydria turned up in my hotel room, someone had
switched them."

"So the hydria in my carabinieri station was also a
fake, in this hypothesis anyway," Lucca said.

"Almost certainly," I said. "That, in fact, was the
problem for the snake. I'm using the singular, but I
believe there were four people involved. The fake was
never meant to end up in a police station. Someone—
and it had to be someone who knew nothing of the
lion's intent to intercept the hydria before it could be
delivered—substituted the fake and probably killed Leclerc, who by this time had figured out way more than
these people wanted him to, and given his propensity
to blackmail, had let them know he knew. Then this
same person put the fake hydria back on track to be
delivered as usual to the Società."

"This snake group, then, wants *a* hydria—I emphasize *a*, rather than *the*—to arrive here today," Lucca said. "But why?"

"Good grief," Lake said. "Does everything have to be spelled out for you? Because, as Lara said, this is all about trafficking in antiquities. The snake's plan is to steal the real hydria, is that not correct?" I nodded. "No one is to know because the fake will be put in the Rosati Collection. Also correct?"

"Yes," I said.

"Poor Cesar," Dottie said. "Isn't that awful!"

"Could you hold your comments until the end, please, madame," Lake said irritably. "So the snake gets, probably buys, the real hydria back from Leclerc, and does what with it?"

"Sells it," Lucca said. "Probably someone with an order in for it already. It's in another country by now, I'm certain. Leclerc figures that out and tries to blackmail them. As we've already heard, he did have a tendency in that direction. The snake agrees to meet him at the Tanella di Pitagora. Leclerc is murdered on the spot. The fake has already been substituted and sent on its way. But unbeknownst to the snake, the lion enters the picture, and the fake hydria ends up in the police station."

"But why steal it from the station?" Eugenia said. "It's a fake."

"So no one will know the original has been stolen, of course," Lucca said. "It's a disaster that it's in the police station because someone, another expert, is going to take a good look at it during Signora Lola's trial, and they're going to figure out it's a fake. Correct, no?"

"Correct, yes," I said. "They have to get it out of

the station before it is tested by someone else."

"Then you're saying one of us stole the fake from the carabinieri station," Hank said.

"I have this picture in my mind of Nicola," Lucca said. "Now that I think about it. In my carabinieri station, holding a large sports bag. Big enough to hold an Etruscan hydria, is what I'm thinking."

"That's ridiculous," Nicola said.

"Was this a one-off?" Lake said to me. "Or something more organized?"

"My guess is it's organized," I said.

"Then they got a little ahead of themselves this time," Lucca said. "Probably an impatient buyer, or merely an opportunity that presented itself, thanks to that fellow Leclerc. Normally, the fake would be substituted after it got to the Rosati Collection, would it not?"

"I think so. There's one way to find out."

"Have another look at our previous finds, the nenfro sphinx and that bronze warrior, you mean," Lucca said.

"What would be wrong with them?" Dottie said.

"Fakes, too," Lucca said.

"But the Bearded Sphinx kylix was stolen. Did someone steal a fake?"

"I'd say the snake stole it for the same reason the hydria was taken from the police station," I said. "The kylix was destined to go to another museum, where it would have been subjected to the same authentication procedures as the chimera hydria would in court."

"So the logical people to be involved in this are Rosati and Mondragon," Lake said. "They are the dealers in the group."

"That is balderdash," Mondragon said.

"I know nothing about this!" Cesar exclaimed. "I just have an art collection, that's all. I wanted to show the world beautiful things."

"How did you manage to make your money, Cesar, after Lake ran you out of business?" Hank said. "That's what I want to know. By selling the stuff we went to a lot of trouble and expense to bring back to Italy? Good deal, isn't it? You pay a one-thirteenth portion of the buying price and sell it for the full price, maybe even a higher one."

"I don't know what you're talking about," Cesar said. "I am as much a dupe in all of this as the rest of you. Nicola has betrayed my trust."

"Just a minute here," Nicola said.

"Did you say the hydria was in another country?" Gianni said. "We bring it back into the country, and then they send it out again? How is that done?"

"I believe Alfred Mondragon is the expert in that," I said. "Indeed, Pierre Leclerc already caught him at it once before. According to Alfred's partner Ryan, Leclerc tried to blackmail him for it."

"I made a mistake, that's all," Mondragon said.

"And what about the insurance?" Gino said. "I'll wager you did even better than Hank thinks you did. Did you sell the kylix *and* collect insurance on the fake?"

"Didn't you insure that kylix?" Eugenia said to Palladini. "You said you had to pay out a fortune on it."

Palladini swallowed. "Yes, I did. That's terrible. I had no idea."

"Did you not say you thought there were four members of this committee?" Eugenia said to me.

I nodded.

"And didn't you say you'd inherited money from your mother, Vittorio?" Eugenia said. "Didn't you tell me the apartment in Rome was hers?"

"It wasn't," I said. "He bought it a couple of years ago, just about the time the kylix went missing."

"Oh, dear," Dottie said. "Poor Eugenia. Us girls are learning more than we ever wanted to know. Where'd they get the fakes?"

"That would require an accomplished artist. Almost as good as the Micali painter, wouldn't you say, Nicola?"

Nicola started to say something but stopped.

"I brought your painting to show everyone," I said. "It's in my bag. I'm sure if an expert took a look at both the hydria and the painting, we'd know one way or the other."

"Hey, I'm thinking here," Gino said. "Didn't Nicola authenticate the hydria in the police station?"

"He did," Lucca said. "Quite definitely."

"Naturally, I wouldn't take the kinds of risks that Lara here did, breaking the hydria," Nicola said.

"Oh, right," Gino said.

"But you were talking about murder," Anna said. "Not forgery, and not insurance fraud."

"Antonio and I were friends," I said. "We looked out for each other. He saved me from robbers. I saved him from being misconstrued. I think he was much smarter than people gave him credit for. He followed me everywhere. He saw everything. I think he saw me put the hydria back in Leclerc's trunk, saw Leclerc meet with the person who would later be his killer, maybe even tripped over Leclerc's body the way I did, and put two and two together. Almost certainly he saw the fake hydria delivered to my hotel room."

"He phoned me, you know," Mario said. "I was supposed to go to the Melone to pick up the hydria from Lara. He called and told me not to come. He said something very strange was going on. He liked you very much, Lara. He didn't want anything bad to happen to you. He said he would go to make sure you were all right."

"So which one of these four miscreants killed Antonio?" Lake asked.

"Whichever one drives the red Lamborghini with a bright yellow umbrella in the back," I said. "Whoever drives that car was in both Nice and Volterra, dealing, I suspect, with Leclerc. There's a distinct possibility it was the car I almost ran into in the fog near Cortona the day I found Leclerc."

Perhaps we hadn't noticed, in the chaos, who was moving where, but as I said this, the miscreants, as Lake called them, made a run for it, dashing toward, and then up, the steps, roughly shoving several people aside as they went. In the turmoil, the bottle of grappa on the table was knocked over, and the liquid oozed across the red cloth.

"Stop them!" Lucca cried, and everyone went after them. Lake, remarkably agile, was already on his way up the steps.

"You creeps," Dottie yelled, taking off her shoes and hurtling up the steps. I stepped aside to let the thundering hordes go by.

I was starting to follow them, when I thought, *How many of them did I see leave?* I turned back and looked about the tomb. It was empty. I walked toward the table at the back of it but saw nothing.

I heard something, though, when it was too late. Cesar Rosati stepped out of the darkness of the side room and grabbed me from behind, a blade, the cheese knife, at my throat.

"Now," he said. "We are going to walk very slowly out of here. You will be ahead of me. We will go to the parking lot and get into my car and drive away. If you do everything I say, absolutely everything, then I will consider letting you go when I get to my destination. Is that clear?"

"Yes," I said. I was looking at the table for some reason, the large dark stain on the cloth and little pools of liquid around the cheese. *Grappa,* I thought, and then I knew what I had to do. I slid my hand slowly to one side, and then, in one swift move, knocked the two nearest candlesticks over.

It was a long shot. The first one spluttered and died. There must have been someone looking out for me, because the second, after a moment's hesitation, ignited the liqueur. It flared like a torch. We both, I think, screamed. I ducked and knocked the knife from his hand.

It may not have been the worst fire in the world, but it was astonishing how fast that tomb filled up with smoke. It was dark, hot, and the air was so bad my lungs hurt. Rosati grabbed me, put his hands around my throat, and squeezed. I fought back, scratching and clawing. His jacket sleeve caught fire, and we both went down. I think I hit my head, I know I saw stars, and for a moment, I may have blacked out. I couldn't breathe, I could hardly move, and for a moment I just lay on the floor. I didn't know where Rosati was, and I knew I would die if I stayed there. I just couldn't seem to summon the energy to do anything.

Then I felt strong arms pulling at me, and Lake's voice in my ear. "You've come this far," he said. "It would be rather silly to give up now." Somehow I stumbled to my feet and followed him up the stairs.

Outside, I lay in the grass, gasping. Dottie and Eugenia sat beside me. "Hold on," Dottie said, patting my hand. "The doctor is coming. I'd like to say in my defense, though, that I thought maybe there were overriding principles, something more important than friendship. Like saving a nation's heritage." I just looked at her. "Maybe not," she said. "I'm sorry."

"I suppose we each made tiny compromises," Eugenia said. "But taken together . . ." Her voice trailed off.

"I've got Rosati," Lucca shouted, pulling a limp body out of the hole in the earth. "Where are the others?"

We looked around and then back toward the house. Nicola Marzolini, Vittorio Palladini, and Alfred Mondragon were trussed like chickens to the columns that stood to each side of the loggia. Crawford Lake was gone.

EPILOGUE

CRAWFORD LAKE IS DEAD. HE SPENT more money than most of us can even imagine on a fancy yacht, sailed it out into the Mediterranean, and on a clear day, when no one was looking and the sea was like glass, the sun reflected in it so bright it was almost painful, quietly slipped away.

There has been much speculation about why someone with all the advantages he had—wealth, intelligence, and a much brighter future than the rest of us can look forward to—could do such a thing.

I know he just got tired of sitting alone in the dark. I'm mad at him, though. He wouldn't let me give up. Why did he?

Cesar Rosati is gone, too. Smoke inhalation. Nicola Marzolini, Vittorio Palladini, and Alfred Mondragon have managed to have their sentences reduced by testifying against Rosati, who couldn't defend himself for obvious reasons, placing him at the scene of both murders, and by telling the authorities where the hydria had gone: a buyer in Hong Kong. Italy has initiated proceedings to try to get the chimera hydria back.

The Società della Chimera has been disbanded. Lola and Salvatore seem to be having a good time scouring the countryside together looking for Lars Posena's tomb. Dottie has found a new man to bankroll her store. Antonio's Teresa has married someone else.

My little 1887 worker's cottage with its white picket fence and tiny garden looked so nice when I got home that I just stood out front and stared at it for a few minutes. The lights were on. Perhaps I thought, Alex, my friend and neighbor, had gone over to turn them on to greet me.

I opened the door. I could see there was a fire in the fireplace. Rob was sitting on a stool at the kitchen counter. "Hi," he said.

"Hi," I said. "I'm glad you're here."

"Me, too," he said. He looked tired, and discouraged, and older, somehow. "Did you have a good time?"

"Not really," I said. "Your job done?"

"Yes."

"I read about it in the newspaper on the plane," I said.

"Then you know?"

"Yes," I said. "You arrested a fellow officer in a sting operation. Drugs."

"I worked with that guy for fifteen years," Rob said. "We were even partners for a couple of them. When I finally figured out who it was, I felt as if I'd been kicked in the gut by a horse."

"That's too bad," I said.

"I'm thinking of quitting," he said. "I'm sure there's something else I could do."

"I'm sure there is," I said. "But you're an awfully good policeman."

"Maybe I could start up a security company, or something. I mean, would that be all right with you?"

I looked at him for a minute. "Whatever you want is okay with me. But I know what you need," I said, going up behind him and putting my arms around his neck and nuzzling his ear. "First," I said, "grappa, which, as it happens, I have in this duty-free bag." I opened the box, placed a glass in front of him, and poured.

"Second," I said. "Pasta. Not just any pasta, mind you. *Pasta con aglio*, *olio*, and *peperoncini*, garlic, oil, and hot peppers. I've been taught by an expert." I opened the kitchen cupboard and brought down the ingredients, then filled a large pot at the sink. "That should fortify you.

"And third," I said, walking over to the Indonesian armoire I use to house my stereo equipment, "Music. Verdi. *Otello*. Because whatever else there is to learn from it, it's about finding out the hard way whom to trust."

ACKNOWLEDGMENTS

THERE ARE MANY PEOPLE WHO HELPED with the research and writing of this book. Thank you to Celia Fairclough, Jan Rush, Carol Kirsh and Roy Abrahamson, Betty Cushing, Jim Polk, Bella Pomer, and, as always, my sister Cheryl.